M000305533

SOUR LAKE

Or,

The Beast

Being a True Account of the Atcheson Horror
and its Rampage through an East Texas Town,
Based on Eyewitness Testimony and
Previously Unpublished Documents

By

Bruce McCandless III

Published by Ninth Planet Press, Inc., Austin, Texas.

Cover design by Shaun Venish.

ISBN: 061554486X
ISBN-13: 9780615544861

Many thanks to Roger G. Worthington, Bill Bingham, Dr. Michael T. McCann, Jack Wilkinson, and Lloyd Bates for their assistance with technical aspects of the manuscript. They pointed the way. The mistakes, alas, are mine.

For Tracy

I looked over Jordan and what did I see?
A band of angels comin' after me.

American Spiritual, c. 1840

* * *

We were surrounded by a great forest of viny trees in which we could almost hear the slither of a million copperheads. We wanted to get out of this mansion of the snake, this mireful drooping dark, and zoom on back to familiar American ground and cow towns. There was a smell of oil and dead water in the air. This was a manuscript of the night we couldn't read.

Jack Kerouac, *On the Road*

SOUR LAKE

1.

Pray

The first blow nearly killed him.

If he'd been a doctor, he might have realized that his larynx was crushed. That he'd never speak, or declaim, or recite again. But Leonard Dalchau was a schoolteacher, and what little he knew of human physiology vanished along with the rest of his rational mind in a sudden dark bloom of panic and pain. The young man concluded without thinking that his inability to scream was simply part of his nightmare, some further and fitting aspect of whatever grotesque retribution was being visited upon him for no reason he could understand.

Not that it mattered. The thing was on him again. This time Leonard lost his left ear and a leaf-sized swath of his forehead, the skin ripped away from his skull with a sound like burlap being torn in two. The schoolteacher found himself face down in a clump of wild rye. He was no longer capable even of dread. His life was seeping out the holes in his head and his throat and there was nothing to do in this darkness but run.

Stumble forward.

Find shelter.

Hide.

The young man pulled himself up and staggered toward the line of trees in front of him. He knew he couldn't outrun his attacker. He had to find someplace he could fall and make himself still. He tried to move faster, but the blood in his eyes blinded him. He tripped and landed heavily on his chest. Still, the weeds grew high here, and he was shaded from the moonlight by the limbs of a giant sycamore tree. It would have to do. Leonard dug a book out of the leather bag he'd been carrying. For a moment, the only sounds he could hear were the pounding of his heart and the wet rasp of his own breath. *Be small,* he told himself. *Be silent.* But he couldn't. He hurt too much, and his mind refused to sit up straight.

And then, even worse, he heard it again.

> *There. That sound. But closer. Coming back now.*
> *Whatever it is. Coming to finish me.*

Leonard Dalchau deserved a better death. He was born in 1890 in Schulenburg, a sleepy farm town halfway between Houston and San Antonio. His father was a farmer of German descent. His mother was Irish, and bore the unlikely given name of Brightful. The youngest of nine children, Leonard was the only one to show any aptitude at school. It was a good thing, too, as he showed little aptitude for anything else. He learned to read not long after he could walk. He knew the Lutheran hymnal by heart by the time he was seven and at the age of ten he won a county-wide contest for composition of a poem honoring the state's Confederate war dead. "They Followed the Flag to Glory" appeared in newspapers in Houston, Victoria, and Columbus. It earned the tender poet a silver-plated cup commissioned by the local chapter of the Daughters of the Confederacy, and helped convince him he might someday be the equal of his idol, Lord Tennyson. He'd been writing ever since. In fact he was writing *now,* trying desperately with the stylus of his own stained finger to convey to himself or the stars or whoever cared to know a sense of what was happening to him.

> *So hard to make letters. But make them. Concentrate.*
> *Shut out the haze. Closer, now. It's coming back.*

Leonard graduated from high school in 1907 and attended college in Rusk for two years. When wheat prices collapsed in 1909 his family had to withdraw its financial support, and Leonard reluctantly sought gainful employment. He found it as one of four instructors at the Brabham Academy in Kirbyville, where he gave lessons in Reading, Composition, History, and Latin. In the evenings he wrote epic poems about enchanted swords and haunted glades, doomed Saxon warriors and the maidens who mourned them. His verse was frequently published in the local newspaper, and Leonard had earned a minor celebrity among the ladies of Kirbyville and nearby Voclaw for his exercises in loosely-metered melancholia.

But Jesus I have done nothing to deserve this.
Dear God protect me for its face is not of this earth and....

He was a tall, sparrow-chested young man with spidery hands and the habit of standing with his hips slightly forward, as if modernity itself had looped a rope around his slender waist and was trying to drag him unwillingly into its angular embrace. He had a dimpled, underdeveloped chin, and he wore his curly blonde hair a little longer than was thought respectable. Though he kept odd hours and had a known aversion to both horses and dogs, schoolteachers were known to have odd habits. His neighbors forgave him.

Please don't let me die like this.
Great God, not like this. Not like this. Not like—

Mr. Dalchau could be strict. He was fond of displaying a well-cured hickory switch that his youngest pupils found terrifying. Still, corporal punishment was routine in the public schools of East Texas in the early years of the twentieth century, and Leonard was no more sadistic than most. He could recite verse in three different languages, and he made a point of memorizing his pupils' names before the first week of school was over. Even his less accomplished students developed a grudging respect for the man, dandified though he was. The schoolteacher was twenty years old when the pain went away and the world went dark and he gave up fighting the thing that held him. He'd crawled up under a tangle of blackberry bushes. The thing yanked him out by one leg. Leonard didn't struggle much by this point. He could barely breathe. Just before he lost consciousness, he heard the snap and crunch of bone as his rib cage was torn open. Then his heart was ripped from his chest, and Leonard Dalchau's killer started to feed.

✳ ✳ ✳

Joe Fuller found the body. He was searching for a lost Holstein and ended up not far from the weedy east bank of Sour Lake. One look at the bloody remains of Leonard Dalchau sent the bowlegged dairy farmer reeling back the way he'd come. He walked the seventy-five yards to the Atcheson road, where he hitched a ride with a young Cajun hauling fresh-cut pine. Though he was generally talkative, especially on the subject of seeds, Fuller didn't say a word the entire trip. He clamped his hands together to keep them from trembling, and he jumped off the wagon as soon as he saw the jailhouse.

He'd never talked to the law before. Bad luck, his father had always said, to spend time talking to lawmen or undertakers. Now he felt he had no choice. Sheriff Reeves Duncan offered him a seat and a dipper of lukewarm water. Fuller refused them both. He told the story as quickly as he could. The Sheriff's face went from mildly interested to downright grim as the farmer described what he'd seen. Joe Fuller couldn't help noticing that the Sheriff's eyes had started examining his hands and clothing. It was an uncomfortable realization.

Surely he hadn't made himself a suspect simply by reporting a dead body? But nothing further came of it. Still holding the dipper, Sheriff Duncan promised to ride out to Sour Lake forthwith to see for himself. And because Reeves Duncan always did what he said he would do, he was on the scene a little over an hour later.

✳ ✳ ✳

Leonard Dalchau's corpse was a mess. The young teacher's entrails lay about him as if he'd swallowed an artillery round. His throat was torn away, leaving the pale bone of the vertebral column exposed to the sun. Though still attached to the body, the head lay at an unnatural angle, almost parallel to the slope of the left shoulder. The face was scored as if by a number of knife wounds. One blue eye stared up at the sky. The trunk and limbs were a fishlike white, a result of the fact that the poor man's vital fluids had been drained from his body. Various organs—the heart; both kidneys; the liver—were absent from the remains.

A ragged piece of paper with two crude brown letters painted on it was found near the corpse. The paper had evidently been torn from a book. The two letters were "MO." At first the Sheriff reckoned it was the victim's pathetic last cry to the woman who'd brought him into the world. Clearly he'd started on the third letter, as evidenced by the vertical finial. It might have been an M, or part of a T.

Deputy Jared Sweet found the remainder of the tome a few minutes later, half-buried in a clump of buffalo grass forty yards from the body. The book was Charles Darwin's *On the Origin of Species*—a clue that Leonard Dalchau's outlook on the world might have been starting to change. Scrawled on the title page was the rest of what the unfortunate young man had been trying to communicate. The Sheriff held the pieces of the book together so the letters lined up. Shakily, in a paste of dirt and blood, Leonard Dalchau had written a single word: MONSTE. Reeves Duncan stared at the word for a good long while. He sniffed once, as if to blow an unpleasant scent out of his nose. He held the remains of the book in both hands and wondered if there was any way to feel vibrations captured in an unspeaking object, emotions trapped inside these grass-stained pages. He checked to see if his deputy was watching. He wasn't. Jared was busy trying to swat a yellow jacket. Quietly, carefully, without quite knowing why, Sheriff Duncan placed the pieces of the book in his worn saddlebag, separate from the rest of the dismal debris he'd collected from the murder site. This was going to require some thought. No one knew it yet, but in his last frantic attempt at taxonomy, the unfortunate schoolteacher was, as it turned out, precisely correct.

2.

Walter and Jake

Some people said the death of his wife sent Walter McDivitt to the bottle. Others disagreed, noting that he'd shown a weakness for spirits even in college.

Whatever its origins, Walter McDivitt's alcoholism became dramatically worse during his service as a military surgeon in the Philippines at the turn of the century. Physicians were in short supply in the South Pacific. Though he was a commissioned Army officer, Walter McDivitt was assigned to accompany General Jacob Smith's Marines on their mission to pacify the island of Samar during the winter of 1902.

American history textbooks are silent on the subject of Samar. This is undoubtedly because the story lacks redemptive qualities. The island is remembered now, if at all, as a footnote to the Spanish-American War. In that conflict, the United States overpowered a feeble Spain and took control of her far-flung colonies, including the Philippines. But there was a snag. The Filipinos didn't want to be controlled anymore—by Spain, or the United States, or anyone else for that matter. A nasty insurgency developed. It erupted into full-fledged war with the massacre of U.S. Army regulars by Filipino insurgents in a village called Balangiga, on the southern coast of Samar, in September of 1901. Forty-four American soldiers perished, most of them hacked to pieces. It was the Army's worst defeat since Little Bighorn.

General Smith sent his Marines to retaliate. His stated aim was the extermination of all male inhabitants of Samar capable of bearing arms against the United States. And quite likely some who were not—Smith set the minimum age for killing at ten. The Marines moved across the island with bayonets fixed to their heavy Krag-Jorgenson rifles. They burned villages and fields and blasted holes in men, boys, and random *carabaos*, the natives' cattle, wherever they found them. No one knows how many Filipinos died on the little island. Estimates range from twenty-five hundred to fifty thousand. The scourging of Samar may have been the closest thing to hell any American of that era experienced. Or created.

Walter McDivitt emerged from the jungle to face an additional threat to his temperament. He was handed a telegram that regretted to inform him his wife had passed away the previous evening in a San Francisco hospital. The cause of death was blood poisoning. The telegram, he learned, was three weeks old.

* * *

The horrors Walter McDivitt saw during the Samar campaign faded from his waking mind, but they never quite disappeared from his dreams. He carried psychic splinters from the struggle like some men carried casing fragments lodged in their bones. Back in the States, McDivitt alternated between stints of private practice and bouts of malarial fever. He also developed a taste for absinthe, the extract of wormwood long favored by English aesthetes and European whores. The stuff nearly killed him in 1905 when, three weeks after his most recent release from Walter Reed Hospital, half mad with grief and self-hatred, he woke up on a pier in Baltimore with a broken wrist, a punctured lung, and a missing wallet. He had no idea where he'd spent the days in between, though he later determined the money had gone to buy two Chinese prostitutes—a mother and daughter, it turned out—and enough opium to stupefy a moose.

The young physician wrestled himself into a period of sobriety after that. He found work in a sanatorium in

Virginia for a time, but this was only a way station. He ended up in the Big Thicket region of Texas in late 1906, largely by happenstance. He was bequeathed a two-story Victorian house and three acres of land in the town of Atcheson by a Richmond widow named Gray whom he'd treated, tenderly but unsuccessfully, for consumption. Walter often remained at the sanatorium overnight. He did so for fear of where he'd end up if he left. But the widow Gray thought it was out of concern for her, and he never tried to disabuse her of the notion. He tended her for three months. They talked until dawn on several occasions. During one of these conversations, as he watched his auburn-haired patient cough up bloody shreds of her own lungs, Walter learned that Elizabeth Gray's late husband had been a botanist. The federal government sent him to East Texas to propagate and propagandize for the Chinese tallow tree, a deciduous native of Southeast Asia that was envisioned by some in the Department of Agriculture as a way to provide the raw materials for a domestic soap industry in the rural South. The unfortunate Mr. Gray died due to complications arising from approximately eighty bee stings he suffered on one of his many trips into the Thicket to spread *sapium sebiferum* seeds in clear-cut timber tracts. Though Silas Gray had displayed admirable initiative, there was no noticeable uptick in the Southern soap industry occasioned by his efforts.

The widow Gray moved back to Virginia to be with her family after her husband died, and the couple's handsome Victorian two-story in Atcheson stood empty for almost five years. None of Elizabeth Gray's kinfolk wished to move to East Texas. She didn't blame them. Her letters home had contained long, despairing descriptions of the insects and fevers and tyrannical heat she lived with in the Big Thicket. But Elizabeth recognized in Walter McDivitt a wounded spirit. She wondered aloud if a life in the back end of nowhere might be just what he needed to help him put the temptations of hard liquor and loose women behind him.

The sad-eyed doctor shrugged, as he often did, and put the matter aside. He was surprised to find that she'd actually left him the house when she died. He was even more surprised when he decided to take it.

* * *

Now Walter McDivitt—"Doc," as he was inevitably called by his neighbors and patients—had a general practice that took up only half his time. He delivered babies and sometimes collected a chicken or two as payment. He set broken bones. He patched cuts and scrapes, now and then pulled a tooth if there was no barber handy. And he performed autopsies for the county at the rate of two dollars a death. It was in pursuit of this princely sum that he rode on a brutally hot afternoon in late September.

Two men stood in the shade of a huge live oak, watching the doctor's slow approach as men in other places will watch ships inch into a wind-starved harbor. Sheriff Reeves Duncan was a barrel-shaped man with a head the size of a prize ham and no clear separation between his jowls and his neck. Despite the fact that he'd stripped down to his shirt, he was sweating profusely in the afternoon heat. Doc noticed the Sheriff's thick face had taken on an unhealthy blush. His body didn't belong here, and was well into its revolt.

Beside the Sheriff stood Jared Sweet, a twenty-two year-old widower who acted as Duncan's deputy. Sweet was calm, moonfaced, as blonde as fresh-split oak. The Sheriff often said he was about as useful as tits on a bull but he kept him on the payroll anyway, possibly because he was a distant cousin and there wasn't much else the kid could do.

"Sheriff," Doc called. "Jared."

It was so humid that the sound of his voice seemed to sink before it could get anywhere. Doc didn't have to rein up. He was riding a bay gelding named Cherokee who was almost twenty years old. Cherokee's mane was flecked with gray, and his flanks were dark with sweat. The horse had already decided he wasn't walking much further.

"Evenin', Doc," said the Sheriff. "Jared, you fall asleep on me? Take them reins, son."

McDivitt dismounted and set about unfastening the saddle bags that held his medical equipment and supplies: scalpel and forceps, glass vials of calomel, glycerine, and chloral hydrate. At six foot three inches, he was uncommonly tall for the era, with a prominent, beaky nose and dark hair he rarely cut. His close-set eyes were blue, and he had a mole at the base of his right nostril. He'd lost his left thumb in a shooting accident some years before. It was said the disfiguration served him well in his obstetric practice because it allowed him to reach further up inside the birth canal of expectant mothers. Doc himself never made this claim, though he never denied it either. He occasionally wore a beard, though it was unclear whether this was a matter of choice or simply a reflection of his absent-mindedness. A mercurial man, he was sometimes vocally impatient with what he saw as nonsense, at other times morose and almost impossible to engage in conversation. He was known to have trouble sleeping, and some of his patients claimed they could smell liquor beneath the anise he chewed. He wore a proper celluloid collar, but close inspection revealed that it was spattered with specks of blood and mucosa. Walter McDivitt was not the beloved, avuncular figure some country doctors become. He was too moody for that, too forbiddingly tall and dour and prone to bouts of silence. Still, he came when he was called, day or night, and he was tireless when caring for a patient. He preferred cash. Anyone did. But he would take goods in exchange for services, and the more goods you had, the more he was willing to take. In the Thicket, this was enough.

Doc took off his battered black top hat and wiped his hair away from his forehead with a shirtsleeve. The sky was a faded blue, as if too much sun had worn it out. Massive cumulus clouds from the Gulf of Mexico drifted north at regular intervals like floats in a lazy parade. Objects in the middle distance shimmered in waves of refracted heat. September was still summer in Texas.

"Ready, Sheriff," said Doc. "Lead on."

Reeves Duncan nodded, but remained where he was.

"It ain't pretty," said the lawman. The whine of cicadas filled the still air.

"Never is," said the doctor.

"Body's pretty tore up. Looks like a mill accident, if you ask me."

"A mill accident." McDivitt searched the Sheriff's face for a long moment. "There's not a mill within five miles of here."

"Exactly. There's not much a' nothin' within five miles of here."

Doc showed he understood with a little grunt. The lawman turned and started walking. "Just over yonder a ways. Watch your step."

McDivitt paused to examine the brown and pink mess that lay in the grass. It seemed to be clotted with maggots. No. Not maggots. *Rice.*

"Jared ain't got much of a stomach," the Sheriff explained.

* * *

It wasn't as bad as Reeves Duncan said.

Hell.

It was *worse.* McDivitt didn't know what to make of the carnage. He spent almost an hour examining the body and studiously ignoring the Sheriff's comments about the feeding habits of various predatory animals that lived in the Thicket. Then he filled out the county's death certificate. From the condition of the semi-digested food he found in the victim's stomach, Doc estimated the death had occurred within the past twenty-four hours. This was about all he was prepared to say.

"Any idea who it is?" Doc asked.

"Not yet. Looks like a he, though."

"I gathered that."

McDivitt was aware the Sheriff was reading over his shoulder.

"What's this?" said Reeves Duncan. He pointed at the section of the report that said *Cause of Death*. A bead of sweat dropped from the Sheriff's stubby finger onto the page, smearing the ink of Doc's signature. Both men were drenched in their own perspiration.

"Says 'UNKNOWN'," Doc answered. He blotted the sweat against his shirt. "Means *I don't know*."

The Sheriff hated that word. It offended him. He'd been a lawman for nineteen years. He knew just about every family in Ochiltree County and quite a few outside it. Not much happened around Atcheson that surprised him.

"Not goin' with the dogs, huh?" he said.

Packs of wild dogs occasionally killed livestock in the Big Thicket. They had been rumored to take children as well, though this was a legend that circulated in many rural communities and no one was ever able to verify it. The packs had been especially bad this year. They were blamed for the deaths of cattle and pigs in northern Ochiltree County and as far west as Telegraph Hill. Reeves Duncan and his deputy had set out poisoned sheep carcasses in April. They managed to kill two of the few remaining red wolves in the area, but it seemed like maybe they'd got the wrong animals because the killings continued.

Doc shrugged. "Dogs. Bear. Panther. All just about as likely. Or unlikely. Too dry to make out much in the way of tracks. You check down toward the lake?"

"What? A gator?"

"I didn't say that, Sheriff. I was just asking."

The two men gazed west at the expanse of black water and moss-shrouded cypress trees that was Sour Lake. It wasn't really much of a lake. A broad, low-lying backwater of the Anahuac River, it was more of a swamp—and not one many folks cared to explore. As the two men watched, a giant crane labored up out of the spatterdock pads and flapped its way into the shadows of the giant trees.

The Sheriff spat a stream of tobacco juice at a dragonfly hovering nearby. He missed. "Well, hell. I don't know either. Might call Ed Petticord out to see if he can scratch up some kind of a trail."

"Who found the body?"

"Joe Fuller. Out huntin' for one of his milk cows. Come up from the south, evidently. Got to right about where that little mayhaw's stickin' up. Saw the mess and turned smack dab around."

"Smart cow," said Doc.

"I meant Joe." The Sheriff ran a hand back through his damp hair, leaned his head back to survey the sky. "God knows what happened to the cow."

* * *

The Sheriff and Deputy Sweet waited around for Tom Watson, Atcheson's undertaker, to ride out with his wagon to collect the body. The plan was to wrap as much of the corpse as they could find in a sheet of canvas and send the parcel to Gosford for burial in the county cemetery. At least this was the plan unless someone showed up to claim the dead man's remains. That was going to present a whole different set of problems. A request for an *explanation*, for one thing.

Doc was on his way home by five o'clock. He rode with his head bowed, his reins sagging below Cherokee's sweat-stained neck. Walter McDivitt had seen plenty of death. He'd lived through a dirty war, after all, and war has an awful way with bodies. He'd seen men blown apart in the Philippines. He'd stumbled upon a human head lying in a ditch with a length of the trachea still attached. He'd examined bodies hacked to pieces by the *bolo*, the natives' fighting knife, and watched children vomit up their own semi-digested blood as they lay wasting with yellow fever. Most days he could keep his visions filed under the proper sanitized headings: Blunt Trauma. Third-Degree Burn. Massive Organ Failure. This was different. The carnage of war, even the shadowy, obscene war in the Philippines, was random and pointless. Something about the mutilation of the young man he'd seen this afternoon struck him as intentional. It seemed like an act of vengeance, vicious and cold. It seemed like murder.

☆ ☆ ☆

Doc was sitting at his dining room table with half a fried chicken—bones and gristle; dark meat and grease— congealing on the plate in front of him when his nephew arrived home. It was late, well after dark. Doc's housekeeper, Mrs. Grady, had left half an hour ago.

Jake Hennessey expected a scolding. Heck. He *deserved* a scolding. He'd spent the afternoon and early evening with Eben Melton out at the farm, and they'd finally gotten the Fair Field Flyer back in the air. Only about thirty feet in the air, and only for a couple of minutes, but that's all they were aiming for anyway. The new ailerons they'd installed were going to work fine—much better than the old wing-warping cables. They planned to run the machine out again over the weekend and put a few miles of real airtime on her.

But while he was working with Eben, Jake had forgotten the chores waiting for him at home. He'd neglected to fill Cherokee's water bucket. The chickens probably needed water too. He'd failed to split a single one of the oak logs piled in the backyard, and he stank of sweat and grease and cottonseed oil. It was almost nine o'clock. He prepared for the worst.

"Jake," said his uncle.

The boy, slender, raven-haired, paused at the foot of the stairs. He'd been caught. He padded over to the doorway to the dining room and glanced inside.

"Sir?" said Jake.

Walter McDivitt poured himself another three fingers of whisky. The way his head swayed on his neck told Jake his uncle was already drunk. That hadn't happened much lately. Jake was sorry to see it now. He didn't understand the attraction of liquor and hoped he never would. It turned his uncle from a reserved but intelligent man into a self-pitying idiot, prey to night terrors and fits of baseless panic.

"Jake?" said Doc. Louder this time.

"I'm right here, Doc. Right in front of you."

Doc lifted his head and squinted through the lamplight. He pushed his plate of chicken parts and cold potatoes further down the table. His dark eyes suddenly found his nephew and bore into him.

"Son," he said. "Be a *lawyer.*"

MURDER VICTIM
WAS AREA TEACHER

Suspect Sought in
Sour Lake Massacre
Duncan Mum on Details,
Requests Information

Atcheson Teller
October 2, 1911
Page 1, Col. 3

3.

The Inquest

Atcheson's civic and financial prospects were debated regularly in Sheriff Duncan's office by a group of men who swore they had more important things to do. They cut and chewed plugs of Lone Pine tobacco, "the Taste of the South." They watched the Sheriff mend tack (a secondary source of income for him, though not by much), and argued the issues of the day till passersby wondered aloud when Ochiltree County was going to get itself an anti-loitering ordinance.

Generally the subject was politics. Most of Atcheson's leading citizens were Jim Hogg Democrats, staunch supporters of the Robertson Insurance Law and the federal government's break-up of Standard Oil. But there were a few old Greenbackers and Populists among them, and even mention of the name William Jennings Bryan could start the spit flying. George Nolte, the German blacksmith, was an unapologetic socialist who'd campaigned for E.R. Meitzen of Hallettsville in the 1910 gubernatorial election. When the bald German bothered to speak, he was capable of defending even the activities of the Finnish union organizers and syndicalists who were causing so much trouble in the Pacific Northwest. Everyone knew the International Workers of the World, the "Wobblies," as they called themselves, were looking to worm their way into the South. They seemed to have started their advance with the railroad workers. Avowedly anti-capitalist, scornful of religion in all its varieties, the Wobblies were said to have instigated the Texas brakemen's strike in the spring of that year. They were also rumored to have been behind the labor violence in Quitman in July that led to three deaths. It was generally agreed that the Wobblies—hell, trade unionists in general—were dangerous, demented, and about as trustworthy as a bag full of snakes. After all, it was the Wobblie McNamara brothers who'd dynamited the *Los Angeles Times* building only the year before, killing twenty-one innocent office workers in what was quickly dubbed the crime of the century. A fire in New York City earlier in 1911 had killed 141 workers in a shirt factory, and the unionists' calls for violence were growing more vehement.

On the other end of the Ochiltree County political spectrum, no one would confess to knowing a Republican, but it was understood that the coloreds backed the G.O.P. as a solid bloc and a man couldn't blame them for voting their interests.

Besides, they never won anyway.

This afternoon, though, the topic under discussion in the jailhouse was the same one that had been discussed the previous three days: Leonard Dalchau. Reeves Duncan had finally confirmed the identity of the murdered man. He'd sent wires to the nearest towns asking if anyone was missing. He included details about the victim's height and hair color and the battered book found near the body. When word came back from Kirbyville that one of the Brabham Academy's teachers was unaccounted for, Duncan had Jared Sweet ride over with scraps of the clothing they'd recovered. The superintendent of the Academy confirmed the scraps belonged to Leonard Dalchau's hiking get-up, right down to the burgundy *lederhosen*. The superintendent also identified two tattered pages of *On the Origin of Species*, adding in a note to Sheriff Duncan that he had warned Mr. Dalchau repeatedly about displaying the book in public. He sent along an address for the young man's next of kin. Now the Sheriff was doing his best to avoid writing the letter he knew he needed to send.

Evidently Leonard had been out playing poet in the woods and managed to get himself lost. Afternoon faded to evening. Evening turned to night. The locals could have told him better. The Big Thicket was no place for gathering daffodils. Deep in southeast Texas, roughly centered along the muddy Neches River, the area was given its name by Scots-Irish settlers who found it too densely forested to penetrate. Most went around it. The Thicket was several hundred square miles of live trees, dead trees, and blackwater swamp, a world where the flora and fauna of a dozen different ecologies had been shoved together by the last Ice Age and now lived side by side in a sort of biological never land, locked in perpetual combat, preying on and over each other. Home to bears, panthers, and enough snakes to fill some Asiatic circle of Hell, the Thicket was more shadow than sun, more water than earth, a dark, damp place the scientists said couldn't exist. Here even the flowers—the pitcher plant and bladderwort— hungered for flesh. The Thicket was carnivorous.

"Don't know why we're speculatin'," said Ed Aiken that afternoon, shifting positions in the chair nearest the jailhouse's lone window. Ed was known to have complaints about his personal regions. The elder brother of Atcheson's banker, little Mose Aiken, he was a sallow, slack-skinned man who possessed none of his sibling's industriousness. He was also the local sales representative of the Loyal Order of Pendo, a Lufkin-based fraternal benefit life assurance society that seemed likely to go bust any day now, casting the usual number of widows and orphans into financial ruin. "Clarence East killed that boy, sure as night's dark."

The Sheriff glanced over his spectacles at his interlocutor. "Well, hell, Ed. Maybe I'll just go fishin' today. You mind enlightenin' the rest of us as to how you solved the crime?"

Aiken straightened in his chair. "'Course I don't mind. East said he was gonna kill the next white sonofabitch who looked at him cross-eyed. I heard it."

"Threatenin' to kill Willard Mills if he hit him with a *log chain*," said the lawman, "ain't threatenin' to kill white men in general."

This was an unassailable fact, and disappointment settled over the room. Sheriff Duncan heard a horse stamp its foot on the dirt road outside, as if to put a period to the conversation. But it wasn't to be.

"Maybe not," said Aiken. "But I still don't like to hear that kind of talk. Gets them other niggers stirred up, for one thing. And that's a fact."

Duncan tested the strength of the bridle he'd mended. He pulled it one way, then the other. "Man like Willard is what gets the niggers stirred up," he said. "East ought not to have said it. I'll give you that. On the other hand, Willard ought not to have gone to hit the man with a log chain. Lucky East saw he was drunk. Mighta had two more bodies on our hands by now."

Dr. Walter McDivitt opened the door to the jailhouse and stepped inside. He smelled mildew and leather and unwashed men.

"Sheriff," said Doc. "Ed. Boys."

Reeves Duncan smiled with relief. "Doc, come on in and join the grand jury. We was just about to send out for a rope."

"You got any better idea who done it?" said Bracy Ames. Bracy was a quiet man, given to long bouts of mournful whittling. This was the first thing he'd said all day. Chances were good he'd be asleep by noon.

"Did what?" said McDivitt, squinting to make out faces in the dim room. "Or am I better off not asking?"

"Not asking," the Sheriff responded. "Always."

"That schoolteacher," explained Ed Aiken. "Shut the door, Doc. You'll let out the flies."

"What schoolteacher?"

"Body we looked at the other day," said the Sheriff. Something about the way he said "body"—the implication that the collection of parts they'd looked at was enough to constitute a *body*—put Walter McDivitt on guard. "Turns out he was with the school up in Kirbyville. Hot enough for you?"

Doc nodded. "Gonna get up near a hundred again today, I suspect."

"We was just askin' the Sheriff," said Dim Evans, "if he had any better idea of who done it."

"Got no idea, period," said Reeves Duncan. He spat into the brass pitcher at his feet. "I've never seen anything quite like this one."

"Say what you know, Reeves."

The Sheriff took his spectacles off and pulled a kerchief from one pocket to wipe the lenses. He knew his audience wanted details. Blood on the grass. Guts in the brambles. But he wasn't going to give 'em any. Not today, at least. There was no sense getting people upset. "Just...don't make no *sense*, is all. Fella was a schoolteacher. Didn't have any money to speak of. He wasn't trespassin'. Ain't no *stills* out there. That I know of, anyhow."

Here Duncan flashed a glance at Dimmitt Evans. Dim was dark and good-looking, a carpenter by trade but a manufacturer of grain alcohol by avocation, with a shock of jet-black hair that never quite stayed out of his eyes. Now he shook his head in agreement with the Sheriff's assertion, maybe a little too fast. The Sheriff made a mental note of it.

"That boy keep his pants on over in Kirbyville?" said Fielding Cobb. Cobb was the town barber, a slight, ferrety man with a hunted look and the slightest half-circle of hair around his head. It was an act of faith to close your eyes on Fielding Cobb when he was holding a straight razor. Most folks took the haircut but passed on the shave.

"What's that supposed to mean?" said Ed Akin.

The Sheriff shrugged. "I know what he means, Ed. He's askin' if there's a jealous husband out there somewhere. I sent a note up with Jared askin' that question myself. Looks like our schoolteacher wasn't much for the ladies."

"What about dogs?"

"Didn't seem to like dogs much neither," said the Sheriff. General hilarity ensued. But shortly ebbed.

"You know what I mean, Reeves," said Aiken. "There's wild dogs all up in them woods."

"I know it. And it coulda been dogs, 'cept for one thing. He wasn't et up."

Not exactly, Doc thought. With the exception of a few organs, the schoolteacher's flesh was mostly intact, though considerably damaged. It was the blood that was gone. The victim had, in a sense, been *drunk up*.

"Panther?"

"Now Dim," said the Sheriff. "When's the last time you heard of a panther killing a grown man?"

"What about Monk Gibson?" asked Cobb. Henry "Monk" Gibson was a sixteen-year-old field hand who raped and killed the four female members of a white farm laborer's family in Edna in 1904. The victims, who were stabbed repeatedly and had their skulls broken open, ranged in age from six to thirty-seven. Monk Gibson was arrested, then escaped and flat-out *disappeared*, sending spasms of panic and paranoia through the southern half of the state. Governor Lanham called out the militia. A fortune teller was consulted. Several counties sent their best scent hounds, and the story of Monk Gibson's mysterious dematerialization was front-page news as far away as Shreveport. Authorities speculated on the possibility of a gang of Negroes and Northern sympathizers sheltering the fugitive. A local newspaper reported that Mexican bandits had helped the dusky fiend find freedom over the border. After two weeks of false leads and mistaken arrests, though, the kid was discovered hiding in a nearby barn. The authorities pumped his stomach to see what he'd been eating. They were certain he'd had accomplices bringing him food, but it turned out all he had in his belly was raw feed corn, and not a lot of that.

Gibson was convicted by an all-white jury in Cuero five months later, then hanged in front of the DeWitt County courthouse as several thousand picnicking locals looked on. The Monk Gibson case stood for the proposition that colored men were dangerous livestock with an insatiable lust for white females. It wasn't the only evidence someone like Fielding Cobb could cite for this proposition, but it was one of the most compelling illustrations.

"Monk Gibson got himself strung up five years ago," said the Sheriff. "Somehow I don't think he's responsible for this one."

"I mean someone *like* that," Cobb persisted. "You know. Someone with a temper."

Sheriff Duncan put his work aside and leaned back in his chair, which squealed beneath his considerable bulk. He sighed as he craned his neck to the right, then the left. They weren't going to leave this one alone.

"Hell," he conceded. "I suppose ol' Clarence might a' done it. If he got mad enough. Or drunk enough."

"Now you're talkin' sense, Sheriff. He's a mean drunk. I've seen him."

"Oh, I've seen him too. He laid out two Irishmen in Saratoga last year with his bare hands. Big men, too. Went down hard. That don't mean he's a murderer."

"No, but…." The shifty little barber paused to spit.

"But what?"

"But it does mean he *coulda* done it."

"Coulda been some hobo done it too," said the Sheriff. "I told y'all about that yegg killed a woman in Beaumont last year. Run her through the throat with a ice pick. Broke into a drilling supply warehouse the next night and blew himself sky high trying to jimmy open a locker full a' nitro. Top half of his head landed in a bakery wagon three blocks away. They found one of his legs with the pants still on it. Dead lady's comb was right there in his pocket."

Reeves Duncan was hoping to distract his questioners. The tactic nearly always worked. Everyone had a nitroglycerine story to tell. The oil men used it to snuff well fires, and anyone who handled it was at considerable risk of ending life as a carbon-based mist. Ordinarily in a circle like this a colloquy of rumored and recollected carnage would ensue.

Not today, though.

No one said a word.

"Come to think of it, has anybody seen East around lately?" said Ed Aiken.

"Not for a coupla weeks," Dim Evans chimed in, his face showing studied bewilderment.

The lawman breathed out through his nose. He knew he was cornered. The fact was, the men in his office weren't simply idlers. They had been appointed, or they had appointed themselves, to make sure Reeves Duncan was doing his job. Not everyone in Ochiltree County thought he was as aggressive as he ought to be. The publisher of the Atcheson *Teller*, for example (motto: *Thou Shalt Not Muzzle the Ox that Treadeth Out the Corn.*), thought he'd been far too lenient with John Bickley, a local oil engineer who had a habit of beating his wife with a weighted razor strap. It was the worst-kept secret in town. Reeves Duncan had talked to the man twice, threatened to lock him up, listened patiently to the expressions of remorse and grief that poured forth from John Bickley and the quieter urgings of Mrs. Edda Bickley that he, the Sheriff, leave things be. But the man never changed. The beatings continued, and one day Edda Bickley walked into the Anahuac River with her pockets full of ball bearings and put her own pathetic end to the violence. Of course it wasn't Reeves Duncan's fault that she'd drowned herself. Nobody said it was; not in those terms, anyway. But there were plenty of people who said he'd been a little too patient with the engineer, a little too willing to trust the promises of a known bully. Bickley left town not long afterward, thoroughly despised by his neighbors. The *Teller* printed an editorial the next day. While mentioning no names, the editorial called upon the good citizens of Atcheson to "teach their neighbors their Christian duty—by force, if necessary, if the servants of civil authority seem not more willing to take up the rod of discipline."

Reeves Duncan roused himself from his memories of the affair. "I suppose that's a fair question, Ed," he said. "Reckon I'll wander over toward Freedom tomorrow and see if I can roust him."

"You need you some deputies, Sheriff?"

"I said *roust* him, not *roast* him. Surely you solid citizens have got better things to do than tail around after a broke-dick old lawman. Hell, that's Jared's job." *There. That was better.* The mention of Jared Sweet broke the tension. A couple of men chuckled. "Doc, you wanted to see me about somethin'?"

Walter McDivitt glanced around the room. He started to speak, then caught himself. The death of Leonard Dalchau was probably not a subject Sheriff Duncan wanted discussed much more, if at all. Especially not in front of this bunch. Dim Evans. Ed Aiken. Fletcher Cobb. Anything he said here would be repeated at supper tables all over the county by sunset. *And what did he have to say, exactly?* He wasn't even sure why he'd come to Reeves Duncan's office. He had plenty to do, after all. He had three calls to make by the end of the day, though fortunately none of them was particularly urgent. To make things worse, he'd gotten good and drunk again last night and he still felt like someone had laid his head on an anvil and tried to flatten it with a twelve-pound hammer. *So why,* he asked himself again, *was he loitering here in the jailhouse with the county's most notorious bunch of speculators and layabouts?* He just needed to talk, he told himself.

About the body.

About *something*.

The men in the room were staring at him now. They were gauging his expression, watching his every move. Doc wasn't the kind of man to stop in for a casual visit. The men seemed to sense there was something out of the ordinary in his appearance.

"Didn't want anything in particular," Doc finally said. The words came out as a croak. Doc wasn't used to editing himself. It felt uncomfortable. But he rocked back on his heels and did his best to give the room a companionable shrug. "I just dropped in to shoot the breeze."

4.

Baby Josh

Josh Turner stood just a hair over five feet tall.

There was white blood in his veins, as evidenced by the freckles on his cheeks and across the bridge of his nose, but in this and many other ways he was unremarkable. He liked clean shirts and new shoes and he favored the color green, which was the color of his eyes and therefore, in his view, lucky. Women considered him gentle and much put-upon, a perpetual victim of circumstance. They called him *Baby Josh*. And yet their Baby Josh gambled incessantly, and drank when he could, and fought other men with a ferocity that seemed the product of some inner hell. Joshua Freeman Turner was always trying to get somewhere else, but he always ended up right back at his own side, in his own coffee-colored skin, unable to evade the man he hated most.

He was trying to escape again on this warm night in early October. There was just a sliver of yellow moon in the sky and thus little light on the road from Gosford to Freedom. It didn't matter. Josh knew the way. He knew it like the back of his hand, and the darkness suited his purpose. He'd been in Memphis, halfway to the new home he hoped to make in Chicago, when he stuck a blade in the belly of a Beale Street bar owner named Gator Moore. Josh didn't regret the killing. Gator was cheating him at blackjack. But Gator Moore dabbled in prostitution and loan sharking, and was said to have friends on the local police force. *Important friends.* So when Gator died in a puddle of his own blood in front of three witnesses, stabbed thirteen times in the groin and abdomen by an enraged and thoroughly intoxicated Josh Turner, Baby Josh thought it best to rethink his travel plans. A week later he found himself carrying the dust of four states on the nape of his neck. He was back in goddamned Ochiltree County, Texas. He was back where he'd started, hungry and tired and wearing out his best pair of brogans in search of the suitcase-sized ass of his sometime lady friend Etta Anderson. Etta had a soft bed and a generous bosom, both of which she was frequently willing to share. She also had a weakness for hard luck stories. With her he could catch his breath, eat a couple of hot meals, figure out his next step. He'd heard good things about the West. Denver, maybe. Or San Francisco. *Etta was the key. Etta was salvation. For tonight, anyway. He'd find another slice of salvation tomorrow.*

As the night wore on, Josh Turner found himself quickening his pace without quite knowing why. Or even, come to think of it, *how.* He was as tired as he'd ever been in his life. His knees hurt and his back was stiff. His stomach was making uneasy, gurgling sounds. He put his sense of unease down to fatigue and hunger. It was well after midnight before he admitted to himself that he was walking faster because something was following him. He tried slowing down. Then, realizing he was within a mile of Etta's place, hard on Turkey Creek, he broke into a trot. But now the sounds of pursuit—branches breaking, birds startled from sleep—circled around until they were in front of him.

Josh Turner stopped and listened to the woods. *Nothing. There was nothing there.* Well, not quite nothing. The bugs were out there. Crickets. Cicadas. Night in the Thicket was louder than a Memphis street at noon. But nothing else was out there. Nothing big enough to care about, leastways. He was probably imagining things. The Thicket was a tricky place. Few people traveled it at night, and even fewer traveled alone. The animals were bad enough. Josh himself had heard the odd, babyish shrieks of panthers in the bottoms around Sour Lake. It was a sound that could make your hair stand on end. But there were stranger things in the Thicket too. His grandmother had told him of *hants* in these woods— grim, bedraggled dead men who walked in the moonlight searching for living beings to share their torments with. Some people spoke of seeing blue and green lights hovering above the swamps. *Lost souls,* his grandmother would whisper. *The Devil's play-pretties. Stop your ears to the songs they sing, lest they take holt of your ankles and drag you to hell.* Josh chuckled to himself, thinking about the old woman's earnest warnings. He'd turned out meaner than any goddamned *hant* in these woods.

Josh resumed his walk. The Freedom road was mostly sand, and it was quiet again but only for a few moments. Now the noises were closer. This made him angry rather than scared—so angry that the veins in his temples started to throb. He took his knife out of his pants and unfolded the blade.

"That's right," he said. "I'm right HERE!"

Nothing responded. Josh moved forward, and the noises followed him. He stopped and everything went silent. This cycle repeated itself until finally the little man screamed challenges into the Thicket and in good time the challenge was answered.

Something large and unrealizable peeled itself from the darkness. It moved so quietly that for several moments Josh thought it was a trick of his own devising, a figment from one of his grandmother's crazy old stories of deep woods specters and mournful swamp spirits. One moment the thing was absent and the next it was there, like a fog, moving slowly toward him. The thing walked like a man. It was almost seven feet tall, and it had lifeless black eyes set low on a smallish head. They stood facing each other on the sandy, moon-dappled road for several seconds, as if attempting to establish through shared memory or the spurs of instinct some script to guide the terms of what they both knew must follow. Then there was a gentle whooshing sound as a set of wings unfurled behind and above the creature. Josh raised his eyes to look at the wings and at the same instant, the creature struck. Josh was thrown several feet by the blow. Now his rage returned, intensified by fear. In the scant moonlight he'd thought he might be dreaming, but the taste of his own blood set him straight. *Not that it mattered.* Anger, indifference, panic, despair. The thing had a face that couldn't be a face at all, since it moved and changed and reconstructed itself as it fended off Josh Turner's attacks.

Baby Josh fought. He fought the creature as hard as anyone ever had: with his knife; with the straight razor he kept in his sock, with his fingernails and his teeth and his feet. He screamed and swore and scratched at the damned thing's lurid unblinking black eyes. And yet the result was the same. Death came quickly, if not easily. His shrieks reached almost to the clay-floored house where Etta Anderson spoke small somethings to a gentleman caller from Huntsville. The bloodless fragments of Joshua Freeman Turner's body lay beneath the stars for six nights, draped in the remains of his lucky green shirt, before anyone found them.

5

The Suspect

Like most Southern peace officers, Reeves Duncan worried about the prospects of lynching. He was determined not to have mob justice break out on his watch. He had plenty of reasons. For one thing, people got hurt—and as often as not, one of the casualties was the lawman who'd humped his hindquarters out and apprehended some no-count sumbitch in the first place. But lots of other folks got hurt as well, and frequently the ones who bled weren't the ones who'd committed the crime. Then too there was the inescapable fact for a lawman that, for at least a few hours, you'd lost control of a situation you were supposed to be keeping a hold of. For a few hours, in other words, you'd been *beat*.

Reeves Duncan was a placid man. Heavy since the age of four, a copious sweater who smelled, somehow, like potato soup, he moved as slowly as the world and his official duties let him. He frequently found himself contemplating scripture as he rode the tangled woodlands around Atcheson. He liked to hum, and he considered himself a better-than-average dancer, despite his bulk. But like most men in the Thicket, he had a hard side. And Reeves Duncan flat-out didn't like getting *beat*.

Lynching was rare in this corner of the world. It wasn't that the residents of Ochiltree County had any extraordinary generosity of spirit. Nor was it, as Reeves Duncan was generally prepared to concede, that his constituents had any great fear of him personally. It was more because the Thicket was so predominantly white, folks didn't feel like the coloreds were a threat in the same way people in other regions of the South did.

But this sense of security wasn't an entirely reliable safeguard. One of the worst lynchings the sheriff had ever heard about took place in Dillon, a day's ride to the north. Dillon had fewer than thirty black residents. But one evening in the summer of 1906 a retarded colored teenager was arrested on charges of raping a widow woman and her blind sister. After a night of intense questioning, some of it involving the butt end of a revolver, the kid confessed. When word got out, a mob of white men and boys disarmed the local deputy and took the kid—Rance Carter, his name was— to the town square. There they built a bonfire and drank corn liquor to work up their courage. Eventually they pulled down Rance Carter's britches and castrated him with a set of bolt cutters. They sawed off his feet and ears and hoisted him up on a chain over a bonfire. When the shrieking captive climbed up the links of his chain to get away from the fire, they sliced off his fingers as well. They called it the Dillon Barbecue. You could still get postcards of Rance Carter's torso dangling from a cottonwood tree in the town square. In the photograph a dozen blank-faced, vaguely imbecilic citizens of Dillon smiled into the camera. What was left of Rance Carter looked like a charred tree trunk.

Some folks mailed postcards with scenes like this to kinfolk and friends. Reeves Duncan occasionally mused on this fact. He couldn't imagine sending his Aunt Kathleen in Shreveport a postcard of a burnt-up black man to help her pass the time of day. But there were plenty of people who could, and these were the people who would be leading the mob Reeves Duncan was going to have to face if things ever got out of hand in Atcheson. He could name at least a few of them. Sneaky little Fielding Cobb. J.R. Holsan, over at the *Teller*. Black-tempered Willard Mills. But you could never know *all* of them. Violence had an alchemy all its own.

It could turn druggists into demagogues. It could change hostlers and soda jerks into cut-rate White Leaguers, howling for the blood of any nigger they could get their fists on.

Reeves Duncan was brooding so deeply on the prospect of vigilante justice that he was surprised when he looked up and found himself at the little dog run cabin where Clarence East had, until recently, lived with his mother. A lean, white–haired woman with huge, flat feet, Ona East was born a slave in southern Alabama. The Sheriff had never quite known how to take her. She could be as gentle as a kitten when delivering babies, and in fact was Doc McDivitt's chief competition in that line of business. But you could also imagine her skinning a dog with a railroad spike. She was a day or two older than dirt and as tough as boiled leather, a woman with almost no teeth but no problem talking. The problem was, the longer she talked, the louder she got. The sound of her own voice seemed to agitate her. She'd finally grown so angry at an itinerant peddler three months ago that she had a conniption fit. Something broke in her head. Blood started seeping out of her eyes. She died just a few minutes later in her own front yard, a soup spoon clutched in one hand.

Told that Ona's son Clarence was devoted to his mother, and that he was bigger than certain types of tree, the offending peddler took off at a fast walk and hadn't been spied since. Reeves Duncan was glad not to see the old woman around—though he half-expected to hear her voice even now.

The Sheriff reined his sorrel mare through the slash pines in the front yard and rode around Ona East's cabin. There on the back steps, in the shade of a hackberry that had grown up over the spavined roofline of the house, sat Clarence East. He was peeling potatoes and sipping a murky amber liquid from a fruit jar. Even sitting, he was a formidable sight—a sort of minor topological feature. Clarence East weighed two hundred sixty pounds and could bend a horseshoe with his hands. His arms were bigger than most men's legs. He made a living digging ditches and cess pits, but he also cut lumber and had helped build many of the oil derricks that now stood rotting in the swamps of Sour Lake. He was not a man to be trifled with. His skull bore a silver dollar-size indentation where a man named Cleon Anderson once hit him with an axle hammer. People said the blow would have killed an ordinary man. It only irritated East. Cleon Anderson was hauled off in a wheelbarrow twenty minutes later, two of his fingers crushed, his right wrist and left leg snapped like kindling wood. Doc McDivitt thought at first that the man had been run over by a milk wagon. That was the sort of story that got around. Though he wasn't the kind to pick a fight, East scared people. And *that*, Reeves Duncan knew, wasn't good. Scared people held a grudge.

"Hey there, Clarence," said the Sheriff.

East looked up. Reeves Duncan had the sun behind his back, and it took the sitting man a few moments to make out who was speaking. Finally East gave a slow, almost imperceptible nod.

"You keepin' yourself out of trouble?" said the lawman.

"Who wants to know?"

Reeves Duncan was a good judge of men. He generally knew when to talk and when to shut up, when to ramble and when to get to the point. He thought for a moment about mentioning East's momma. Offering his condolences. *Fine Christian woman; meet her at the gates of heaven.* But that might be a mistake. He wasn't sorry Ona was gone. And he sensed—had always sensed—that Clarence East was a man of intelligence. Duncan didn't like the challenge in the big man's voice. But that wasn't what he'd come for. He knew he could play games now and get to the point later or just get it over with. The Sheriff felt another bead of sweat break and roll down the small of his back. This made up his mind. It was too goddamned *hot* for games.

"You cut up a white man out on Sour Lake?" said the Sheriff. "Skinny fella? Little gingery moustache?"

The Negro flinched. He studied Duncan for several long moments, his mouth shut tight. Then he laughed—a bitter, humorless sound. "I ain't never cut nobody," he said. His voice might have come from the earth itself, so deep it was, and elemental.

Duncan nodded. He suspected East was telling the truth. He seemed calm, for one thing—though the corn liquor he was drinking might be responsible for that. *Besides, why would Clarence East need to use a knife?* He could have snapped Leonard Dalchau's neck with his bare hands if he'd chosen to. Could have broken his skull with his fists.

The Sheriff pointed with his chin at the ancient shotgun that stood leaning against the door frame. "Been out lately?"

"This mornin'. Didn't see nothin' though."

"There's people in these parts would just as soon see you dead, Clarence. You know that, don't you?"

The Sheriff paused a moment. He listened to the buzz of the cicadas in the trees and from somewhere not far off, the caw of a blue jay. But his gaze never left East. Now the big man looked up. He had weepy red eyes and a set of high cheekbones, like a Cherokee, though there hadn't been any Cherokees in these parts in over sixty years.

"You ain't so popular yourself, Sheriff," he said. That voice again. Like volcanic rock.

"That's a fact. But the county *pays* me to be unpopular. And my skin's a little lighter'n yours."

East rubbed a hand over the contours of his own jaw. "What else you come for?"

"You heard anything about that killing?" asked the Sheriff.

"People talkin', sure."

"That boy was bled out about as bad as I ever saw. I know you ain't a cutter, so I don't know as I've got a beef with you. But let me tell you this. Nobody gets done like that in my county."

East looked down at his jar. The Sheriff shifted on his saddle and wished he could find some shade. He clawed at the knot of his necktie. It was already loose.

"You hear me, Clarence?" said the lawman. Not that he was scolding Clarence East in particular. He was getting tired of this conversation.

"I hear you."

"So I need to know who done it."

East stared straight at him. He leaned forward, and his massive legs shifted, and Reeves Duncan's hands drew back on the reins before he'd realized what he was doing. The black man was just rearranging his great bulk on the rickety wooden step. He didn't notice the Sheriff's reflexive retreat, or pretended not to.

The Sheriff paused to give his heart a chance to slow. "And you *need* for me to know, too. If you take my meaning."

East nodded. "I heard dogs got your man."

"Could be," the Sheriff conceded.

"Chewed him up pretty good."

Reeves Duncan looked off at Ona East's vegetable garden. It was overgrown, obviously untended. East was drinking too much. You could tell plenty from the state of a man's garden. When he looked back, East was still studying him.

"Law don't think so, huh?" said the black man.

"Never mind what I think. You seen your friend Turner around these parts lately?"

East leaned over and spat to one side of the steps.

"Well?" said the Sheriff.

"Josh Turner ain't no friend of mine. Went on up to Chicago, last I heard. Prob'ly dead by now. 'Less his mouth shrunked up when he left."

"He was handy with a knife, as I recall."

"Knife or a razor. Either one."

"All right. You plannin' on goin' anywhere anytime soon?"

East shrugged. It meant: *Got no place to go.*

"Good," said the Sheriff. "You stick around. And let me know if you hear anything."

With this, Reeves Duncan reined his horse around and headed out of the yard. East didn't bother to watch him leave. He took another sip from the fruit jar. The Sheriff was just out of earshot when the big Negro spoke again.

"Heard plenty already," he muttered. East scanned the tree line beyond his momma's tomato and squash plants, now brown and ruined and hemmed in by stink weed and stickleback. *Woods is movin' closer,* he thought. He could sense without articulating it the deep unspeaking malice that pulsed in the green ranks around him. The Thicket never stopped trying to reclaim its territory, to recapture even the narrow swathes of land it had been beaten and hacked and burned out of. The Thicket was creeping back by inches. By hours. It was stretching out its slender green fingers, looping them around whatever flimsy man-made structures it could touch, pulling itself forward on its ravenous belly. Cicadas hidden in the forest canopy ran through the series of clicks that started their monotonous song, then buzzed again in chorus like tiny demons urging creation on in its incremental dance of chaos and resurgence. Heat shimmied up through the oaks and hackberries into an empty blue sky. Clarence East glanced behind him at the battered shotgun that stood against the doorway. He reached back and grabbed it, sighted down its barrel at the mass of vegetation that surrounded the cabin. It was a wall, he thought. *A green wall.* And it kept moving closer.

"Heard plenty already," he repeated.

6.

Friends of Amos Newton

Four years after his arrival in Texas, Jake Hennessey was still trying to figure out if he was home. His uncle, Walter McDivitt, was not an affectionate man. In fact Jake often wondered if Doc was looking forward to the day when his nephew left the drafty, oversized house they shared. He knew *he* was. Jake had had his fill of his uncle's brooding silences and unexplained shouts in the night. He remembered enough about family life to know it occasionally involved laughter. He knew that a simple conversation shouldn't have to feel like a test, or an interrogation.

Jake had returned to America in July of 1907. Like most eleven year-olds, he was in love with his parents—with his father's splendid moustache, which reminded the boy of a furry bird; with his mother's soaring, sweet voice—and he desperately wanted to stay with them. But that spring his sister Sarah died of cholera in Brazzaville. Brazzaville was on the west coast of the sweltering, mud-choked country then known as the Middle Congo, where Jake's father served as a missionary for the Great Plains Baptist Congress of Churches. Little Sarah's death nearly killed her mother. Sally Hennessey was a perpetually worried, starved-looking woman with a strong chin and weak eyes. She mourned her daughter for almost a month, during which time she ate nothing but cassava and boiled eggs. Her demeanor grew somber, as if she'd been told a troubling secret. As indeed she had. Sally advised her husband that Africa was going to kill them all. She told him the continent was cursed by God and that if he wouldn't help her get her son back to the United States, she would take him there herself. This decided Calvin Hennessey on the spot. If Calvin was anything, he was practical. Sally Hennessey cooked and cleaned and cared for the family. This was important enough. But she also helped him compose his sermons, and she more or less single-handedly wrote up the monthly reports he was required to send home to the elders of the Great Plains Baptist Missionary Convention in Topeka. Calvin knew that without his wife's enormous energy, he would have nothing at all to rely on in that strange and unedifying land. His mission would suffer. The Lord's fields would go untilled. And so little Jake Hennessey—dark-haired, somber, painfully shy—was packed off to America.

As it turned out, Sally Hennessey's presentiments proved accurate. Five months after Jake set sail for New York, Calvin and Sally died when the ferry *Ville de Marseilles* capsized on the Congo River. Sixty-eight Africans perished in the calamity as well—some, it was reported, devoured by the crocodiles that infested the waters just upstream from Brazzaville. In those days the newspapers wouldn't have reported an unseemly detail like this about white passengers. But since the bodies of Calvin and Sally Hennessey were never found, it was difficult to say what actually happened.

* * *

Jake Hennessey seldom dwelt on his discomfort with his uncle. In fact he did a passable job of not thinking about Doc at all. He spent every hour he could at Eben Melton's sprawling pig farm just off the Gosford road. There he and Eben built motors and repaired the drive shafts of windmills and tried to figure out how to improve the various items of machinery they happened upon, traded for, or were flat-out given. Their current projects included two bicycles, a motorcycle, and wireless telegraphy. Eben had vague ambitions of constructing a submarine, but was stumped for some place to test it. Besides, both he and Jake were nervous around water. The two prized above all else an airplane they'd built from a set of plans published in *Modern Mechanix* magazine. It was a rickety six-wheeled contraption obviously modeled on the Wright Brothers' Model B racing aircraft. Eben had christened it the "Fair Field Flyer," though in truth it spent more time rolling, bouncing, and disintegrating than actually flying.

Eben was a heavy-set forty-six year-old bachelor with a milky left eye and a pronounced limp. He had a shock of thick black hair and large, usually grimy hands, and he wore a more or less constant three-day growth of beard. He'd spent five years as chief mechanic for the Gulf, Beaumont & Kansas City Railroad Company in Missouri. He worked for a time supervising construction of the streetcar system in Austin before an accident involving an exploding steam sled left him crippled and partly blind. His attorneys won him a financial settlement from the City of Austin, and Eben returned home to take care of his arthritic mother and run the family farm. He'd always had a head for machines. When he came back to East Texas, he found he liked pigs almost as much. Business was good. Eben expanded operations. In his own way he was the happiest man in the county, though he looked like hell and generally smelled like something that lived under a bridge.

In his mania for invention, Eben Melton was typical of the country. It was the golden age of contraptions. Henry Ford had started pumping out Model Ts in 1901 using his assembly line method, but most machines were less uniformly made. It was only a few years since Orville and Wilbur Wright had fashioned an aircraft out of sailcloth, spruce and a twelve-horsepower engine of their own design. Now tinkerers across the country were devising steam-driven motorbikes and collapsible velocipedes, basement submersibles and mechanical single-row stalk cutters. The mania wasn't solely American. Men in Europe too had come to believe that the right configuration of pistons and pulleys could be made to do just about anything. A Brazilian in France invented an airplane he stood up in to fly—then shattered both his legs in an attempt to demonstrate it. In Bavaria, a man named Wolf invented a hop-harvesting machine that boasted the ability to replace up to 150 migrant workers, mainly gypsies. The Italian Army invaded Turkey in 1910 and outflanked Sultan Mehmed V's forces with a series of lightning-fast maneuvers carried out on bicycles. A young Russian engineer named Igor Sikorsky devised propeller-driven snow sleds capable of carrying men and materiel at tremendous speeds across ice and snow—an invention with obvious military implications for the Czar's northern neighbors. For a young man with mechanical inclinations, the future looked bright indeed. It was apparently going to be loud. And made of metal.

Though he'd started out as Eben Melton's apprentice—grease monkey, wrench-fetcher, chief cook and bottle washer—Jake Hennessey was increasingly the theorist of the two. He was the pencil jockey, the one who could hardly wait to rough out his ideas on a sheet of coarse packing paper or the surface of a pine plank. Eben took the boy's visions and translated them into struts and rivets, muslin and baling wire. There was no question of seniority or rank. It was an aristocracy of ingenuity. Jake had come to love Eben's ramshackle kingdom of pig pens and crescent wrenches and felt most fully himself in it.

Jake only spent time with Doc when his uncle forced him to. This was a rare event, but it did happen. Doc wasn't sure why he required it. On occasion he felt something he recognized as being akin to jealousy. He liked Eben Melton. Eben was one of Ochiltree County's most interesting residents, an intelligent and endlessly curious man who was more or less immune to the snares of small-town propriety. But Doc sometimes resented the pig farmer's hold on his nephew. When this happened, he told Jake to come straight home after school. He'd have the boy bring the buckboard around and he'd take his time as he checked his medical bags. He'd pack everything he could think of, just in case: kerosene for cuts and scrapes; quinine for malarial symptoms and nascent pneumonia; a home-made cherry bark cough syrup; loose-leaf chewing tobacco to treat wasp and bee stings. Then Doc and Jake would ride out together so Doc could check on a newborn, or set a broken arm.

* * *

It was on one of these days in early October that they visited Lydia Terrell. Lydia was a scrawny thing, pale and shy and given to mumbling, and quite obviously perplexed by the challenges of keeping her family fed and healthy in surroundings that flat-out declined to help. But like many women in these parts, Lydia's biggest problems involved the attentions of her husband, who sought out the moist place between her legs with aching regularity. Doc had driven out to check on Lydia's youngest boy, a four-month-old with a nagging fever, and to leave the family with two jars of mayhaw jelly he'd been paid by Evelyn Ash the previous winter. The child was fine. His fever had broken. But Lydia was another matter. She looked worse than Doc had ever seen her: dull hair, bloodshot eyes, fingernails cracked and bleeding. Just twenty-two years old, she could have passed for forty. It was always ticklish to try to give a Terrell anything. They were a furtive, wormy clan, quick to take offense at a slight, difficult to appease thereafter. Doc finessed it this time by insisting that sugar was important to a nursing mother. The jelly, he averred, was a form of medicinal supplement. She'd need it. He pulled out his little prescription tablet and said aloud, "Two bottles...*serum.*" Then he looked up at Jess Terrell. "You'll be able to pay me come spring?"

"Pay you what?" said the farmer.

"A man's gotta eat. Pay me in sweet potatoes. Pumpkins."

Jess Terrell rubbed a rough hand over his beard. Doc could hear the scrape of skin on the coarse hair. "Don't grow no pumpkins in the spring."

"Cucumbers, then," said Doc. "Tomatoes. Long as I can stick a fork in it."

Terrell surveyed the lopsided lines of his home. "You eat eggs?"

"All the time. That's why I keep my leghorns. I'd just as soon wait for the tomatoes. You've got a nice place here, Jess. Thanks for letting me come out."

The little man gazed at his own bare feet, which were covered with the red dirt of the farmyard. "You know better than that, Doc. You're welcome anytime." Jess Terrell glanced back beyond Walter McDivitt toward the buckboard he'd ridden out on. "Hey! Rose Anne, you quit pesterin' that boy."

Doc looked over to see a little red-headed girl climbing down off the wagon. Jake was blushing. He held a spray of daisies in one hand.

The farmer was happy to leave the subject of payment. "Sorry to embarrass your boy there, Doc. Rose Anne's a little friendlier than she needs to be sometimes."

"Nonsense." Doc tried to work up a smile for the little girl. It wasn't easy. Doc didn't smile much. He knew he sometimes frightened toddlers. The funereal frock coat. The greasy black top hat. But Rose Ann seemed to expect adoration. She must have been about six—a skinny little thing but bright-eyed beneath her plentiful freckles, and living proof that flowers could bloom in even the harshest desert. "I've never seen a man yet who didn't like getting a gift from a beautiful gal."

Jess Terrell put a hand in his daughter's hair and drew her close. "This here's a good one," he said. "She helps her mama out. Don't you, peanut?"

"Yes, daddy."

"Wants to go off to school next year though."

Doc saw the spark in the little girl's eyes. She grinned, showing a gap where she was missing two of her upper incisors.

"Best thing for her," said Doc, trying to strike a professorial air. *Unless she wants to look like her mother in the space of a few years. Teeth falling out. Furrows in her brow deep enough to plant corn in.*

"Is he your son?" said Rose Anne, gazing at Jake.

"No, darling. That's my late sister's boy. My nephew, Jacob. He doesn't say a whole lot."

Now they all gazed at the boy. Jake stared down at the reins in his hands, trying to ignore the attention.

"Maybe he's hungry," said the girl.

Doc chuckled. "Oh, he's always hungry. But I think he's a little awkward around the ladies, too."

"Ladies like me?"

"Yes, ma'am," said Doc. This time the smile came a little easier. "Exactly like you."

With this, Rose Anne Terrell executed a crude but unmistakable curtsey in Jake's direction. Then she giggled and went skittering off toward her mother. Lydia Terrell was watching from the little house, hanging on to one of the posts of the front porch as if to hold herself up.

* * *

It was a long ride home, and Doc spent the first half-hour of it brooding. He wondered if Lydia Terrell was going to survive the winter—and what was going to happen to her children if she didn't. *Might ought to tell Jess Terrell to spend a few months sleeping with his hogs till Lydia regains her strength,* he thought. *Give the woman some rest. Give the pigs some excitement.* He hated to see Lydia in such straits. Rife with vermin and thick with pestilence, hot in the summer and wet all winter, the Thicket was no place for a woman—especially a woman as frail and pretty as Lydia Terrell. This conclusion got Doc thinking about his own wife.

Lily had died six months after he left San Francisco for the Philippines. The culprit was blood poisoning from the prick of a rose thorn. The wound was minor, barely noticeable. But it became infected, and the infection went untreated, eventually developing into massive sepsis. Lily's kidneys failed. She died before Doc, three thousand miles away, even knew she was sick. There had been no chance for last words, no opportunity to tell her how much he'd loved her. He wondered if he might have felt better if he'd had that opportunity. *Would the grief have been any less intense?* He doubted it. Doc still missed her when his rounds were done and dinner was over and there was nothing to do but stare out the windows into the night. Sometimes in the darkness he could see them together, Walter and Lily, back in that old place before the war when rooms were filled with light and there was a tall, dark-haired man with a mole at the base of his right nostril who laughed as he held his elegant, thin-boned wife in his arms and smelled the sweet scent of her chestnut hair.

And here he was now, a gray-faced old wading bird, sepulchral in his stained black vestments, brooding over the past, skeptical of the future. Doc noticed he'd infected his nephew with his own sour mood, and he resolved to lift his spirits.

"You keeping up with your lessons?" he asked. Out of the blue.

Jake was watching the sky. It took him a moment to gather his thoughts. "Most of 'em. Mr. Dawkins says he's not sure he can teach me much more mathematics."

"Not if you don't show up at school, he can't."

Jake shrugged. This was an old argument.

Doc continued. "Your mother was a whiz-bang student, you know. Knew every verse Longfellow ever wrote. Used to enjoy showing me up when we did recitations."

"You told me that story," said the young man. He was mildly annoyed about having to utter more than a grunt, but he had to head his uncle off somehow.

"She was a good woman. How she got wrapped up in…
what your father was doing, I don't know."

Jake's usual inclination to defend his father was absent
today, a casualty of the heat.

"Don't get me wrong," Doc continued. "I liked your father
too. He was a good-lookin' cuss, I'll give him that. Wingspan like
a whooping crane. Moustache as big as a broom. I just don't go
in for the Bible thumpin'. I guess you know that by now. And I
don't see why they had to go halfway around the world to do it."

They rode in silence for a minute.

"Guess I've said that before too," said Doc.

"Once or twice," Jake confirmed.

"Why Africa, is what I'm asking. Plenty of sonsabitches
need savin' right here at home. Did I say *that*?"

Jake let out an embarrassed laugh.

"How are you and Eben coming on your motorized
bicycle?"

"We *were* comin' on pretty good," said Jake. "Till Eben
ran it into a fence post."

"Hurt, much?"

"Shoulder's a little sore. He said he was gonna pack it
in mud."

"Pack it in mud," Doc scoffed. "Good Lord. Tell him to
have a gypsy smite him three times with a black cat while he's
at it. In a graveyard. At midnight."

"I think he was afraid to tell anyone. People laugh at him
already."

"That's just because of the flying machine."

Jake paused. This too was an old argument. He tried to
leave it alone, but couldn't. "I don't know why they'd laugh
about that. People been flyin' for eight years now."

"People *have been* flying," Doc corrected him.

"People *have been* flying. For years. Maybe before the
Wright Brothers, dependin' on who you believe. Heck,
there's a *woman* with a pilot's license now, up in New York.
Glenn Curtiss is dropping bombs outta planes for the Navy."

Doc emitted a pinched, humorless laugh. "There's progress for you. Bombs delivered right down your goddamned chimney. My point is, nobody in *Atcheson's* been flying, and they're not going to believe it till they see it. Or until Reverend Keech *tells* 'em they've seen it, at least three times."

"I've seen it. There's plenty of others have too. Josie Guy. Ed Petticord."

"*Mister* Guy and *Mister* Petticord. You've seen it fly?"

"It flies," said Jake. "You could see for yourself if you came out to the farm."

"Eben flew it?" Doc persisted.

"He won't exactly fly it himself. Scared a' heights."

Doc started to ask the logical next questions—*Well, who does fly it, and why on earth would anyone do a damn fool thing like that?*—but the words died in his throat. Two men sat watching them from the shade of a hackberry tree just a few yards off the road. By the time Doc noticed them, it was too late for what he felt the irrational but unmistakable urge to do: turn back.

One of the men was lanky and pale, with angular features and thinning black hair he wore slicked back from his forehead. He had full red lips and a prominent, hawkish nose, and there were dark circles around his eyes, as if they were bruised. He wore a stained black jacket, a white shirt, and heavy, expensive-looking dark pants. There were gold chains around his neck and left wrist, and he wore a ring of the same material on his right hand, set with an emerald the size of an almond.

The man perched beside him was swarthy and thickly built. He had long black hair gathered in a ponytail, and Jake wondered briefly if he was an Indian. But he was bigger than any Indian he'd seen. He had thick eyebrows, a bushy moustache, and deep-set, glittering yellow eyes. His neck and the backs of his large hands were tattooed in blue and red, though Jake couldn't make out any particular design.

"Afternoon," said Doc. Cherokee was happy to stand for a few moments. The old horse whipped his tail around to chase the flies.

The men sat on the bench of an ancient but ornate green coach. The vehicle had a carved wooden pillar at each corner, as if to provide the framework for a protective canopy, and there was a windowless door on the near side of the odd, rounded passenger compartment. *Like a ship's clock on wheels*, mused Jake about the shape of the vehicle. On the door he could see a faded gold emblem depicting some type of bird, with a fiery sunset behind it. No, not a sunset. Those were *feathers*. The bird was a peacock—and a particularly fierce-looking one at that. The conveyance was pulled by a pair of listless gray mares that stared at the dusty earth at their feet. The animals were in sorry shape: manes tangled, coats crusted with mud on the flanks and fetlocks. The smaller horse had an open sore on one shoulder that glistened in the afternoon sun.

"Evening," said one of the strangers.

"Evenin'," said Doc. His voice was louder than normal. He inclined his head to the right, where an overgrown logging trail led across a scrubby field into the Thicket. "Been back to see ol' Amos?"

"We have," said the pale man. Jake struggled to place the accent. It was something refined and Eastern sounding, like the voice of a man who'd spoken to him once on the ship that brought him back to America. This wasn't much of a classification, but Jake seldom met anyone from outside Ochiltree County. It was the best he could do. "We work with Mr. Newton."

"Not from around here?" asked Doc.

The two men considered the question for a good long time. Jake had the feeling they wanted to consult each other. But they stayed still.

"Who's asking, friend?" said the tall man.

"Just me, I guess."

"And who might you be?"

"Walter McDivitt. I'm what passes for the town doctor."

The long-haired man finally spoke. His voice was harsh, rasping—as if it had been damaged on the trip through his throat. "Maybe you should keep passing, then."

Doc gave a polite laugh.

Now the pale one spoke again, as if to make up for his companion's awkward remark. "What news from the medical world, Doctor?"

Doc shrugged. "Medical world's pretty quiet right about now. Some yellow fever over in Lake Charles. Nothing hereabouts, though. How's Amos doing?"

"Mr. Newton is fine, thank you."

"Still drilling back there?" Doc persisted.

"Oh yes," said the pale man. "Yes indeed. Still drilling."

"Bound to turn up something sooner or later, I guess. Haven't seen him around much lately. His back holdin' up?"

The two men seemed to have been struck by a spell of silence.

"Back was hurting last time I saw him," Doc explained. "Thought it might be a disk."

"He says it's doing better," said the pale man. Suddenly he sounded annoyed. "He's very busy."

"You all waiting on someone out here?"

"That's right. Waiting."

Doc paused, expecting more information. When it didn't come, he nodded. "Well, you tell him we said hello."

The swarthy man leaned over and spat. "Who's 'we?'" he said.

"Just me. Doc McDivitt. No need to bother about the boy."

But the swarthy man did exactly that. For the first time he stared Jake full in the face, studying his features like a beast marking its prey. He smirked.

"We'll tell him," said the pale one.

The sun went behind a big bank of cumulus clouds and a breeze seemed to spring up from nowhere, chilling the sweat on Jake's back and arms. The two men sat motionless, staring at Walter and his nephew. It seemed to Jake that their looks were nakedly aggressive, as if they had already begun the process of cutting the meat from their bones. The boy felt his flesh crawling under his shirt. He had an urge to jump out of the buckboard and run for the woods. But Doc just pursed his lips and gave a noncommittal bob of his head. "Much obliged," he said. He gave Cherokee a flick with the traces and the horse took a lazy step sideways, then leaned in and the vehicle started forward. The movement couldn't come soon enough for Jake. There was something *off* about the pale man, he thought—something as rotten and soft as mushrooms growing from the trunk of a fallen tree. *What kind of a coach were the two strangers driving? And what were those blazing peacock feathers meant to represent?* Jake forced himself to keep his eyes on the road, but for twenty yards he imagined he could feel the man's gaze on the back of his head.

"What all's back there?" Jake asked his uncle, nodding at the woods.

"Old lumber mill the Nichols brothers built when they first settled here in the 1870s. Mostly ruined now. Couple of outbuildings. Little warehouse, as best as I can recall. Never amounted to much. The Nichols brothers pulled up stakes and moved to Colorado. Place was deserted the only time I was out there, maybe four years ago. Hard to believe, but not so long ago, Atcheson was a real up-and-comer. Gonna be the next Beaumont, they said. Next *Chicago.*"

Jake sniffed. "I don't think we made it."

"Reckon we didn't," said Doc. "Couldn't even hold on to the county seat."

"Who's Amos Newton?" the boy asked.

"You mean the Great Amos X. Newton? He's the oil tycoon brought in the strike out near Telegraph Hill in 1904. Real gusher, till she played out a few weeks later. But that was only after a couple thousand men, women, and children converged on Atcheson to make their fortune. Amos encouraged it all, of course. Sold stock in his company for fifty bucks a share. Amos is an old carnival huckster. He knows how to make a pitch. They say he made himself a rich man. But not a very popular one, after everything went bust. There are still folks around here who think the whole thing was a fraud—that he salted the well, or maybe bribed the geologist just to make a killing on the stock. I know a few people who'd as soon put a bullet in Amos Newton's belly as give him the time of day."

"What's he doing now?"

Doc shrugged. "Well, like I said. Last I heard, he was still drilling. Bought up a couple thousand acres around Sour Lake, including the Mill, and said he was going to bring in something bigger than Spindletop. Has a few men out there, evidently, though you don't see much of 'em in town."

"Who were those two?"

"Never seen 'em," said Doc. "Can't say I'm sorry, either."

"What do you mean?"

"Something not quite right about 'em, if you ask me."

Jake was relieved to hear Doc shared his apprehensions. A squirrel darted out of the woods in front of the buckboard, but Cherokee never broke stride.

"Why do you say that?" asked the boy.

He and Doc both turned in their seats to look back along the way they'd come. There was no one in sight. The older man gave his nephew a sidelong glance. His voice was lower now. "Amos Newton's back is fine, son. It's his knee gives him problems."

NEGRO BODY FOUND
Law Fears Animal Depredation
Remains Disfigured

The scattered remains of a recently deceased Negro male were found late Tuesday near Atascosa Creek by a pair of youthful hunters, Lucius and Lawrence Wisdom, of Atcheson. A well-placed observer, whose reputation for truthfulness is impeccable, states that the dusky corpus, which bore the marks of animal attack and partial consumption, is that of Josh F. Turner, believed to be 26 years of age, a porter, most recently of Gosford. Sheriff Reeves Duncan indicates that the most strenuous efforts are being made to find the culprits responsible for the attack, most likely wolves or dogs, and to trap and destroy them. There is speculation that the gruesome killing may be related to the recent death of schoolteacher L.S. Dalchau of Kirbyville, aged 20, though Sheriff Duncan thus far denies any link.

Atcheson Teller
October 5, 1911
Page 3, Col. 2

7

Where Men Go

One of Walter McDivitt's peculiarities was his insistence on treating colored people as if they were human beings. He came by the trait honestly. He was the grandson of Joshua and Martha Barnes Hill, Quaker abolitionists who ably and openly assisted the operations of the Underground Railroad in central Ohio in the years before the Civil War. The Hills were said to have helped some three hundred fugitive slaves find freedom in Canada and New England. They operated so openly, and so successfully, that members of the Mississippi Legislature established a $300 bounty for the capture and delivery of Dr. and Mrs. Hill to Jackson.

Taught as a child to respect the inner divinity of all men, Walter remembered the lesson all his life—even as he eventually left other tenets of Quaker teaching behind. Indeed, Doc's only close friend was a Negro physician from St. Kitts named Daris Kendrick. The two met in medical school in 1892 and nurtured their friendship with regular correspondence through the years. Daris had wound up through the entanglements of matrimony in Houston, where he ran a thriving general practice in the neighborhoods of the 4th Ward, west of downtown. Frequently featured in the Red Book, Houston's registry of prominent colored citizens, Daris Kendrick was one of seven colored physicians in the muddy little city. In 1908, he became the first black man in Harris County to own an automobile. It is entirely possible that his friend's presence less than a hundred miles away was the principal reason why Walter McDivitt moved to East Texas rather than sell the house he was bequeathed by the widow Gray.

October 8

My Dear Daris:

Thank you first for asking after Jake. He sends greetings—or would, if he were capable of standing still long enough to consider the matter. He is as ever engaged in various feats of amateur engineering, both practical and speculative, and cannot be hindered by such pedestrian matters as eating, bathing, or forming personal attachments. I fear we are no closer now than when he first came to stay with me. He thinks me queer, no doubt—and seems repulsed by my occasional fits of melancholia. I for my part could be more enthusiastic about the boy's faith in mechanics. He claims now to have fabricated a working aeroplane with his friend and mentor, the sometime pig farmer. No word yet on who is to pilot the apparatus. Perhaps one of the porkers— though the pig is said to be an intelligent beast!

But forgive me if I touch for a moment on darker matters. There is considerable unpleasantness hereabouts. Percy Wisdom's boys were running raccoons on Monday evening and found human remains two miles outside of town along Atascosa Creek, also known as "Turkey Creek," not far from where the locals say a man named Jasper Bivens was killed by a feral hog a few years back. The dead man was a mulatto, in his early twenties and somewhat undernourished. His name was Josh Turner. He had a reputation in the county for petty theft and physical violence and indeed in death he held a straight razor, purportedly his weapon of choice. It seems to have availed him but little.

The victim's throat was torn away. There was evidence of massive hemorrhage and a fierce struggle—fingernails broken, forearms and forehead scored to the bone. The hemispheres of the rib cage had been forced apart and the viscera scooped out through the thorax. I found portions of the scalp and neck lodged in a fork of a nearby sweetgum tree, which suggests the work of one of the big cats that still live hereabouts. Body several days dead, to judge from the state of decomposition, but less bothered than you might imagine by the local wildlife. Indeed, I could find no sign whatever of postmortem predation—strange in a land so teeming with animal life, from red ant to black bear, as the Thicket.

I mentioned a similar incident when I wrote you last: a young schoolteacher from Kirbyville caught out in the thicket north of here and by someone or something torn asunder. Prevalent theory is dogs and no doubt they could be the culprits in the first death but not I think in this, given my recovery of body parts from the tree. The worst of it is, I suspect there may have been other deaths in the region of which no one will ever know.

I believe I have told you about the small community of Croats who lived a few miles southwest of here, on the other side of the Anahuac River. They came as stave cutters— arrived sometime in 1906—several worked in the mill down in Batson. They were never many, maybe twenty souls, loosely organized in a village of one-room pine cabins and at last count no more than a dozen strong. They sold their goods to Eddie Stephens over in Whitehall, traded for sundries here at an establishment called Wally Moon's. Folks rarely saw them then and their visits eventually ceased altogether. They were Roman Catholic of course and a sorry lot: pallid, half-starved, and probably wishing they had never left the Olde Country. They were largely shunned in our thriving metropolis on account of their undeniable odor and generally furtive air—not to mention what our Baptist minister, Mr. Keech, calls their "papish insolence."

Our Keech is a great reader of Reformation propaganda and finds much to disapprove in the Roman traditions, which seem to him to involve various flavors of idolatry and fetishism. To my mind, the Catholicism is a pretext. If Moses himself were to wander out of the Thicket with a tribe of Hebrews in tow, searching for flammable shrubbery, he would be subjected to similar disdain. Though even the most established families in Ochiltree County have been here only seventy years, the locals resent newcomers. As you know this was land only the poorest whites chose to settle. The Thicket presents almost insurmountable barriers to large-scale agriculture, which meant among other things that there were few slaves in the area. In fact the little colored settlement of Freedom, eight miles west of here, was founded by a group of optimistic ex-slaves in the first years of Reconstruction in hopes that the soil of East Texas might support a colony of yeoman farmers. Those hopes have not been borne out and there are only a few souls still on the original survey, though there are numerous reasons for this, not all of which you would be surprised to hear.

But back to the point: the Croatian settlement seems to be deserted now, and no one is around to tell us where the inhabitants went. This second killing has some of us on edge, and perhaps it is nerves that has me thinking about this so monotonously. Is there some more sinister agency of violence at loose in the dark corners of the Thicket? I hesitate even to say these things, not knowing whether to dread more that they are shown to be true, or that it is my mind that works so unreliably again. I am sorry if I have clouded your consciousness today. Forgive me, old friend. I have no one else to confide in. The Thicket is a strange place, still in many precincts physically impassable. I wish it yielded its secrets more readily. I wish I knew where men go when they leave.

Yours etc.
Walter

8.

Petticord

Edmund Alfonse Petticord had the lively blue eyes of a child. He was slender and soft-spoken, a wraith of a man with sloping shoulders and a loafing, hangdog gate. Though his head was slightly too small for his body, his face was pleasant enough, handsome even, and surmounted by a shock of cloud-white hair that would have done credit to a Georgia senator. Not that he cared. Edmund Petticord had no concern for his appearance or the appearance of others. He held no gainful employment and had no apparent desire to obtain any. He was, in short, a happy man. This made him unpopular. He lived with his two spinster aunts and helped them financially whenever he could. He occasionally sold his knowledge of the whereabouts of a promising bee hive for a few cents. He collected mayhaws and sassafras root for Wally Moon to sell at the mercantile, and he had been known to show up in town with a cloth sack full of Solomon's seal or valerian that he sold to Henry Gayle at the drugstore for fifty cents. But mostly what Edmund Petticord did was ramble. When the weather was fine he would set out from home with a sandwich in a pocket of his overalls and stay gone for days. The aims of his wanderings were unclear, but he'd been spotted as far north as Palestine and as far south as the Bolivar Peninsula. He slept in trees and ate honey and acorns, blackberries and wild onions. He was also said to snack on grasshoppers, like some unruly Old Testament prophet. It was a rumor that fascinated the nine-year-olds of Atcheson.

Petticord showed up at Doc's house one afternoon as the shadows of the live oaks were growing longer in the overgrown back yard. Mrs. Grady had set out ham sandwiches and buttermilk, and Doc and Jake were finishing their supper at the little table in the kitchen. Invited in and warmly welcomed, Petticord emptied one of his pockets to reveal a dead cicada wasp, a baby corn snake, three acorns, a snail shell, and a fistful of St. John's wort wrapped in a blue kerchief. Doc took a closer look. He frequently prescribed the plant as an antidote for melancholia. He'd heard old Ona East had used it as an abortifacient, mixed with her usual concoctions of tansy and pennyroyal. Ethical scruples aside, Doc sometimes wondered if he should give it a try. Lydia Terrell might be thankful for a dose or two. But he was letting his thoughts wander. He purchased this new bunch for thirty-five cents. More than it was worth, probably, but Doc added the premium to encourage his supplier. He offered to pour his visitor a cup of coffee, but the offer was declined.

"Headed home?" said Doc.

Petticord nodded. He stuffed the little snake back in his pocket.

"You're welcome to bunk here for the night," Doc offered. "If you don't mind a little shady company, that is."

Doc had forgotten that Edmund had trouble with jokes. The slender man was silent for almost a minute before he said, "I don't figure you and Jake to be shady company."

Doc transferred the herbs to a clean white cup towel. "Well, thank you, Edmund. The feeling's mutual. You've been on the tramp, I presume?"

"East a ways. Up Sand Creek. Gonna be cold this winter."

"That right?"

"Oaks still puttin' on bark," Petticord said.

"Any rain in store?"

"Not yet."

Jake looked up from his notebook. "You ain't scared bein' out in the Thicket by yourself?"

"*Aren't* scared," said Doc.

Petticord looked from one face to the other. "Not generally, no. I aren't scared."

"Say there's wild dogs hereabouts," Doc interjected.

The visitor glanced out the doorway into the yard. "Ain't seen dogs—a pack of 'em, anyhow—in a couple of years."

Doc went to the stove to light a cigar. "Well, you would know, I suppose. But..." He too looked outside. There wasn't much to see: oaks and sweetgums standing amidst their own brown ruins as night crept in from the Thicket, a few spindly Chinese tallows starting to turn orange for the fall. "I suppose I should tell you. There have been some... there's been a couple of bodies found recently. Possible dog-attack victims. Maybe some other animal. I guess I'm trying to advise you to be careful out there."

"Appreciate that, Doc. You be careful too." Petticord turned to the boy. "Be home by dark."

Something in the little man's voice was different. Even Jake noticed it. He set his pencil down.

"You trying to tell us something, Edmund?" said Doc.

Petticord hummed a little to himself. He was a man who couldn't be rushed. He stared straight ahead, as if the wall across from him was the future and he was looking into it as easy as he pleased.

"I seen it," he said.

"Seen what?"

"Thing that did them killings. I seen it from a tree."

"What kind of thing?" said Jake.

"What tree?" said Doc. He spoke calmly, so as not to spook the quiet loner. "Where were you?"

"Out on the Trace, about a month ago. Lookin' for bees. Around about six-thirty—around suppertime—I had one of my spells. When I come to, it was full dark. I knew I was in a bad spot. Too far from town. Too weak to walk. And there was a smell in the air I didn't much like. So I found myself a tree—big old red oak, maybe fifty foot tall—and climbed up as high as I could. Nothing happened for the longest time. Just night in the Thicket. Heard an owl out huntin'. Hogs about a quarter mile off, just after the moon come up. Must have slept some, now that I think about it. But around four, just as the east was startin' to light up, the whole woods went still. Not a breeze. Not a skeeter. Nothing. That's when I woke up. I spotted him maybe forty yards off, across the edge of the clearing. He knew I was there. He could smell me, maybe, but he couldn't get a fix on me. So he stood there, watchin', and I lay there watchin', and neither of us moved a muscle. I knew if I even shifted my weight, he'd a' seen me. I can be still, Doc. Still enough to watch deer feed and never spook 'em, and that's what I was."

Petticord seemed to want some sort of acknowledgement.

Doc chimed in: "You can be mighty still, Edmund. That's for sure."

"Might as well a' been dead. He didn't like it. Wasn't used to it, I reckon. He thought he'd flush me, and I could feel him pulling me out. Sort of froze my heart, like. I could feel him searchin', feel him comin' like mist drifting through the trees. It was just a matter of time, and I thank the Lord he run out of it. Soon as the sun started to break through them trees, he disappeared. I waited a bit. I waited a good long while, I guess. Then I climbed down and walked to town."

"Walked?" said Jake.

"Yessir."

"You didn't run?"

"I didn't."

"Why not?"

Petticord bit his lip. "Wouldn't a' made no difference," he said.

Doc sat down at the table. "What makes you think this—was it a *man?*"

"Wasn't a man. I don't know what it was. Big, though. And quiet. Like a walking shadow, is the best I can say it. I just call it a he."

"What makes you think it had anything to do with the killings?"

Petticord set down the leaf he'd pulled out of his pocket. Though Doc had asked the question, Petticord looked Jake straight in the eyes for longer than the boy cared to look back. Jake had bent his head to his drawing when Petticord spoke again.

"Doc, I been out in them woods a long time. I know what kills and what don't. This thing kills."

"It walks? Upright?"

"Like a man. Mostly."

"What does that mean?"

"*Jerky* somehow," said Petticord. He seemed puzzled by his own recollection. "Like a mantis. Stiff."

"Did you happen to tell the Sheriff about this?" said Doc.

"He didn't ask."

"Can *I* tell the Sheriff?"

"Sure you can." Petticord thought about it a minute. "Prob'ly should. But I'd best get movin'. I got ground to cover. We'll talk again if you want."

"I wish you'd stay," said Doc.

The little man stood and folded his blue kerchief. "I'll be all right. Gotta get goin' though."

"I'll come see you. If you don't mind talking some more about this thing you saw."

"I don't mind. You know where I live."

With this, Edmund Petticord walked out the door and headed off into the oaks. Jake watched him go. There was open field just past the trees, then pasture land and a road after that. Petticord's home was out there somewhere, thought Jake, though he'd never seen it. The little man disappeared into the gloom under the trees in less than a minute. The sky was a deep blue now—almost purple, like a bruise. The first stars swam into view.

"Might lock that door," said Doc.

Jake was already turning the latch.

9.

Letters

Houston October 12, 1911

Dear Walter:

I am sorry to hear of your animal problem which has so far gone unreported in Houston, even in the pages of such estimable Fourth Ward journals as Jeffrey Jackson's Jimpelcute. I say "animal problem" because I cannot but dismiss as misguided your other avenue of speculation— i.e., the "more sinister agency of violence"—if indeed you were serious about it.

We are in good health and tolerable spirits here, feeling finally as if we have crawled out from under the heat and general oppression of summer on the bayou. Do you remember the feel of October in Cambridge? Despite the general sogginess of the Gulf Coast, I can always recall the smell of the Charles and the wood smoke of the first few hearth fires burning. Possibly that will become for me an unreachable perfect past and I will never know anything as sweet again. Ah, but I wander the lanes of a land long lost to us. Back to work, my friend—always for me a panacea. Would a visit from yours truly be taken amiss? It has been too long. As you know I am reluctant to tarry in the Thicket but for your sake I will venture all.

With greatest affection,
Daris

P.S.   I am enclosing a copy of Bram Stoker's Dracula, suitable for long evenings by the fireside and cultivation of phantasmagorical flights of fancy.   I daresay it will prove safer than your former avenue.

Atcheson
October 16

My Dear Daris–

I am aware that Mr. Stoker's book is fiction, and not particularly good fiction at that, because I read it several years ago. A good deal of it is in the form of letters—letters like these, actually—and so the narrative takes twice as long to move the expository furniture about as it ought. It is a slap-dash, lurid, and wholly vulgar work (a work for women, clearly). And yet I'm glad you sent it. My interest is not in the novel itself but in the legends that inspired it.

Legends are almost always based on facts. These facts may become distorted by subsequent artifice, but if one digs through enough fat the bone is exposed at last. The bone in this case is the Eastern European belief (mirrored, I should say, by the beliefs of numerous other races, in various regions of the world) in the existence of creatures that nourish themselves on human blood. They are said to rise from their graves to walk at night, and can only be dispatched by being beheaded and buried upside down at a crossroads. Indeed to this day in the Carpathian region certain corpses are ritually rid of their skulls before burial. On quite the opposite side of the globe, Andean peasants tell of the pishtaco, an undead ghoul who eats the fat of human children. Filipino villagers fear the aswang, a vampirical creature that craves the taste of human liver and female fetuses; it can assume the shape of a bat, a pig, or a black dog. There are numerous Chinamen on the islands and they have brought with them from their homeland an extensive pantheon of ghosts and

*vengeful succubi. In the legends of some races the vampire is
a demon, set on earth to torment the unwary and unwise. In
other cultures the things were once human, but have become,
through some pathology I cannot pretend to understand,
different—strange—monstrous.*

*A six-year-old girl named Rose Ann Terrell has gone
missing here. She is the daughter of a local farmer, and not
the sort to wander. A pretty thing—bright as a penny—
proof the human spirit can blossom though sown in meager
soil. She was last seen four days ago. Neighbors have been
scouring the Thicket and nearby farmlands. The county's
hounds have been employed, thus far to no effect, and the
child's mother is beyond despair. Davis, I know you think
me hysterical. Perhaps I would think the same of you, were
our positions reversed. But I assure you my speculation is
grounded in sober observation. Consider the record: this
disappearance, along with two violent deaths in the past
several weeks, without a single piece of evidence adduced
by anyone to identify the killer. And yet we know the deaths
are not random. The modus operandi is clear. In each case
the victim has been found with his throat ripped away and
the corpse almost completely drained of blood. In each case
too the remains have gone unmolested by the local wildlife—
even insects.*

*A local man, a sort of idiot savant named Edmund
Petticord, told me recently that he had encountered what he
described as a walking shadow, and the one clue we have
from a victim—that unfortunate schoolteacher I wrote you
of—is the word "MONSTE" daubed on the flyleaf of a book
he carried.*

*Speculation about the killer has focused on some sort
of wild beast—a bear or large cat or even, as you say (and
as I myself first tended to believe), a pack or packs of dogs.
Unfortunately the few faint tracks found near the bodies
seem unlike the prints of any known animal predator. This
is a fact that the local sheriff has so far managed to keep*

sub rosa, so have a care. I should add also that a vocal minority in the community think the deaths attributable to a colored man named Clarence East, a hulking semi-mute of immense strength, evidently cretinous or nearly so. Most of these people have had no opportunity to examine the bodies, as I have. Thus they cannot know the extent of the damage done to them.

Now whether our killer is truly a creature of the underworld or, as is considerably more likely, some misguided soul who <u>believes</u> himself to be a creature of the underworld—a wight; a fiend; a vampire or lycanthrope—I know not. But it seems clear to me that it can only assist us in our efforts to apprehend this monster if we attempt to understand both its pathology and its psychology. I therefore intend

[Additional pages missing]

October 21, 1911

My Dear Walter,

I hardly know whether to feel alarm or amusement at your musings. I share your puzzlement at the deaths you report, and I understand though of course I cannot completely share your increasing concern for the people around you. But Walter this is no cause for abandoning discipline and the power of rational thought.

As you know I perform the not inconsiderable number of autopsies called for in connection with Houston's population of Negros, as the esteemed Dr. Henry DeGroot, our county coroner, does not care to associate with members of our dusky race even when we are safely dead, and thus unable to cast our predacious glances upon the chicken-like throats of his womenfolk. Over the course of the past several years I have seen the grisly results of perhaps sixty shootings, a similar number of knife and razor fights, four arsenic poisonings, a dozen bodies burned beyond recognition, several hangings and numerous drownings. I have seen grown women starved to death by men who professed undying love for them and I have catalogued children's skulls split open with axes, hammers, and the butts of revolvers. I therefore feel qualified to assure you that human beings are perfectly capable of finding ways to exterminate each other without assistance from the supernatural.

I suppose this is all by way of saying that whatever otherworldly agency you imagine is active in Ochiltree County, dismiss it from your mind. If ferae naturae are not to blame for these maulings, you are dealing with the handiwork of a particularly industrious maniac—nothing more nor less. History is replete with examples of the breed. London had its Jack the Ripper, known, as you will recall, for slashing the throats of his victims and hacking out of their torsos various internal organs, including, in two of the murders, the uterus. Closer to home, you may have heard of the so-called "Servant Girl Annihilator," who brutally murdered (as if a murder could be anything but brutal) several young women in Austin in the winter months of 1884-85. Neither man—for I think we can safely assume that in both cases it is a man rather than a member of the fair sex we are discussing—was ever apprehended. For all we know the Austin killer is now serving in our state legislature.

If your local constable (and I picture here a particularly uninspiring specimen of the breed, block-headed and somewhat slow of speech) cannot cope with the task at hand, I suggest you write posthaste to Austin. I am no great admirer of our state police, but by reputation each Ranger comes fully licensed to kill vermin of various descriptions, along with any unfortunate bean-eater, however virtuous, who happens to find himself in the vicinity. Whatever else *can be said of this type, it is familiar with the workings of the shotgun. Ghost stories are one thing. I have yet to see the killer who cannot be made to see reason when it comes clad in lead.*

Steady, old friend. You have long since overcome your demons. Do not let them loose in the castle again. Look to your semi-mute hulk—your swarthy Caliban!—and I suspect you will have found your murderer.

Daris

October 27

Daris:

I cannot blame you for your skepticism but I have no time to argue. I am more than ever convinced that there is something at large in the woods hereabouts and it must be killed or caught before we have more bodies to bury. I have located three of the reference works I am seeking through correspondence with a bookseller in New Orleans, recommended to me by a source from whom I buy other products on occasion. I am not a stupid man; I trust no one from Louisiana. In this instance however I have no choice. I have struck my bargain, dear as it is, and await delivery. I will write again as soon as I have additional information: or theories.

I beg you keep me in your thoughts and prayers. Best wishes also and love to Miriam and Liza. May we meet again old friend may Providence protect and defend us all.

Walter

NOVEMBER 1, 3:28 P.M.

WALTER:

YOUR LETTERS LEAVE ME UNEASY STOP LEAVE HOUSTON SATURDAY A.M. BY TRAIN ARRIVE ATCHESON EVENING STOP STAND FAST STOP

10.

McDivitt's Research

The books arrived the next day. There were three of them: *Empire of Shadows*, by Lucius von Kreisler; *A Thesis on Certain Occurrences in the Gujarat Province, 1852-54*, by Alistair St. John; and an 1844 translation into English of the *Phenomenologica Obscurae* by St. Anselm of Ondkirk. Jake saw the package on the dining room table and ripped it open without even glancing at the address. He grabbed *Empire of Shadows* from the stack, flipped the yellowed pages, and started reading:

> *The night walker is a beast of enormous cunning. Like the wolf or the lion, it chooses its victims from the weakest of the community that furnishes its sustenance, generally at such times as, through happenstance, the victim is alone. Nighttime offers the beast its preferred hunting conditions. It sees with exceptional acuity in the darkness, and is furthermore untroubled by the superstitions of men, which render us easily cozened and intimidated in the hours after sundown. Indeed the vampire is a creature of shadow entirely. Because it is evil, and tainted by sin, it is sickened unto death by exposure to sunlight and evidence of the greatness of God's creation. For this reason confrontation of the undead is only to be undertaken during daylight hours, when the creature's strength is greatly vitiated. The testimony of the cleric Alfonse of Brno illustrates this point. In July of 1615 a vampire killed two maidens in the village of Otrabirsk and left behind only portions of their naked young bodies,*

strewn like the petals of daisies in the mud. A group of men tracked the creature to a cave in the forest only a few rods from the village. They thought to take the vampire in this cave but misjudged the length of the day, and so approached the lair of the beast at dusk. One man grew fearful and retreated to the village, for which act, he later reported, he was roundly ridiculed by his companions. However, of those who continued on, not one made it home alive. One night a week later their severed heads were returned to the village, with each grisly trophy set upon the doorstep of the dwelling its owner formerly occupied. This testimony was vouched for under oath by fourteen good men of the parish. A monument to the dead stood in the churchyard of Otrabirsk until 1636, when Protestants wantonly—may God have mercy on their souls—destroyed it, along with all the glass contained in the church itself, and many of its most holy possessions, including a strap from the sandal of John the Baptist. By then the parish was much reduced, having suffered the deaths of 108 persons through violent or unexplained causes over the course of the previous seventeen years. Many moved away from the accursed place, and today wolves prowl the ruins of both village and church. Such is the power of these unholy creatures, who walk in the shadow of the Evil One and without mercy prey upon the faithful.

"Jake!" said Doc. He stood at the doorway, holding his coat. "What are you doing?"

Jake jumped involuntarily. "I don't know," the boy responded. It took him a moment to collect himself. He stepped away from the book. He wasn't sure whether to laugh or to run. "Reading."

"Those aren't your books."

Jake nodded. "That's for sure."

"Son, this is none of your affair. Do you understand?"

"What's none of my affair? Are you thinking the killings...?"

Doc swept the book up and placed it under one arm. His face was bright red. Convinced though he was of his intuitions, and of his need to follow them, Walter McDivitt was nevertheless aware that the tomes he'd received harkened back to a primitive and irrational age. "I said, *it's none of your affair*. And I'll thank you not to interfere with my things. Get to your room, sir."

Jake didn't argue. He took the stairs two at a time. Doc slammed his fist on the table, then gripped the back of the nearest chair till the blood drained from his head. It was bad enough, he thought, that his fears were starting to master him. He was *not* going to have his nephew brought into this... *investigation*. In fact, it might be time to send him away. Jake had relatives on his father's side somewhere in Oklahoma. Ardmore? Was that it? Doc gathered they were block-headed, Bible-thumping relatives, but they were relatives just the same. And nothing happened in Oklahoma. It might be the perfect place for the boy. *Get him out the Thicket*, at any rate. Doc stared at the leather-bound volumes on the table. He'd been informed by the New Orleans dealer that the books were exceedingly difficult to come by. This meant, of course, that they were horribly expensive. But this was no time for pinching pennies. There was something evil in the woods around Atcheson. Doc wasn't sure what it was, but he knew it was out there. There were the bodies, first of all, violated beyond anything Doc had ever seen. *All the blood gone. What else could that mean? Why would something drain the blood from a man except for sustenance?* He thought about Edmund Petticord's story. *This thing walks like a man.* But Edmund had known at once that despite its outward seeming, the creature was something other than human. *MONSTE, the schoolteacher had written.* The Sheriff hadn't particularly wanted to disclose this detail, but he felt like he had to tell someone—especially after Doc had related the story of Ed Petticord's encounter in the woods. Walter McDivitt surveyed his stack of books again. He knew ninety percent of what he was about to read was hokum. *But what about the small percentage that remained? What about the deaths no one ever accounted for? What about the shadows no one could explain?* He heard Jake's footsteps thump across the floor above him. At almost the same time, the clock in the parlor struck ten. The sound jarred Doc from his musings. He took a bottle of whiskey down from the top shelf of the armoire in the corner and set it on the table in front of him. He had work to do.

He'd do it, too.

As soon as he had a drink.

11.

Daris Kendrick

He was a short, bald black man with a snow-white beard, an enormously wide, flat nose, and a rolling lopsided walk. He was struggling with the weight of two large valises. Jake opened the front door and the man stopped in front of him on the porch.

"You can just put them bags in the first room upstairs," said Jake.

The stranger set the valises down with a heavy sigh. He produced a red handkerchief from a pocket in his jacket and mopped at his face, though the afternoon was cool. Jake figured the man couldn't have made it much more than another step or two.

"You must be Jacob. A Hennessey, if I'm not mistaken." The stranger's English was flawless. Sonorous. Elegant. Jake blinked, trying to account for what he was hearing.

"Jacob Hennessey?" the Negro repeated.

"Just Jake's fine. Where's Dr. Kendrick? He was supposed to be here for dinner."

"Dr. Kendrick."

"You didn't come with Dr. Kendrick?"

"Not exactly. No."

The boy opened his hands, arched his eyebrows.

A half-smile appeared on the black man's lips. It disappeared just as quickly, as if this was a joke he'd grown tired of long ago.

"I *am* Dr. Kendrick."

Jake struggled for words. The man looked past him into the house.

"Is your uncle around?" said the doctor.

"He went to see to Miss Terrell. He should be back directly, though. She's staying in town." Jake paused. "She has…you know. Her head hurts."

"Ah, yes. *Cephalgia.* I'm familiar with the beast. You said *Terrell?* Lydia Terrell? The woman whose daughter has gone missing?"

"That's right. Not much hope, is what they're saying. Not to her face, though."

The black man nodded. "The longer the hunt, the less likely the prospect of success. First room up the stairs? That still the plan?"

"What's that? Oh. The bags. Um, yeah. I mean, yessir. First room."

Daris stepped past Jake into the house. He left his suitcases for the boy to carry. Might give him something to do, the doctor figured, besides *gape.*

        ✼ ✼ ✼

Somehow Doc knew Daris had arrived. He swept into the house a few minutes later, calling his old friend's name as if it was a battle cry. Daris came pounding down the stairs from his second-story room and the two men laughed and hugged and thumped each other on the back. They made an odd, ungainly pair, Doc tall and pale and haggard, his black friend short and plump and white-maned.

Jake pretended to read the *Teller* in the parlor as Doc brewed a pot of coffee. The two men carried on their conversation in the kitchen. Doc sometimes read his letters aloud to his nephew as he composed them, so Jake knew most of the stories: Medical school. Cambridge. Old friends and misadventures. But there was a liveliness in his uncle's voice he hadn't heard in a long time. Jake wasn't sure what caused it, but he enjoyed the sound nonetheless. It was like a glimpse of blue sky after a long spell of showers. After the opening round of inquiries about family and business and classmates, Doc and Daris spent twenty minutes commiserating over Harvard's decision to let two-year men into the medical program. It was a disastrous move, they agreed. Hasty. Ill-advised. Bound to dilute the quality of both student and studies. Not that the students were all that impressive in the first place, Daris said drily. This remark set them off again, and the conversation careened back into the past. Now they reviewed the various misadventures of their classmates, from Hudspeth's Missing Monkey to Thompson Wakes Among the Cadavers. Fresh gales of hilarity ensued. Daris Kendrick's hearty, booming laughter, like small explosions in a distant boiler, mingled with Doc's reedy, almost girlish giggles. It was an hour before the talk slowed and Daris's face grew serious at last.

"Walter," he said, leaning back against the kitchen wall. "All levity aside. I'd like to take a look at you."

Doc chuckled. "I wondered when you were going to get to that. The letters, right? You can examine me to your heart's content, Dr. Kendrick. But you'll be wasting your time."

"We'll just take a look anyway. Somewhere with a little more light. You don't mind?"

"Two lamps in the parlor," said Doc. "That's where I see my patients, once they've demonstrated they have the means to compensate me for my services. If they've managed to steal a chicken, for example."

"How have you been eating?" asked Daris, as they returned to the room where Jake was seated.

"Orally," said Doc. He seated himself at the edge of his flat-top desk.

"Funny."

"Like a horse."

Doc's eyes flicked over to meet those of his nephew. This wasn't true, but Jake bit his tongue.

"Any sleep?" asked Daris.

"I sleep."

"How much?"

"A little less, lately. But so will you. You shouldn't have come."

Daris placed his thumbs on Doc's cheeks, stretching the skin to expose the membranes of the eyes. "Right. The Monster of Ochiltree County. Some inflammation here. You've consumed alcohol in the past day or two?"

"Damn straight I have."

Kendrick made a little movement with his hands: *Let's hear it.*

"Whiskey, Daris. Enough to pickle a pachyderm."

"No dances with the green fairy?"

"None," said Doc. "I gave that up years ago. You know that."

"I know what you tell me. But why the whiskey, if you've committed to sobriety?"

"I've committed to no such thing. Whiskey takes the edge off. Blurs the dreams. The absinthe used to make them more vivid."

"So. Nothing hallucinogenic since…when? Since your nephew came to live with you?"

Dr. Kendrick glanced over at Jake.

"The boy," said Walter. "Yes."

"The boy?"

"What?" said Doc.

"I don't know if you've noticed, Walter, but that's no boy. That's a young man."

Jake blushed. He knew he was being patronized, but he appreciated the words just the same. He took another sip of coffee. Doc was staring at him, but he didn't say anything.

"So," said Daris, milking his white beard. "Are we able to eliminate alcohol as the cause of your…*anxieties* lately?"

Doc shook his head. The bravado he'd shown earlier was gone. "You keep thinking this is all in my head, Daris. It's not.

Some of the same things I started drinking to forget. They've come *back*. Only worse."

"The Philippines," said Daris. "It plagues you still."

Doc held up his hands. "That's enough."

"I get it," said Daris. "Don't want the *boy* to hear, eh? Fine. We'll continue this later. First, I'd like to see you get some rest."

"Rest," said Doc. He laid his forehead in one palm. "Maybe you're right."

Doc didn't really mean it. He needed sleep. That was true enough. He needed a week's worth of sleep. In the final analysis, though, *rest* wasn't going to solve anything. But he'd had enough argument. He'd grown weary of this conversation and its general direction. He felt claustrophobic, out of sorts. It occurred to him that his oldest friend was well on his way to becoming, with the best of intentions, his biggest obstacle.

* * *

For supper they ate baked ham and boiled cabbage delivered by Doc's housekeeper, Mrs. Grady. Kathleen Grady lived with her invalid husband a few minutes outside of town. She was a dour, tight-lipped Presbyterian from northern Ireland who muttered to herself as she worked. Mrs. Grady cleaned better than she cooked, but she was maniacally punctual and she knew better than to touch Doc's books or to discuss his affairs. She cocked an eyebrow to see Daris Kendrick sitting at the same table with Doc and Jake, but Doc ignored her.

* * *

Later that evening, Daris found Jake sitting at the cherry wood dining table, a dark and immensely heavy Victorian construction Doc had inherited along with the house. The boy had a copy of *Scientific American* open in front of him, and was sketching wing designs on a piece of brown paper.

Kendrick sat down across the table. He studied the magazine through a pair of gold-framed spectacles.

"Anything interesting in there?"

"Not really," said Jake.

"Something about aeroplanes, though. I can see that. Your uncle tells me you're quite the engineer. Even built your own flying machine."

The boy shrugged. "Eben does most of the building."

Daris placed a stubby finger on one of the illustrations. "Yes? And your machine looks something like this?"

Jake turned the magazine around so the black man could see it better. "That's the *June Bug*," he said.

"Indeed. Does look a bit like an insect, I suppose."

Jake grinned in spite of himself. "That's just the name. It's got one of Glenn Curtiss's engines in it. He was the pilot too. It made the first American flight longer than one kilometer."

Daris produced a meerschaum pipe from his vest pocket and examined the bowl. "I thought they were flying further than that these days."

"Sure they are. This magazine is a couple years old. There's a man flying clean across the country this summer."

"Is that the soda pop plane?"

Jake glanced up. Daris Kendrick clearly knew something about aviation, though he didn't care to admit it. "That's right. The *Vin Fiz*. Company's giving him fifty cents for every mile he travels. He's following the railroad lines. He's already crashed it three times, though."

"Imagine that." Kendrick took a long look at the illustration. Then he leaned back in his chair. He retrieved a tin of tobacco from his jacket and started filling the bowl of his pipe. "No wonder I'm not interested in aeroplanes."

"You will be, though. Everyone will."

Daris jutted his bottom lip, paused to consider the notion. "I'll take your word for it. But let me ask you something. Something on a different subject entirely. Are you and your uncle getting on alright?"

Jake shrugged. He wasn't sure he knew how to answer a question like this—or whether he even wanted to answer it. Aside from their occasional arguments, it wasn't like living with Doc was *uncomfortable.* Jake just felt lonely sometimes. Isolated. He knew Doc was unhappy and he figured the biggest favor he could do for his uncle would be to leave Atcheson once and for all. Find work. Or go off to college. Just…*go.* He looked up and caught Daris studying his face. Sweet-smelling smoke from the black man's pipe curled toward the ceiling.

"I hope you aren't offended by my interest," said Daris. "I've known your uncle for a long time now. I worry about him. He had some bad times in the service. We weren't sure he was going to make it. I'm not sure all of him did."

"I don't know what you mean by that."

Daris Kendrick used his thumb and index finger to massage his own temples. For a short man he had very large hands. "It means we old-timers worry too much, I suppose. Your uncle and I were in medical school together. You know that. You're probably sick of hearing it. But what you may not know is that your uncle was one of the few students who would have anything to do with me.   Defended me once, from a valiant Kentuckian who thought I'd slighted him by entering a dining room before he did. There was talk of a duel." Here Daris made an antic face. "A *duel!* Can you imagine? Pistols at dawn. That sort of thing. Your uncle offered to be my second. It never happened, of course. I wouldn't be standing here if it had. This fellow I insulted by walking in front of finally decided there was no profit in dueling with a black man, and I didn't try to convince him otherwise. But your uncle and I became friends after that, and we've stayed friends now for eighteen years." He looked at the floor. "Like I said. I worry about him."

Jake nodded. The silence was broken only by the ticking of Doc's grandfather clock. "He ain't sleepin'."

"Isn't sleeping."

"Okay. Isn't sleeping. I know he said he was, but he ain't. I can tell you that."

Daris nodded. "I figured as much. But I suspect tonight will be different. I've given him something that should help."

"Medicine?" said Jake.

"Of a sort."

Daris stood up and wandered into the kitchen. He dumped the contents of his pipe in an empty sauce pan, poured himself a cup of cold coffee from the pot that stood on the cupboard, and added several spoonfuls of sugar. He stirred the coffee absentmindedly and was surprised to see the boy enter the room just a few moments later.

"What's the green fairy?" asked Jake.

"The what?"

"I heard you say *green fairy* before. When you were talking to Doc."

"You heard right. And maybe I shouldn't have…but never mind. What's true is true. The green fairy is absinthe. It's a narcotic beverage produced in Europe from a plant called wormwood. Like whiskey, I suppose, only more potent—and more addictive. It makes people see things that aren't there. Makes 'em think there's not much of a point to life except taking that next sip. It can kill a man. Has killed plenty. And now your uncle, he—. He had a fondness for absinthe. It was a distraction for him and at one point it got worse than what he was trying to distract himself from. It was an ugly war, Jake. The Philippines. I don't know how much you know about it, but our military did some terrible things over there. Your uncle was with a platoon of Marines that wiped out the male population of several villages on Samar. They were cursed roundly, and many times over, by the survivors. They're probably *still* being cursed. One set of imprecations they heard at the time was uttered by an old woman who was said to be a witch. The story sounds ridiculous. The Marines had just arrived at some fly-blown hamlet when the woman confronted them. She spattered them with pig blood. Then she sliced off one of her own fingers, and there was a great deal of screaming and confusion. Walter tried to ignore the whole thing. He knew exactly why he and every other white soul on that island was being cursed. But one of the Marines, a particularly violent sergeant who hailed from Oklahoma, was offended. He dispatched the witch with a pistol shot to the forehead. Walter told me he didn't think much of the incident at the time. He'd seen so much death, the atrocities tended to blur. But his platoon got lost when it tried to rendezvous with its company on the other side of the island. Nineteen men went into the jungle. Only four came out, including your uncle. He's never told me exactly what happened during the couple of weeks he was lost. I'm not sure he even remembers it all, and what he does recall makes very little sense. He says the jungle tried to *keep* them. One man died of a snake bite, four others of fever. Two drowned. One of them—the sergeant I mentioned—cut his own throat with a bayonet, and two more were hacked to death by the natives. It's unclear what happened to the others. There are men who can go through that sort of thing and forget it— or at least bury it deep enough to where it doesn't bother them. Not your uncle. He's not completely different. The Walter I knew in medical school is still in there. Still kind; still inquisitive; still amused by the world. But he's fenced in by the man who grew around him. The man who seems determined not to let life sneak up on him. The man who drinks himself to sleep at night, dreaming about..."

"Dreaming about vampires," said Jake.

"Then you know."

"He's gone queer about it. Ordered some books and all."

"*The Empire of Shadows*. I took a look a bit earlier. Strange book, wouldn't you say? I mean, in an age of phonographs and flying machines?"

"I don't guess that's my business."

Daris rose and walked to the doorway of the dining room. He cocked his head to listen for any sound coming from upstairs. Satisfied that there was none, he turned to face the boy. This time his voice was low and urgent.

"Jake, I'm not going to lie to you. Your uncle is unwell. I'll admit the deaths here are disturbing, as is the disappearance of this little girl. *Rose Ann?* Is that her name? But the combination of events seems to have completely upset your uncle's sense of reason, which I suspect has been somewhat fragile in the past few years. I need your help in convincing him that this is a criminal matter, not a supernatural one. Yesterday I sent a telegram to my state senator about the situation here in Atcheson. The killings. The suspicions. I've asked him to request dispatch—"

Jake glanced out the screen door. A colored boy stood on the back porch, all elbows and knee caps, bouncing from one foot to the other. They hadn't heard him arrive.

"Miss Mills," he stammered. "She got k-k-killed. Killed *bad*. Sheriff says for Doc to come quick."

Jake and Daris exchanged glances. Daris spoke first. "Doctor McDivitt is resting," he said to the boy on the porch. "But I can come. Can you wait?"

The boy shrugged as if the question was in a foreign language.

"Where is she?" asked Jake.

"Out on the Saratoga road. Just past the Tuckers'."

"We can walk that. Go ahead, Jimmy. Tell the sheriff we're on our way."

※ ※ ※

Reeves Duncan set kerosene lanterns on the red earth of the road, and placed a borrowed bed sheet and a saddle blanket over the several portions of the body. Jared Sweet tried his soft-spoken best to keep the bystanders—there must have been a dozen of them; mostly adults, still in their nightclothes, but two children as well—a respectable distance away. *Shame to see the little ones up so late,* thought the Sheriff.

Then he caught himself. This was a thought for ordinary times. Nothing about this situation was ordinary. Another murder. No. Strike that. Another *vivisection*. He realized he didn't care who was still up or how late it was.

"Where's Doc?" said the Sheriff, when he saw Jake.

"Dr. McDivitt is indisposed at present," said Daris. The portly little man was out of breath from the walk to the crime scene.

"The hell he is," the lawman said. "You go back and tell him this can't wait."

Daris glanced down at a tuft of hair that lay at his feet. "I could tell him repeatedly and it wouldn't make a difference. I've given him a dose of laudanum to calm his nerves."

"You what?"

"Four drops under the tongue. I'm a physician, sir."

"You? You're–?"

Kendrick extended his hand. "Daris Kendrick," he said. "I'm an old friend of Walter's. From medical school."

The Sheriff finally extended his hand in response. "Medical school. You ever done somethin' like this before?"

The black doctor knelt beside the saddle blanket. "Sir, I have performed over a hundred and fifty autopsies in the counties of Harris and Brazoria over the course of the past eight years." He peeled back the saddle blanket to reveal the body beneath. "I'm sure I, uh—. Good Heavens. This is...this is unusual."

"That's one way to put it," said the lawman.

"I'm going to need to see the head."

"Over yonder, under the sheet." The sheriff looked beyond Daris at Jake. "You're gonna have to step back, son. This ain't a picnic."

Jake closed his eyes and stepped away.

Daris tried to keep his composure. "What happened here, Sheriff?"

"You tell me. The Haltoms, about fifty yards down the road, was gettin' in bed when they heard the screams. John come out to look and saw one of his dogs tearin' down this a' way. He followed it and found *this*. Woman named Liz Mills. She lives on the other side of town, but she's got kin up the road a piece. I figure maybe she was...."

Daris moved over to the bed sheet. He lifted it to reveal most of the woman's head and face. The skull had been cracked open, and the poor woman's brains were spilled out on the road. *Some of them*, anyway. To Daris's practiced eye it looked as if a portion of the mental organ was absent—consumed, perhaps. The victim lay in a puddle of her own blood. Both of her eyes were missing.

Daris Kendrick was a man of science. An acolyte in the church of empirical reasoning, he was capable of describing in elaborate detail Koch's pioneering work in the area of tubercular bacteriology and the prospects of the new Wassermann test for retarding the spread of syphilis. Science gave his life a solid mooring, a fixed connection to a world that was color-blind and completely rational and thus immensely comforting. He forgot about that mooring now. His heart was thudding inside his chest like one of those bass drums the Salvation Army band played in downtown Houston at Christmas time. His stomach lurched and churned, and he found himself repeating words he didn't know he remembered. *Yea*, he murmured, *though I walk through the valley of the shadow of Death, I shall fear no evil.* And yet he did fear evil. Just now, gazing out at the dark walls of the Thicket, Daris Kendrick feared it profoundly.

☆ ☆ ☆

Reeves Duncan needed a drink.

Part of it was the shock of seeing Elizabeth Mills dead. She was a decent woman—a better woman than her husband deserved, for certain. Short, stout, and fast-moving, like a summer squall, Liz Mills always had a friendly greeting and a genuine smile when she met you on the street. She was known as an easy mark for whatever relief effort anyone happened to be collecting for. African heathens. Orphans in China. They all deserved a nickel or two. Atcheson would miss her. But worse than the passing itself was seeing the *way* she'd died: torn apart like a cheap parcel by something the Sheriff couldn't even categorize, much less identify. Compounding all this was the Sheriff's realization that he was going to have to break the news to Liz's husband. He'd sent for Willard Mills even before he sent for Doc McDivitt. Now he heard the sound of hooves pounding along the dark road, coming closer, and figured this would be him. The new widower. Willard would blame the niggers for this...God. *Whatever it was.* Willard Mills always blamed the niggers. And at the moment there was one particular nigger standing smack-dab in the middle of the gun sight. There was bad blood between Mills and Clarence East already. It was about to get worse. Reeves Duncan felt reflexively for the handle of his sidearm. He was alarmed to realize he wasn't wearing it. *Time to change that habit,* he thought. A chilly breeze shook the trees south of the road. The sheriff chafed his arms, blew into the wind. It was going to be a brutal winter.

Willard Mills rode bareback. He'd stuffed his nightshirt into a pair of brown trousers, but his thick black hair was uncombed and his eyes had a wild, unfocused look. He dropped his reins and slid off his horse just shy of where Jared Sweet stood. He took two steps forward, then stopped to survey the scene: the flickering lanterns; the empty shoes and clumps of hair. Daris Kendrick—a black man in a white man's suit. And the covered lumps on the road. He stood like a man struck dumb by the hand of God.

When he spoke, the words were the same Reeves Duncan had heard only a few minutes before.

"What happened?" said Willard Mills.

The Sheriff took another deep breath.

Mills Death
Linked to
Previous Killings
Theory of Animal Predation
Called into Question
Local Man Witnessed
Figure Fleeing Scene

There can be but little doubt remaining in the minds of any unbiased observer that the recent murders in this area are related in type and intent. We use the word "murder" advisedly and with full understanding of its implications; indeed the eyewitness account of Vernon Haltom, 36, compels us to do so. Mr. Haltom, who lives at some remove from the city's westernmost limit, along the Liberty road, was first upon the scene of the most recent carnage to shock this community. He describes seeing a figure moving across the fields north of the road using bipedal locomotion—that is, walking upright, with a stiff, but steady, gait. Though Haltom was at some distance from the figure and therefore cannot be entirely certain of the figure's dimensions or physiognomy, and though Sheriff Duncan has raised the possibility that the figure was a bear, we think it established beyond a reasonable doubt that some human agency is at work in perpetrating the recent killings that good citizens, and this publication, have heretofore been content to ascribe to animal predation. This raises the disturbing prospect that the killer walks among us—is a member of our community–and that his bloody work may continue, if not actively and indeed forcibly curtailed by the civil authorities elected to protect us. We therefore call upon those authorities to devote themselves steadfastly and single-mindedly to the task of rooting out and destroying the person or persons responsible for these outrages on our lives and very souls.

Atcheson Teller
November 3, 1911
Page 1, Col. 3

12.

The Ranger

Captain Jewel T. Lightfoot arrived that Saturday on the four o'clock train.

Sheriff Duncan told him everything he knew. He conceded he'd had three bodies turn up in and around Atcheson since late September and yes, there were peculiarities common to the deaths. He patiently explained the mutilations. He named the few known miscreants in the area and their possible links to the crimes (tenuous at best), and he provided as much detail as he could about the crime scenes themselves. Seven-year-old Rose Ann Terrell was missing too, but the Sheriff had no reason to think her disappearance was related to the murders. The girl's family farmed a thirty-acre spread on Grape Creek. Rose Anne Terrell had last been seen on the creek's muddy south bank, trying to talk to a turtle. Despite an extensive search, no body had turned up. Reeves Duncan figured she'd probably drowned.

Damn shame, really. She was a pistol.

Jewel Lightfoot listened carefully. He even took a few notes in a little red book he carried in his shirt pocket, occasionally licking the lead of a stubby black pencil as he did so. Reeves Duncan was going to have to reflect on this development. He'd never known a Texas Ranger to take notes. He'd never known a Ranger who could *write notes*, now that he thought about it. So maybe it was true that the Rangers were trying to reinvent themselves. He recalled hearing that Captain Bill McDonald, the most famous of the state's vaunted police force, had led the Monk Gibson investigation a few years back. He gathered photographic evidence at the crime scene, measured the bloody footprints on the floor, and testified for the State of Texas at the trial. He wasn't just tracking criminals. He'd set himself up as a sort of expert on *criminality in general.* It made sense when you thought about it. There wasn't much of a frontier left to patrol these days. The Apaches were dead or trying to grow sorghum in Oklahoma; more or less the same thing, to an Apache. The Mexicans were fighting each other again, stirred up this time by the socialist reformer Madero, late of San Antonio and Dallas, and a flamboyant revolutionary named Zapata, reputedly an avid reader of the Russian anarchist Peter Kropotkin. The Rangers occupied themselves instead with harassing union organizers in Houston and Galveston and killing goat thieves down on the Rio Bravo. It wasn't exactly fighting Comanches, and the Sheriff found himself wondering for a moment if a Ranger ever felt restless. He shook his head and urged himself to focus on the situation at hand. Jewel T. Lightfoot had asked him a question.

The answer was no. The Sheriff felt like an idiot when he said it, but he told the God's honest truth. He had no strong theories about the killings and no real suspects, just a growing feeling of outrage. And apprehension: both of the murderer, whoever he was, and how his constituents were going to react to finding *out* who he was. He didn't mention that last part. The truth was, Reeves Duncan wasn't quite sure how to feel about Captain Lightfoot's arrival. He hadn't asked for help. In fact, he'd tried his damnedest to keep the killings quiet. He wouldn't even admit—to anyone but himself, that is— that they were related.

So how did Jewel Lightfoot know to show up?

And how much was he supposed to defer to him?

Rangers were a mixed blessing for a local lawman. True, they generally got results. But they weren't precise about it, and they didn't much care what kind of mess they left behind when they went back home. Men like Reeves Duncan got to worry about things like that. Men like Reeves Duncan got to mop up the blood. Fill out the forms. And explain, as best they could, to the next-of-kin.

"Who's this?" said Lightfoot. The Ranger stood at the door to the cell block at the rear of the building. He pointed at the massive figure sitting on the floor behind the first set of bars. The afternoon light was failing. It was hard to see the prisoner's face.

"That there's Mr. Clarence East," said the Sheriff. "Not sure I mentioned him."

East looked up from the stool he'd been trying to fix. He gazed at the little Ranger as if someone had asked him to step on a cockroach.

"What'd *he* do?" asked Lightfoot. He was livelier without a pencil in his hand. "Eat somebody's horse?"

"He's a jumbo, that's for sure. Not sure he did anything. Got kind of a bad reputation is all. Stove up a coupla other niggers. Threatened Willard Mills, the husband of the woman who got killed last night. And now that folks is getting' agitated about the killings…."

"You locked him up. Makes sense. Son, you're a lucky nigger."

"Yeah," said East. He reached out to scratch one of his bare feet. "I was just thinkin' that."

Reeves Duncan chuckled a little louder than was called for. "Well, it ain't like I brought him in. He come in on his own this morning after he heard about Liz…about the killing last night. He lives out at his mama's place. He was afraid if someone come out after him, some of the neighbors might get hurt. I figured we'd keep him here for his own good."

"Folks can get ugly. That's a fact. You ain't got nobody else in custody? Two cells back here."

"Quiet town, Captain Lightfoot. Until just lately, seemed like it was gettin' quieter."

"Whole state's quiet," said the Ranger. "Nothin' wrong with that."

Reeves Duncan noticed the little man was staring off at nothing in particular. *I knew it,* he thought. *In twenty years there won't be any Rangers left. Nothin' for 'em to do anymore.* The Sheriff wandered over to the single window in the front of the jailhouse. He watched the sun set behind the roofline of the Baptist church down the street. Through the oleanders in front of the porch, he caught a glimpse of his nephew approaching. Same old shuffling walk, same vaguely dazed expression. *Is Jasper Sweet the future of law enforcement?* Reeves Duncan wondered.

"Quiet is good," agreed the Sheriff. "We was just about rollin' in it till last month. Hey. Here's my deputy coming up the walk. He can spell me, and I'll walk you over to see Doc McDivitt."

✿ ✿ ✿

While Reeves Duncan was ambivalent about the arrival of a Ranger in Atcheson, Jake Hennessey's feelings were simpler. He knew he was in the presence of greatness. Like any Ranger of note, Jewel Lightfoot was a campfire legend. He'd joined the force at the age of sixteen and ridden with Sam "Big Foot" McMurray in Company B of the Frontier Battalion. He'd fought fence cutters in the Panhandle and tracked *Garzistas* up and down the Big River. He battled gunmen who thought the Civil War ought not to have ended quite the way it did, and he'd brought to justice, dead or alive, a rogue's gallery of murderers, rapists, and thieves.

Most famous of all, Jewel Lightfoot was with Bill McDonald when McDonald faced down an entire company of black U.S. Army infantrymen in Brownsville. The soldiers, edgy and aggressive in the face of repeated insults from the local citizenry, had a hundred Springfield rifles; the two Rangers had six-shooters. This was the incident when someone said of McDonald that he'd charge Hell with a bucket of water. True enough. All true. But Jewel T. Lightfoot would have been right there beside him, carrying the bucket. It wasn't clear what he did these days, but the Ranger told Reeves Duncan vaguely that he was doing administrative work—"riding a desk," he called it—in Austin. He'd had to pull a few strings to get back out in the field, he said, and even now his presence was to be kept quiet. East Texas's legislative delegation had been anti-Ranger for years; no one back at headquarters wanted to antagonize the local politicians.

It seemed like a modest request. Jake was prepared to swear secrecy forever. He was still doing his best to believe he was sitting in the cluttered parlor of Doc's home, drinking coffee with his uncle, the Sheriff, Daris Kendrick, and a *bona fide* Texas Ranger. Jake found himself hoping for propriety's sake that Doc had brewed up a pot of the real stuff, not the ground chicory he kept around for everyday use.

Sheriff Duncan wiped the sweat off his forehead with a sleeve of his shirt. *Nerves,* he told himself. He was in an unaccustomed position. Generally he was the one who sat back and let the conversation come to him. Now he was trying to generate some talk between Doc McDivitt and the Ranger, who had so far sat together in silence. Each man seemed to be taking the measure of the other over his porcelain cup. It was dark outside, with a chill in the evening air. Oak logs burned in the fireplace.

"I have to admit," said the Sheriff, a little louder than was necessary. "I was a little surprised to see you in these parts, Captain Lightfoot. Last we heard, you was down in Cameron County, puttin' the clamps on that Rosario feud. And that was…what? Three years ago?"

Jewel Lightfoot was the sort of sawed-off, whip-thin man who made it a point to sit as tall as he could. His hair was a shade somewhere between blonde and gray and he kept it oiled and up out of his eyes. He had a narrow face dominated by close-set gray eyes and a nearly lipless mouth. His bony nose had obviously been broken more than once. Half his right eyebrow was missing, and there was a powder burn, a little cloud of black, low on his cheek on that same side. There was something slightly off about the little Ranger's complexion. The lines of his jaw and cheekbone seemed to be a shade of metallic blue, as if the man had only recently been thawed from a block of ice. He had a habit of looking at someone other than the person he was actually addressing when he spoke.

"I guess those boys was just about feuded out," Lightfoot replied. He took a sip of coffee and fixed his eyes on the tablecloth in front of him.

Reeves Duncan was gripped by a sudden sense of levity. "Hell, they was just about *shooted out,* from what I heard. They say y'all killed five men down there. Men on both sides. Stopped the feudin', all right."

The Ranger raised his head and considered the Sheriff with those storm-cloud gray eyes of his. He just sat there staring, and Jake was reminded of the expression a lizard got when it was watching a bug. There wasn't a trace of emotion on the lawman's face.

Sheriff Duncan felt a sudden strong urge to take his words back. And bury them, maybe. In the *woods.* With a couple of rocks to hold them down.

"Anyone got hisself killed in Cameron County had it comin'." Lightfoot proceeded to lock eyes with every man in the room in turn, including Jake, as if to burn the verdict into the minds of all present. "If it was a Ranger done the killin', I mean."

Then he grinned, and Jake found himself laughing out loud. He wasn't sure why. The boy realized there was nothing funny about the statement. But it was too late. Jake noticed his uncle was watching him.

"Jake," said Doc. "I'm going to have to ask you to leave, son. I have a couple of things I need to discuss with Captain Lightfoot."

Jake tensed in his seat. A flash of anger filled the young man's head, but he knew it wasn't going to make any difference to complain. The Ranger, the Sheriff, and Daris

Kendrick were all studying his reaction. If he wanted to be treated as an adult, complaining was the worst thing he could do. So he stood and walked out of the room. He stomped up the stairs. Then, without even stopping to reflect on what he was doing, he slipped off his brogan shoes and retraced his footsteps—softly, this time. He detoured around the dining table and stood with his back to the wall of the parlor. He could hear the conversation just fine. Reeves Duncan was the first to speak.

"Captain," said the Sheriff. "You didn't come all the way out here to the ass end of nowhere to shoot the breeze. You got any more questions, this here's the man to ask."

"Well, I do have one," said Lightfoot.

Doc nodded, straightening in his chair. "Ask away."

Lightfoot looked at Daris Kendrick. "Who's the nigger?" he said.

The air of expectation seemed to drain from the room.

Walter McDivitt waited a moment to reply. "This is no *nigger*, sir. This is Dr. Daris Kendrick."

The Ranger gave Kendrick another long appraisal. For a moment he looked as if he was trying to figure out it if he'd made a mistake. "Doctor of what?"

Daris himself now spoke. "Doctor of medicine, Captain Lightfoot. I'm a physician."

"Good Lord. Sheriff. How many doctors y'all got in this town?"

Walter's voice was strained. "Dr. Kendrick is from St. Nevis and Kitts, Captain. He now lives in Houston, but he was educated at the Harvard College of Medicine, as was I. He is an old and dear friend of mine, and a very talented colleague who has written at some length on the prospects for use of epidural anesthesia in abdominal surgery—a measure that could provide relief for thousands of men and women at a difficult, indeed critical, time in their lives. I will thank you to show him a proper measure of respect."

A red haze crept into the Ranger's face. It was hard to tell whether it signaled aggression or embarrassment. Or possibly both. Jewel Lightfoot's eyes remained dim, his mouth set. He opened his little notebook, glanced inside, shut it again.

"McDivitt," he said, "the Sheriff tells me you've seen all three of the bodies."

"I have," said Doc, exhaling heavily. "And they all look more or less the same. I should add that Daris—Dr. Kendrick—saw the most recent victim before I did. He was able to sew one of her legs back into place and to replace portions of the viscera. For burial, I mean. Our local mortician is working on the rest of the job."

Daris started to speak, but the Ranger cut him off. "In other words," Lightfoot concluded, "she was tore up."

Doc was glad his nephew was gone.

Daris stated what everyone already knew. "Gutted, Captain. Cut up like bait. And drained of blood."

A heavy wagon creaked past outside—old-growth pine, probably, headed to Beaumont for milling. The window was open and they heard the driver curse at his animals. It was already full dark. If the Ranger had heard Daris Kendrick speak, he didn't let on. He continued to look directly at Doc.

"Anything you know of coulda done it? Any*one*?"

"I'd tell you, but I suspect you'd laugh. Others have."

"Walter," said Daris. "Please."

"Spill the beans, Doc. What are you thinkin'?"

Walter McDivitt blushed, flexed his fingers.

"I can wait," said the Ranger. "I ain't proud."

The Sheriff shifted in his chair. The uncomfortable silence returned.

"I think we're dealing," said Doc, "with some sort of *vampire*."

"A vampire," Lightfoot repeated.

"I know it seems farfetched," Doc conceded.

"That's one way to put it."

"But hear me out, Captain. You'd grant me there's something grotesque about the way these people died."

"If you're sayin' they didn't die of old age, I'll ride that far. But there ain't nothin' new about that. You get east of the Trinity, folks die hard. It ain't like Austin these days. We got ladies up there get themselves embalmed first and die later, when it seems convenient."

The joke fell flat.

"This woman last night...?" said Doc.

"Her name was Mills," interrupted the Sheriff, looking at the Ranger. *He owed her that much.* "Elizabeth Ann Mills. We called her Liz."

"Throat ripped out," Doc continued. "Blood drained from the torso and head. Bones snapped as if they were match sticks...."

Lightfoot worked his tongue in one cheek. "Still don't mean there's a big bat flying around, suckin' the blood outta people's heads."

"Not a *bat*, Captain Lightfoot."

"You said a vampire. They's supposed to turn into bats, ain't they?"

"That's a myth," Doc stated.

The Ranger nodded. "I see. That part's a myth."

"But the vampire is real." Doc walked to the mantel piece and picked up the framed tintype of his sister. He stared at it as if he was waiting for permission to speak. He was struck once again by the resemblance between her and Jake: the same arched eyebrows, the brown eyes and thin nose. He was glad the boy was gone. This wasn't easy to say. "I know I'm not the first to believe this. But I do think I'm among the first to bring a rational, scientific approach to the matter. And I've become convinced that vampires—not just this one, but potentially an entire species—live alongside us. Cultivating us. *Preying* on us. Why does that seem so strange, I wonder? We know South America's vampire bat—*Desmodus rotundus*; a mammal, obviously, and quite similar in some respects to us—lives entirely on animal hemoglobin. Why couldn't a subgroup of man develop a similar diet?"

Reeves Duncan had grown increasingly agitated by Doc's words. It was bad enough that he had no good theories of his own. This was starting to sound like mockery. "You're makin' this too complicated, Doc. This thing ain't no *hemogoblin*. Or—."

"Well played, sir," said Daris.

"You know what I mean. He's a goddamn murderer is what he is, *whoever* he is, and if he thinks the State of Texas is gonna stand around and watch him tear up a decent woman like a dog chews a chicken, he's got another think coming. 'Cause I will find him. And I will see his sorry ass hanged."

Doc crossed his arms. "Ignore Dr. Kendrick, Sheriff. His mind is obviously closed. I agree with you that we need to find this...*killer*, whoever or whatever it is. But don't be hasty. We'll need some time to prepare."

"And how are we gonna do that?" said the Sheriff.

"There are only two ways to kill a vampire. A stake through the heart, or direct sunlight."

Jake leaned forward from his place of concealment in the next room. Craning his neck, he could see portions of the parlor in the mirror that stood in the near corner. Daris was on his feet now, his coffee cup on one side on the table. "Walter," he interjected, "you're delusional! It's as simple as that."

Doc stood to face him. Both men were shouting. "Go home, Daris! Go home if you can't see what's in front of your face!"

"I'll go home when I've seen you in the care of an alienist, my friend. *Two ways to kill a vampire* indeed. I'll tell you how to kill a vampire. It's quite simple. Turn on the light and put down your bottle! You need professional help. You heard him, Captain Lightfoot."

"I heard him clear as a bell," said the Ranger. There was a strange, sly grin on his face. He slid further down into his chair. "And you're right, Dr. Kendrick. There ain't just two ways to kill a vampire."

They stared at him. Something in the fire popped and hissed as the Ranger placed a handful of bullets on the table. They gleamed in the weak light of the room.

"Silver," said Lightfoot. "Kills 'em deader 'n hell."

Then he laughed. The Ranger laughed for a good long while, and even Jake felt a shiver crawl up his spine.

* * *

Jewel Lightfoot took a folded sheet of paper from the pocket of his waistcoat and tossed it on the coffee table. Daris leaned forward, picked up the paper, and read aloud:

> *To Whom It May Concern: Captain Jewel T. Lightfoot travels on special assignment from the State of Texas. He is to be accorded all courtesies and official cooperation. Expenses reasonably incurred at his request will be reimbursed upon submission of suitable documentation (viz. invoices, bills of lading, etc.) to the Comptroller of Public Accounts, Austin, Texas. Any interference with the execution of Capt. Lightfoot's duties, which duties shall be determined in his sole discretion, will be punished to the full extent of the law.*
>
> *Signed under seal this 15th day of October 1911, His Excellency S.W.T. Lanham, Commissioner, Texas Department of Insurance, Statistics, and History*

"All right," said Daris. "I'll bite. What in the name of Caesar's ghost is this supposed to mean?"

Jewel Lightfoot nodded as if he'd been expecting the question. "Just what it says, Doctor. I'm on orders from the Commissioner of Insurance and History himself. And you all are hereby officially deputized to assist me, on account of your superstitious natures, plentiful foodstuffs, and general proximity to the scene of the crimes."

Doc held up his palms. "Deputized for what?"

"I assume you can rustle up a few side arms," said Lightfoot.

"My question was: deputized for *what?*"

The Ranger made a shelf of his bottom lip, bobbed his head. "For finding and killing whatever nasty sonofabitch is running the woods hereabouts, for starters."

"Which is? Are you saying you agree with...?" Daris couldn't even finish the sentence.

"Not exactly," said Lightfoot.

"Then what *do* you think is out there, Captain?"

"It don't matter what I think. My job is to kill it. Whatever it is."

Daris glanced at Doc and Reeves Duncan as if seeking support. The chilliness between Daris and Doc had disappeared, replaced by their mutual suspicion of the Ranger.

"So let me see if I'm following you," said Daris. "The State sent you down here to kill what you call a nasty sonofabitch, but you don't know who the sonofabitch is? You don't even know *what* the sonofabitch is? I think you're not telling us everything."

The Ranger picked something off the heel of his boot. "And I think you talk a lot for a nigger."

Doc hissed in disdain.

"Captain Lightfoot," said Sheriff Duncan. "With respect. What *are* we dealing with here?"

"You're dealing with three dead bodies and a missing little girl, and not one a' you has a theory worth a flying pellet of pig shit as to who done it, or why. Not to mention which, there's a smart-ass nigger the size of a Kodiak bear down at Sheriff Duncan's jailhouse who's gonna get himself hanged if he ain't real careful, and it ain't gonna accomplish nothin' but reducin' the county's feed bills. Now what else do you need to know?"

Daris Kendrick shrugged as if to say: *More.* The Ranger looked around the group and there was a challenge in his eyes. Somewhere not far off, two cats were fighting. The Sheriff got up and closed the window.

"All right," said the Ranger, nodding as if he was trying to talk himself into something he'd rather not do. He pulled his notebook back out of his shirt pocket, flipped through several pages. "You think you want to know, I'll tell you. If I'm right, what we're about to tangle with ain't like nothin' else you've ever seen. They found one of these things in northern Japan four years ago. Place called *Ho-kai-do*. Scientists brought it to the university there and cut it up. Found a pair of wings that don't seem to work too good and a pair of lungs that do. Thing can swell up to half again its size. Jaw is retractable, like a shark's. It can see at night and its skin is sensitive to light." The Ranger glanced down at his notebook again. "Highly sensitive to light. As in, *catchin' fire*–type sensitive."

"You're joking."

The Ranger emitted a hard little snort. "Well, Doc, that's a hell of a thing for *you* to say. No. I ain't joking. Turns out this thing they found in Japan wasn't dead. And it didn't take too kindly to being sliced open like pie at a picnic. Killed everyone in the building but the janitor."

"Maybe *he* did it," said the Sheriff. He was glad of the opportunity to say something again. His stomach was churning, and he'd been resisting the temptation to start humming, which was his usual reaction to stress. "The janitor, I mean."

"Not likely. Janitor was a gal. She was fifty-seven years old and hid in a broom closet. She thinks she might a' passed out for part of it. Things she said didn't make a whole lot of sense. But the bodies….*Nine men.* Four of them soldiers. Couldn't tell one from the other after this thing got through with them. There were photographs. Whatever it was, it disappeared that night and hasn't been seen since."

"Jesus," said one of the men.

"*Jesus* is right," said the Ranger. He was warming up to his story. "But that ain't the worst of it. This thing—or these *things;* it's possible there's more than one—these things we're up against can change their shape. Doc, you was talkin' about a vampire. Folks might think this was a vampire. Hell. These things coulda been every goddamned monster ever reported. Vampire. Banshee. *Chupacrabra.* And lately they're gettin' better at disguisin' themselves. Folks in Washington got a filing cabinet full of reports. Nineteen dead in Bombay from 1886 to 1889. Six in the copper fields up in Idaho in '94. Place called Lan Ju in China, a whole village disappeared. Twenty-nine Chinamen. Gone."

"Good Lord," said Reeves Duncan. "You think one of these things is here in Ochiltree County?"

"I think *something's* here, Sheriff. And it ain't Santy Claus."

"And the State sent you down here to take care of it."

It was Daris Kendrick speaking again. He made the statement sound like an accusation. The little Ranger chose to ignore the sarcasm. He shrugged.

"Way I heard it, killings like this are bad for business. Cut down on the immigration prospects. Scare the railroad men."

"So it's a matter of money," said Daris. "When you get right down to it."

Lightfoot paused to light up a cheroot. He waved the smoking match in the air to extinguish it. Then he sat back and blew out a smoke ring.

"Hell," said the Ranger. "What ain't?"

* * *

Reeves Duncan's hands were working like they held a broken halter. "So what's our first step, Captain? I mean, assuming we're..."

"Assuming you're gonna get off your asses and lend a hand? We reconnoiter. Somebody's got to get a fix on what's out there. That means we go in, unless one of them comes out first."

"Go in where?" said Doc. "What are you taking about?"

"I'm talking about that old mill. Sheriff, what's it called?"

"You mean Nichols Mill?"

"That's right. Nichols."

Doc raised his one palm as if he was trying to slow a runaway horse. "Hold up. Wait a minute. That's Amos Newton's place. It's the site of an active oil drilling operation, as far as I can tell. We're looking for a monster, not a fraudulent stock promoter. In my opinion, we need to start out at the Croat settlement. It's a collection of single-room cabins about ten miles southwest of here, on Honey Creek. As late as last year there was a dozen men living in those shacks. Now nothing. The place is deserted. We need to figure out why."

Lightfoot sucked at his teeth. "Well, you go ahead on, Doc. I've got information points to the mill. How often do y'all see the folks out there?"

The Sheriff shrugged. "Couple of men come in for supplies sometimes. They get salt, sugar, and flour over at Harvey Moon's here in town. A lot of it, according to Harvey. Brought in a big steam drill three or four months ago. And I know they been wearin' out cable and drill bits, 'cause they get 'em through East Texas Oil Supply over in Gosford, and Floyd Drake told me so. But that's about it. Amos's men ain't real loose with their tongues, from what I can gather."

"Don't surprise me none. These boys know what they're doing."

Daris Kendrick looked up from filling his pipe. "Captain, you astonish me. What are you saying? Are we tracking men or a monster?"

"Maybe both. There's a couple of fellas bound up in this thing. Don't know exactly how or why. Some kind of a Arab—fellow named *Na-geeb*. Don't ask me to spell it. Big sonofagun. Specializes in breaking necks. Doesn't let himself be seen much. He operates with a procurer named Solomon, a tall drink a' water they call the Turk. He's the brains of the outfit. Dark hair, dark eyes. Supposed to speak nine languages. Does the outfitting and travel arrangements. Hires the—. What is it, son?"

Jake couldn't resist anymore. He stepped out of the dining room into the parlor. "I've seen them! I mean, *we've* seen them. Doc and me."

"Jake! I told you to get upstairs."

"No you didn't," Daris chuckled. It was a rich, luxurious sound. Jake was grateful for it. "You told him to get out of the room. And so he did. For a little while, anyway."

"You stay out of this," said Doc.

"Who did you see, Jake?" asked the Sheriff.

"Solomon, I guess. And the Arab. The big one. On the road to the Mill."

The Ranger glanced over at Doc.

Doc shrugged. "We saw two men, yes. Conversed with them, even. I don't know that they're the men you mentioned, though."

Jake shook his head at what he was hearing. Doc realized the boy was puzzled. Hell, he was puzzled a bit himself. He knew damn well there was something sinister about the two men he and Jake had met on the way back from Jess Terrell's place that day. And yet Doc was denying any such thing. He wasn't sure why. Maybe it was because he was one of only two physicians in Ochiltree County. He was used to getting his way. He'd convinced himself that there was some dire clue to the recent killings to be found in the mysterious disappearance of the Croat settlement, and now this presumptuous carpet tack of a man, this Texas Ranger, was galloping off down the wrong trail, taking Doc's very few friends and relations along with him.

Lightfoot was rolling another cheroot. "I ain't sayin' they are. All we know is wherever these two *hombres* go, people end up dead—dead, and lookin' a lot like the bodies turnin' up around here. Four women and a baby in Juarez. A priest and a little runaway boy in San Antonio. That's the last place we had the scent. They disappeared for almost a year. Didn't have no clue at all till we got word of the deaths here in Ochiltree County. You say you've seen these two out there, right? Or—okay; hold your horses, Doc—*might have seen* 'em, anyhow. So it sounds like maybe this man Newton's place ain't a bad place to start."

"You thinkin' about trying to get a warrant?" said the Sheriff. "I know Judge Stovall pretty good."

The Ranger cleared his throat. "That wasn't exactly what I was thinking. But now that you mention it, I reckon we oughta do this the legal way. If possible."

"The legal way," said Reeves Duncan approvingly. He looked as if he'd just heard from a long-lost relative. "Good."

CITIZENS' COMMITTEE
TO MEET THIS WEEK
Mills, Others
Call for Justice
Suspicions Center on
Vicious Negro

Voicing dismay at the recent slayings reported in the pages of this publication, several prominent citizens of Atcheson have announced formation of a Committee of Inquest aimed at ferreting out the culprit or culprits responsible for the hideous violence in the vicinity. The leader of the committee will be Mr. J.R. Holsan, who has announced a general meeting to be held two days hence at the home of Willard Mills on Finch Street. Holsan announced that in the meantime, he will call upon Sheriff Reeves Duncan and offer him one final opportunity to locate or produce the killer before the Committee will petition the County Commissioners to be deputized en masse. The Sheriff has continued to assert the hypothesis that the recent deaths are the work of predacious canines. However, suspicions among community leaders currently center on the Negro Clarence East, a known brawler and miscreant with a history of aggressive behavior, who is believed to be in police custody but who thus far remains uncharged. Mills, a co-chair of the nascent committee, has vowed that this situation will soon be rectified; that an impartial investigation will be conducted with the nicest scruples observed; and that the darkie will be brought to justice.

Atcheson Teller
October 21, 1911
Page 1, Col. 3

13.

The Witness

Their first break came two days later, on an overcast Thursday that promised rain. It turned out Judge Stovall was in Austin for the week. As Sheriff Duncan struggled to draft up a warrant that didn't sound dog-slobber crazy, he left word with several local business owners that he was interested in hearing about the movements of anyone associated with Amos Newton's drilling operation. A response came quickly. Late that day, Wally Moon's son showed up with a handwritten note from his father. In it, the grocer reported he'd seen one of the two men from the Newton camp who regularly traded for provisions at his place. The man was riding through Atcheson, and looked to be headed south. The Sheriff couldn't follow him. He had to be in Gosford that evening for the County Commissioners' meeting. But he passed the word to Jewel Lightfoot, and the little Ranger was halfway out the door of his hotel room before Jared Sweet finished giving him the news.

※ ※ ※

Moon's description said the man was a weak-chinned blonde, maybe twenty years old, with ruddy cheeks and a pair of wispy, mutton-chop sideburns. Lightfoot spurred his big sorrel into a canter. Three miles later he had the rider in sight, and had to fall back a bit so as not to be noticed. The kid was easy to follow. He pulled a pint bottle out of his jacket and started swigging from it when he was still an hour outside of Batson. The first thing he did when he hit town was visit a whorehouse called Lola's, where he spent an impressive portion of the evening sporting with a mulatto gal named Crater Lil.

Jewel Lightfoot sat on the porch swing of a bordello two houses down, waiting for his quarry to emerge. The sky turned steel blue before it went dark, and the Ranger smelled a storm in the air. Lights appeared in windows along the street. At nine o'clock, a bearded man with a Cajun accent and a dragon tattoo covering half his face appeared on the porch and ordered Lightfoot to carry his loitering ass down the road. The Ranger observed that it was raining. Not *hard*, admittedly, but he wasn't exactly dressed for the weather. The bouncer would have been a remarkable sight anywhere else in the state. But Batson was smack dab in the middle of the East Texas oil fields, a territory populated by hustlers, hard cases, and numerous freakish specimens of humanity. Dragon Face was just a shade over six feet tall. He wore a gold hoop in his left ear and carried a two-foot club inlaid with brass in a repeating, diamond-shaped pattern. He patted the club against his right leg as he sized up his opponent. When he took another step forward, Lightfoot showed him his badge—the Rangers' iconic five-pointed silver star, carved from a Mexican *cinco pesos* coin. He also showed him his double-action Colt service revolver. It could seem especially large when it was pressed into the soft flesh of your testicles, as this one now was. Lightfoot drew back the hammer.

The Ranger was so quick with his gun, it took the bearded man a moment to figure out what had happened. And what was *about* to happen. Once he'd thought it over for maybe four seconds, Dragon Face allowed as how it might be just fine for Lightfoot to cool his heels a while longer. Lightfoot sniffed. He bobbed his head and thanked the stranger kindly. His face was calm, but there was a glint in his gray eyes that indicated all hell was about to break loose, and that he—the Ranger—was going to enjoy it a sight more than anyone else in the vicinity. "Didn't know you was the law," muttered the bouncer as he backed away.

Lightfoot was left alone after that.

* * *

The blonde kid staggered out the front door of the whorehouse twenty minutes later, drained of certain fluids but full of others, grinning like an idiot with a sack of hard candy. Lightfoot stood, stretched, and followed him down the street. The kid's next stop was a saloon called the Iron Cross, a dimly lit establishment that kept its doors open despite the mist and rain. Lightfoot took up a position on the opposite side of the street, where he could see inside the bar. It was a roughneck's dive, spit-stained and shabby. Lightfoot was familiar with this sort of establishment. He'd seen its counterparts in Nogales and Abilene, Galveston and Laredo. Drop your guard in a place like this and you might end up with a slug of chloral hydrate in your whiskey. You'd see the room start to spin ten minutes later. Since the effects of a Mickey Finn were identical to those of simple drunkenness, you could easily be removed from the premises and dragged out back, then relieved of your wallet and pocket watch. You'd be lucky to lose only your possessions. Fall asleep in the Iron Cross and you might end up at the bottom of one of the blackwater sloughs hereabouts, getting acquainted with the alligators.

Inside the Iron Cross, the kid brushed the rain off his canvas jacket and introduced himself to three different individuals in the space of twenty minutes. From what the Ranger could see, they each told him to mind his goddamned business. Or worse. Lightfoot guessed the game. He crossed the street, entered the dive, and took a seat at a table not far from the bar. He sat down and spread his legs as if he'd just wandered in from Houston on foot. The black man at the piano played "My Old Virginia Home" and periodically wiped his nose on the sleeve of his jacket, a patchwork affair that looked like it had spent time at the bottom of an outhouse. The place smelled of stale grease and beer, armpits and onions. A cracked mirror hung behind the bar, and there was a blood stain the size of a pillow case on the pine planks near Lightfoot's right boot. *Nice place.* But he'd seen worse.

The Ranger took three coins out of his pocket and stacked them in different configurations on the tabletop in front of him. He looked as troubled as he knew how. It didn't take long to get a bite.

"Lookin' for work?"

Lightfoot glanced up at the blonde kid he'd been trailing. The kid stood beside his table, swaying slightly in his boots.

"Could be," said the Ranger. "You got some?"

The stranger settled into a chair on the other side of the dirty table, gazing at Lightfoot with a peculiar intensity. He had wide-set, watery blue eyes, and a jutting jaw. He smirked when he wasn't speaking, and the heel of his right boot bobbed up and down like a piston. *Cocaine?* thought the Ranger. You could get it in Galveston for a dime a box. The stevedores took it to stay alert. The whores at Lola's might have put it to different use. At any rate, the blonde kid was hopped up on something. "She ain't pretty, but she pays."

Lightfoot shrugged. "Keep talkin'."

The kid excused himself for a moment. When he returned, he held two glasses of beer. The Ranger took an experimental sip, swallowing as little as he could. This took will power. He was thirsty. On the other hand, the beer was awful.

"Oilfield work over near Atcheson," said the kid. "Spuddin' and diggin'. You still spry enough to swing a pick?"

"I can swing a pick."

"Ain't afraid to sweat a little?"

"Son, I've been workin' all my life. How much does she pay?"

"You get three dollars a day, plus meals."

Lightfoot straightened in his chair. "You gotta be kiddin'."

The blonde man laid three ten-dollar bills on the table.

"This look like I'm kiddin'? One week's pay in advance—plus a bonus for signin' on. Don't smoke, do ya?"

"I like a smoke, when I got the—"

"Say no. No smoking allowed. No fires neither. Boss won't have it."

Lightfoot frowned.

"Don't think about it too long, friend," said the kid. "You wanna work or not?"

"I'll take it," said the Ranger.

"You ridin'?"

"Horse is right down the street. Beecher's place."

"Same as mine. You got a name?"

Lightfoot shrugged. "Do I need one?"

"Better off without." The blonde man tipped his glass and drained the contents. He surveyed the premises as if to make sure he hadn't forgotten anything. Evidently he hadn't. A grin played over his unshaven face. "Well, hell. Guess I've done everything I come here to do. *Vamonos.*"

"Hey," said the Ranger. "Waitin' on you."

* * *

The rain was coming on. Smeared yellow lights leaked from just a few windows, and the streets were deserted. The two men set off down the rickety pine-plank sidewalk toward the livery stable, holding their hats on their heads. The Ranger wondered how long to go on with his charade. Maybe he could ride it all the way out. Maybe he could head back to Atcheson with the kid, take a first-hand look at the Mill, slip off the premises before dawn. But that seemed a little too complicated—and Jewel Lightfoot was not a complicated man. It would be safer, and a hell of a lot easier, just to make his play here. The kid was even drunker than he'd been when he left the whorehouse, which didn't help his odds. But he wouldn't have had much of a chance anyway. Three blocks from the bar, Lightfoot shouldered his companion into an alley.

"Where we goin'?" said the kid, not quite resisting.

The Ranger lowered his voice to a conspiratorial whisper. "Wanta show you some postcards, *amigo*."

"Postcards? I don't…"

"Sure you do. These come straight from Paris."

When his companion tried to sidestep, Lightfoot grabbed him by one forearm and swung him around hard, smashing his face against the planks of the nearest building. The kid came up swinging. The Ranger got to him first with the butt of his revolver. As soon as the kid could talk through his own blood, Lightfoot showed him the star.

"Who are you workin' for, son?"

The kid spat something off to one side. "You gotta be kiddin' me," he snarled. "You broke my front tooth."

"Over in Atcheson," the Ranger persisted. "You and that bunch out at the Mill. Who you workin' for?"

"I'm workin' for J. P. Morgan, you sawed-off sonofabitch. You broke my damn *tooth*."

Lightfoot relaxed, looked around him, emitted a companionable chuckle. Suddenly he slammed his forehead down like the business end of a claw hammer. He heard the satisfying crunch of cartilage in the younger man's nose. The blonde kid dropped to his knees in the mud, holding his hands to his face, making a high-pitched moaning sound.

"Try again," said the Ranger.

Nothing. The kid seemed to be stuck between inhaling and exhaling.

"Who do you *work for*, goddammit?"

Lightning flashed in the sky, and thunder rolled over them a moment later. The kid looked toward the street, then back at the Ranger. There was a trace of alarm in his eyes.

"That's right," said Lightfoot. "Just you and me, Goldilocks."

"You know who I work for," the kid mumbled.

"Say it."

"The Turk."

"Where's he from? And where is he now?"

"Where's he from? He's from Turkey, you idiot. That's why they call him the Turk."

Now it was Lightfoot's turn. The Ranger glanced around to make sure no one was watching. Then he reared back and put a boot in the kid's ribs. He didn't like being called an idiot. Of course the man was from Turkey, he reminded himself. They called him the *Turk*. Never mind exactly where Turkey was. Or why some damn fool would name a country *Turkey* in the first place.

"Where is he now?" said the Ranger.

"Where's—?" Hell, I don't know."

"Son, you need to start thinkin' harder. Or you ain't gonna have no place to put them sideburns, if you know what I mean."

The kid looked up at the barrel of Lightfoot's six-gun. He blinked the rain out of his eyes, grunted his amusement. "You think I'm afraid of you, shit-kicker? You have no idea what you're messin' with."

"How 'bout you lighten my burden?"

"How 'bout you jump up my ass," said the kid. "And give it a tickle."

Lightfoot hit him again with the butt of the revolver—this time on the back of the neck, just at the base of the skull. He was vaguely aware of the return of that centerless but pleasurable feeling he got when he was beating the living hell out of someone. He knew he wasn't supposed to enjoy it. Wasn't *professional*. Could ruin a shirt. But he couldn't help himself. Indian. Greaser. Irishman. Kraut. Administering a competent beating always felt the same way: good. The Ranger suspected that inflicting pain was, in some elemental sense, what he was born to do. All the better, now that he had a reason for doing so. He remembered the words of those who'd sent him. He had another clear shot at the kid's head, but he restrained himself. Lights out would mean the conversation was over, and he hadn't yet heard anything he didn't already know.

"What are y'all doin' out at the mill?" the Ranger demanded, breathing harder.

"We're diggin'."

"Diggin' for what?"

"For treasure." At this, the kid started laughing. It was a rapid, high, hysterical laugh. It sounded as if he'd been out in the sun for too long. But this time when Lightfoot looked away, the man reached up and grabbed the pistol. Lightfoot refocused just in time to get a fistful of mud in his eyes. He clutched his sidearm as hard as he could. He tucked it into his gut and fell to the ground, cradling the weapon, yanking it away from his attacker. The thought flashed through his brain: *Shame how many lawmen get killed with their own goddamned guns.* The kid stomped him twice on the back of his head, which didn't hurt, then reared back and kicked him in the upper spine. Which did. He had the Ranger in a bad spot and the Ranger knew it. *A shifty opponent. Had to respect that—the kid had some snake in his belly.* But then the Ranger's assailant—*panicky? drunk?*—did an inexplicable thing. An *inexcusable* thing, really.

He ran.

Lightfoot hated to run. Horses ran. Dogs ran. Rangers, in his experience, did *not* run. Unless there wasn't a choice.

And there wasn't. The Ranger chased his quarry for fifteen minutes. The sky spat harder and he followed the kid through curtains of rain and the puddled dark streets at the edge of town. He clambered over a split-rail fence and splashed through the neat rows of a truck farm and out into a spongy field where the rickety derricks stood like a skeleton forest. Two roughnecks speckled black with oil like the dying blood of Mother Earth herself watched the panting chase with exhausted eyes. Lightning split the heavens. The storm was breaking right over them now and the wind nearly blew the Ranger off his feet. Mud clung to his boots but he ran till his lungs burned and his legs were shaking and stiff. The skinny little bastard had disappeared. A possibly crucial witness. In his hands. *Gone.*

Then he heard the high-pitched laughter again.

Goldilocks was standing just ahead of him, on the slight elevation of an embankment of the Hammond East West Train Co.—the *Hell Either Way Taken*, as it was locally known. The kid was soaking wet, and his dirty blonde hair hung down like a curtain over one of his eyes. Blood poured from his shattered nose. He held a length of two-by-four in his hands. He was gasping for air, but it looked like he had some fight left in him.

Lightfoot heard the rumble of an approaching train. He looked west, to his left, and saw the light of the engine. *Damn it all.* No way to tell how many cars it was pulling, but if it was more than a few he was going to lose the kid for sure. He knew he couldn't run any further. The Ranger's head jerked to one side with frustration.

"I don't hafta SHOOT YOU, goddammit!" Lightfoot gasped. "But I gotta tell you. I'm leanin' that way."

"I can't...tell you...*nothin'*," shouted the kid, "if I'm dead!"

It took Lightfoot a moment to understand what his quarry meant. He watched the kid step out onto the tracks and still he didn't quite grasp what his eyes were telling him. The rumble of the train was closer. It filled the air around the Ranger like perpetual thunder, like God's own headache. And then he figured it out.

"Hold on there, son! Hold on just a..."

Then the horn screamed and the metal brakes screeched and it was impossible to say anything else. There was nothing the Ranger could do. The kid kept him locked in his sight. Lightning brightened the world for almost a second and Jewel Lightfoot reflexively stepped backward. He got a good look at the young man's face just before the end. The kid was smiling. He was smiling like the world had just repaid him a sizeable debt as thirty tons of steam and steel cut him clean in half.

14.

Roll Call

The next evening, Jewel Lightfoot took another gulp of Doc's brandy as he glanced around the room. He'd called several men together in the cluttered parlor of Doc's house because he didn't care to repeat himself. He told his story carefully, pausing whenever someone looked puzzled, trying as best he could to explain what he'd seen in the last twenty-four hours. Clearly the kid from Amos Newton's place had gone to Batson to recruit new workers. He'd made his pitch in the sorriest bar in town, looking for down-and-outers who'd sign on with a minimum of questions. In fact, it was when the questions started—Lightfoot left out the part about the pistol-whipping that accompanied them—that the kid seemed to panic. Now he was dead, churned into two unrecognizable hunks of blood and pulp on the tracks of the Hell Either Way Taken. There was no way of knowing exactly when he'd been expected back at the Mill, but his *compadres* were bound to notice him missing sooner or later. And then they were going to start asking questions. Jewel Lightfoot gave the men surrounding him a minute to contemplate this possibility.

It was an odd gathering. On the divan, Reeves Duncan stared at his own plump hands and looked as if he'd rather be somewhere else. Walter McDivitt sat at his desk, thumbing through the yellowed pages of *Empire of Shadows*. His long face was pale and unshaven, not quite concealing what some in the group suspected was a massive hangover. Natty as always, Daris Kendrick wore a full-length rabbit fur coat against the cold. The gaslight reflected off his bald head as he scratched notes on a sheaf of yellow paper, and the sweet smoke of his meerschaum pipe gathered like a fog below the ceiling. Occasionally he glanced up at the Ranger, seeming to focus on the little man's face and neck. He'd already noticed the scrapes on Lightfoot's knuckles. Clearly there had been more to the Ranger's back-alley interrogation of his prisoner than a nod and a handshake. It was not unheard of for a Ranger—or any lawman, for that matter—to kill a captive in the course of his questioning. Daris wondered to himself if the Ranger was telling the whole story of the blonde kid's death.

Big Clarence East worked a length of rope as he listened, twisting it one way, then another, to no apparent purpose. He dwarfed the chair he occupied. Edmund Petticord lounged, barefooted, on the floor by one of the room's two windows, his head cocked as if he could hear the distant heartbeat of the Thicket itself. Jake Hennessey, meanwhile, eyed Jewel Lightfoot's nickel-plated slide-action shotgun. He was visibly perplexed by the Ranger's tale. What kind of a man would toss himself in front of an onrushing train rather than answer to the law? So far he hadn't come up with any answers. A fire popped and sputtered in the fireplace. Mrs. Grady had sent word that she was ill, and plates with the remnants of day-old biscuit and cold side meat sat in front of the men.

"Whatever that kid knew," the Ranger concluded, draining his glass with a careless flick of the wrist, "he wasn't about to share it. Somethin' scared him a helluva lot more than I did, I guess, and I can't say as I've seen that kind of behavior before. Used to be, an Apache'd kill himself just to spite you. But it didn't have nothin' to do with bein' *scared.* I don't know what else there is to say. The way I see it, we need to get our tail ends out to the Mill and see what the hell's going on. Warrant or no warrant."

Sheriff Duncan nodded. He looked as if he wanted to agree, but the Ranger wasn't finished yet.

"'Cause the longer we wait, the more holes y'all are gonna be diggin'."

Doc sat back in his desk chair, his sallow face set in a frown. He folded his arms and considered the little Ranger as if he were an as-yet-uncatalogued species of pathogen. "Again, Captain, we're talking about an oil-drilling operation. Why are you so sure Nichols Mill has anything to do with the killings?"

Lightfoot spoke as if he'd been expecting this one. "Go ask the kid, Doc. Where I come from, folks don't catch a train by steppin' in front of it. And I don't hear no goddamn better ideas."

"And the plan?" said Daris Kendrick, between draws at his pipe.

"The *plan*," said the Ranger, with undisguised contempt. "There ain't no plan. We ride out there tomorrow bright and early and take a look around. See if we can talk to this Amos Newton character. And see how many guns he's got, 'cause if I figure this right, the man's got some odd and unsavory characters workin' with him, and they ain't gonna be holdin' flowers when we go to meet 'em. Who's got a horse?"

"You mean…all of us?"

Lightfoot glanced around the room. "That's right, Sheriff. All of us. That's why I asked Petticord here, and your boy East, to join us. There's strength in numbers—especially when one of your numbers is bigger'n a Pennsylvania shithouse. Excuse my French."

They all looked at the massive Negro as if he'd suddenly materialized in their midst. *God he was big*, Jake reflected. East glanced up from his rope work. He seemed to have a ridge of muscle running straight across his forehead. For some reason Jake felt proud of East's great bulk. It was as if he'd grown the black man himself.

Reeves Duncan shook his head. "Well, that there's a problem. East gets himself seen outside of my jail or this house, Captain, and he's liable to get hisself hanged. Willard

Mills and the folks at the *Teller* have got folks pretty stirred up. The Citizens Committee sent me a note this morning after Liz's funeral. Said they want to question my prisoner. I think he ought to stay hid."

"Nobody's hangin' one of my deputies," the Ranger declared, small sparks flashing in his gray eyes. "He'll come with us."

"No," said Doc. "The Sheriff's right. Some folks have got it in their heads that East is the killer. They're not going to be pleased to see he's on the loose."

Daris spoke softly. "Walter," he said, "I'm surprised at you. You've told me yourself Mr. East is not a credible suspect. Why cater to the whims of the Mob? East is a free man, same as you or me or anyone else in this room. He knows the situation well enough. I suspect he'd like to help. Has anyone asked him?"

The Ranger laughed. "What about it, East? You in? Or you wanna spend the day tomorrow all by your lonesome in that jailhouse?"

East shrugged. "Find me a horse," he said.

"Good." Lightfoot scanned the room. "Petticord? You still here?" Petticord extricated himself from under the couch and sat up. "You're the only one that's seen this thing, and they say you know the land hereabouts as well as anyone. You can ride, can't you?"

"I got a pretty good grip," the little man said.

"We're gonna be ridin' these horses, son, not carryin' 'em. Can you stay in a saddle or not?"

"I believe I can," Petticord answered gravely.

The Ranger shook his head. "Mr. Petticord, I've not seen your like before, and that's all I intend to say. But I'm proud to have you with us. Sheriff, what about your deputy? He gonna be able to tie back all that hair of his and join us?"

"He'll come."

"Not my nephew," said Doc, when he saw the Ranger's eyes sweep the room.

"What's that?" said Lightfoot.

"Jake. I don't want him involved in all this."

"He's old enough to shoot straight, ain't he?"

"No," said Doc. "He *isn't*. And I don't want him with us."

"Well, that ain't completely up to you. I aim to deputize him."

"Captain, don't check me in this matter. He is the only surviving child of my late sister and I will not have him endangered."

The Ranger looked like he wanted to spit. He had a gash just above his right temple that he'd declined to let Daris treat. It was encircled by a livid blue bruise.

"Jake," said Daris, jumping in before the conversation grew too heated, "I see that blush and I know you're angry. But I have to say I agree with your uncle this time. This isn't building flying machines in the backyard. You let us geriatrics take our chances."

"What?" said Jake.

"Us old farts," the Sheriff explained. "We'll get ourselves shot up so you don't have to." Reeves Duncan meant this as a joke. No one laughed.

"You ain't gonna keep that sprout under your wing much longer, Doc," said the Ranger.

Doc seemed to be on the verge of answer, but he held his tongue. It wouldn't have been pleasant.

"I know George Ridley," the Sheriff interrupted, addressing his comments to Jewel Lightfoot. "He owns the livery stable. He'll rent us some horses. 'Course, you already picked out the best one, Captain. But he's got a couple others worth puttin' a saddle on."

"Are you planning to tell Mr. Ridley why we need them?" asked Daris.

The Sheriff frowned.

"Tell him we're goin' huntin'," said Lightfoot, propping one of his square-toed boots on the coffee table. "It might turn out to be true."

Letter from Daris W. Kendrick, B.S., M.A., M.D.

Atcheson
November 10

My Dearest Miriam:

I regret to say Walter fares no better now than when I arrived. His drinking has, indeed, worsened, as has his idée fixe about the possibility of some vaguely defined supernatural menace in the area. I confess that circumstances here are strange in a way I had not previously imagined possible. There is work by a German named Dorfler that suggests hysteria may, in some sense, be contagious. More on this when I return. Walter's delusional tendencies aside, there is certainly some predatory agency at work in Ochiltree County, and I have, through no particular impetus of my own, fallen in with two peace officers, one local, the other a representative of the State, who are endeavoring to halt the bloody work that has manifested itself here recently. The local is intelligent and apparently well-intentioned, but not overly fond of the fruits of industry. Our state officer—I will keep his identity confidential, for the nonce—is entirely uneducated but possessed of an undeniable charisma. He is a sharp little splinter of a man, and it is he who goads us to action. Worry not! I will tend to my safety, as you well know. Your suspicions regarding young Jacob Hennessey were, as usual, correct. His uncle spends but little time with him, and Jake, as he is known, feels unwelcome and unwanted. I have done my best to show him that Walter's problems are not of his doing. He is a bright boy, as pale and dark-eyed as his mother, much given to mechanical pursuits and convinced that little else is worth notice. Please inform our friend Wilson that he may continue to see such of my patients as are content to see him, and that we shall be auditing his accounts to see that no unfair liberties have been taken with my usual fee schedule. With any luck I shall have a practice remaining when I return. In fact, with Wilson at large, the Ward may find that it has more need for my talents than ever before! Allow me another few days to see this matter through. Walter needs me. Not as much as I need you, my love, but his need is real nonetheless. My best, and butterflies, to dear Liza as always.

With love and frequent kisses,
Daris

P.S. I have made a friend. The massive field hand I wrote you of earlier—the one who imprisoned himself, and whom I suspected briefly of the mayhem here—seems grateful for my solicitude. A small price to pay. I merely asked him for his opinion. Apparently such requests are rare in the Thicket. He has also been persuaded to bathe—an even rarer event in the Thicket!

15.

The Sortie

Jake ended up riding with the posse after all.

He hadn't intended to. Saturday dawned cool and overcast beneath an oyster-colored sky. Lightfoot and the Sheriff already had horses. Doc and Ed Petticord rode mares from George Ridley's livery stable, while Daris picked a gelding named Rebel. East was finally mounted on a gigantic mule named Maisie, which was owned by Jake's friend Eben Melton. Reeves Duncan's deputy, Jared Sweet, also had a horse, but he missed the appointed departure time. Though the Ranger had a few choice words to deliver on the subject of dependability, the Sheriff wasn't overly concerned. Jared had a tendency to oversleep. For that matter, it was sometimes difficult to tell when he was fully awake. His usefulness to the posse was questionable.

In fact, though, there was a good reason for Jared Sweet's delay. When he showed up at Doc's back door, not long after Lightfoot and the others rode out of town, Deputy Sweet looked like he'd walked through a cyclone. He said he'd been detained by J.R. Holsan and Willard Mills, who surprised him at the ramshackle boarding house where he lived and asked him more questions than he could truthfully answer. They wanted to know where the hell Clarence East was, and when he'd be back in his cell. Focusing on the second part of the question, Jared answered honestly that he didn't rightly know. The fact was, Reeves Duncan didn't always tell his deputy what he was thinking or had planned. Holsan and Mills weren't pleased to hear this defense, but they seemed to accept it; most everyone knew Deputy Sweet didn't know sorghum from swamp water. They let the deputy go with a few choice words of warning. The town was watching him and Sheriff Duncan both. Blood called for blood.

Whole town's watching, Jared dutifully repeated. *Yessir. Blood calls for blood.*

Ten minutes later, Jared slipped out the back door of the boarding house, circled around George Nolte's smithy, and followed the little creek that led to Doc's place. He'd heard about the Nichols Mill, he admitted to Jake, but he wasn't exactly sure where it was. This was all the excuse Jake needed. He saddled Cherokee and led Jared out the Flood road at a canter—or as close to a canter as Cherokee could muster these days.

They caught up with the Ranger and his companions three miles outside of town, just before they turned onto the overgrown wagon trail that led to Amos Newton's place.

"Nothin' like punctuality," snapped Lightfoot, glancing beyond Jake and Jared back along the way they'd come. The Ranger sat slumped in his saddle on his big sorrel gelding. He'd pulled his flat-brimmed hat low over his eyes, and he looked for all the world like he was about to fall asleep. Yet he was armed for a minor insurrection. He wore his pistol in a cross-draw holster on his weak side, just behind a coffin-handled Bowie knife. His slide-action Winchester shotgun hung in a scabbard beneath his left knee.

"I see two mules tied inside that first line of trees to my right," the Ranger continued. "Don't go lookin' *now,* for Christ's sake. Them boys probably ain't sure what to make of us. But I'm willing to bet they ain't waitin' to hold our hands. Jake, you'd best stay with us."

Doc's face puckered in disapproval. "Stay close," he muttered, when Jake rode near.

Jake looked up at Doc's pressed-silk top hat and figured it might make more sense to keep his distance. But he just nodded.

"Nice and easy," muttered Lightfoot, reining his horse around without any apparent effort. "At a walk."

✿ ✿ ✿

The Mill wasn't much to look at. The main building was a barn-like two-story structure with warped wooden shakes and a noticeable sag in the roofline. In the shade of a huge live oak on the north side of the building stood a bulbous, kelly-green coach—the same coach Jake had seen with Doc a few weeks before. A barbed-wire fence enclosed a few square yards of dirt for several horses, and two wooden sheds housed a welter of mismatched machine parts and lengths of steel cable. Dun-colored canvas tents were visible beneath the trees that ringed the clearing. Shirts and trousers hung limp from a pair of clotheslines, and empty cans and old newspapers lay strewn about the buildings. From somewhere came the throb and clank of mechanical equipment, loud and insistent in the stillness of midday.

Steam drill, thought Jake.

The riders reined up in the open area in front of the main building. Daris Kendrick's horse shouldered into Lightfoot's sorrel. The Ranger took one foot out of his stirrup and gave the offending animal a shove with his boot. "You men keep crowdin' me," he hissed, "and I'm gonna shoot you myself. Spread out."

Daris was unfazed. "Apologies, Captain. I was trying to get a better look at your skin. If I'm not mistaken, sir, your complexion has taken on a bluish tint."

"Much obliged, Doctor. Yours still looks black to me. Now back off about ten paces."

The monotonous racket of the drill suddenly ceased. They all turned when they heard the creak of old hinges from the main building.

The front door opened and stood ajar, showing nothing but darkness within. Then a set of fingers wrapped around the door and someone stared out from the gloom. A moment later, Amos X. Newton himself stepped out onto the dilapidated porch. Amos had never been a handsome man. Now he was downright repellent. He had a large, potato-shaped head, a bulbous nose, and a soft-lipped mouth that took up most of the lower half of his face. Streaks of white scalp showed through the dark hair plastered to his head. His black wool trousers were held up by a pair of grimy red suspenders looped over his shoulders and naked torso. Sweat glistened on his forehead and shoulders, and Jake could see a constellation of crumbs in the pelt of black hair on the man's belly.

A moment later a bald man with a shotgun and a week's worth of beard stepped out on the porch beside him. He wore an unbuttoned green shirt. Like Amos Newton, he was barefooted, as if he'd just stepped out of bed.

"This here's private propity," he announced, in a voice that could have come from the rusty hinges. "What the hell y'all want?"

Lightfoot glanced over at Doc as if to say *Your turn.* Walter McDivitt tried to smile. Doc wasn't much of a smiler even at the best of times. Garbed in black and seated uncomfortably on his horse like some sort of sea-sick buzzard, the expression he made now was more of a wince.

"Just came out to check on Mr. Newton here," he explained. "Haven't seen you around, Amos. Nobody has."

Amos Newton shaded his eyes against the daylight. "Come with a bunch of men, huh? Just for a house call?"

"Well, I suppose there's a few of us. But I did want to check on you. How's the knee?"

"Knee's fine, Doc. If I felt any better, there'd be two of me."

"And the drilling?"

Amos's eyes darted to one side—the side where the man with the shotgun stood. "Comin' on, I reckon."

Doc's horse shied and danced. She was a skittish little roan and the men watched as he tried to calm her down. "Found anything?" he finally said.

"Who wants to know?" Newton demanded, drawing himself up indignantly.

"Nobody wants to know. Don't get tetchy."

"You just asked," Newton persisted. "Sounds like you want to know."

Doc shook his head. "Just making conversation."

"You didn't come out here to say *how do*. Y'all come to see what I *found*, didncha?"

"Amos, I'm your doctor. I am sincerely inquiring as to the state of your health."

Lightfoot interrupted. "You mind if we take a look around your place, Mr. Newton?"

Amos smirked for a moment, as if contemplating the humorous possibilities of such an inspection. Then, as if remembering his situation, his face grew serious again.

His companion pumped the shotgun to chamber a shell. "Yeah, he minds. I told ya, this here is *private propity*. Now I don't know what kinda monkeyshines y'all are up to, and I don't give a rat's ass. Y'all need to move yer butts on down the road before I get to the count of ten or I'm gonna turn one a' y'all into a got-damn bloody *mess*."

Jewel Lightfoot spat something off the tip of his tongue. "I don't recall speakin' to you, friend."

The bald man's eyes bulged in his head. "And I don't recall asking for any a' your lip, you sawed-off hunk a' dog turd. So get off this land. NOW!"

This should have been where it ended. The Ranger knew he didn't have any right to be on the property. This was Texas, after all. Private property meant just that. *Private*. The lawman waited a couple of moments to see if Amos Newton's companion was going to be stupid enough to actually aim that pig-shooter his way. That would be a different story.

Threatening a peace officer. Lightfoot had shot men for less. Considerably less. But the pugnacious bald man stood perfectly still. The Ranger had been asked to leave. He didn't have a warrant, so leave is what he was going to have to do.

By now, though, Amos Newton was grinning at some secret that was too powerful to keep inside. He stepped to the front of the porch and stood in the center of a dark stain on the weathered pine planks. He raised his arms up over his head as if he was addressing a midway crowd of gawking bumpkins. Behind him a chicken strolled out the front door of the mill house as if it was searching for a front-row seat.

"Friends," said Newton, as if he was about to confess. "I've found some things." He chuckled, shook his head. "I've found *wonderful things*!"

"What have you found, Amos?" said Sheriff Duncan.

"I ain't supposed to tell you that," he whispered theatrically. He gave a grotesque sort of wink as he jerked his head in the direction of the man with the shotgun.

"That's enough," said Shotgun, poking Newton in the ribs with the barrel of his weapon. "Get your fat ass back in the house."

"Oil?" prompted Daris Kendrick. "Water?"

"I said that's *enough*," squealed the bald man.

"Better!" shouted Amos, his voice suddenly powerful. He stood on his toes and raised his hands to heaven. "I've found LIFE!"

A single shot rang out from the woods in back of them. A red wound blossomed in the center of the big man's forehead, and his yellow grin, all rotted gums and tobacco-stained teeth, froze in place as he fell backward. Amos X. Newton—showman, stock fraud, wildcat driller—was dead before he hit the porch.

✵ ✵ ✵

It was hard to say exactly what happened next.

Lightfoot drew his revolver. Or, more precisely, Jake Hennessey later reflected, the big Colt *appeared in his hand*, because there seemed to be no intermediate thought or action; it was simply there. The bald man raised his weapon, but the Ranger fired before he could level it. The shotgun fell to the steps and discharged back toward the house and the bald man gripped the hole in his face where his left cheek had been. Blood poured out between his fingers as he staggered down the stained planks and toppled off them into the pile of detritus at the end of the porch. A window shattered. More shots rang out. Jake forced himself to look away from the house: from Amos Newton lying dead on the planks like a small mountain, staring up at the sky, and the bald man writhing on his pile of trash, screaming in pain. The boy saw puffs of smoke rising from at least two different spots in the trees. Doc gave a little grunt and seemed to slump in his saddle. Reeves Duncan was battling his horse and trying to get his sidearm unholstered at the same time. Jewel Lightfoot fired rapidly three times, now four, into the woods.

"Ride!" said the Ranger, and he whipped the sorrel's head around toward the road back to town. In only a moment all the horses were following, each trying to outrun the next. The bullets whined as they passed. Jake grabbed a handful of mane and held on to Comanche as best he could. The old horse had shuffled off the weight of a dozen years and was close to the front of the herd, wheezing with exertion. The motley group of men and animals went thundering up the narrow road like Crusaders charging through a mountain pass. It was exhilarating in that peculiar and irrational way known best to young men. Jake found himself grinning in spite of his terror.

They'd ridden half a mile when Lightfoot reined up. The others followed his example. The Ranger quickly dismounted, threw himself on the ground, and pressed one ear to the earth.

"They're comin'," he growled. "Get off the road."

"Where do we go?" asked Daris.

"I don't care, just *go*! Get back to town and meet up at the house. And get that goddamned sidearm out, Sheriff. Maybe you can throw it at someone."

Jake didn't wait for further instructions. He spurred his horse into the sweetgum and shag bark hickory trees on the south side of the road. Daris was right behind him. He was followed by the Sheriff, Jared Sweet, Clarence East, and Doc. Edmund Petticord brought up the rear. The Ranger shook his head as he watched his posse of mooncalves and misfits disappear into the brush. *This bunch,* he reflected, *wouldn't have lasted a day in the Comancheria.* He stuck his left foot in the near stirrup and vaulted up into the saddle. With a flick of the reins, he turned his horse and plunged off the road in the opposite direction.

❊ ❊ ❊

The Thicket closed in around them. It was dark in the trees, cool and green and as still as a grave. With Jake still in the lead, the men urged their mounts through a muddy slough choked with hackberry and mustang grape, then rode up into a stand of pines where they made better time. The pines gave way to hardwoods again—old-growth stuff, tangled and dark, massive trunks standing like pillars in a disorderly acropolis. Then they crossed a trail running east and Jake bore left to follow it. He looked down, then back at the men following him. He almost ran into the first corpse.

The bodies hung upside-down from a dozen oak limbs, suspended by chains wrapped around their ankles. They were naked, and their flesh was a variety of colors that ranged from a fishy white to the gray-green of Spanish moss. Most of the corpses were headless. The faces of the others were so caked with gore that it was impossible to recognize their features. Their lips curled back from their teeth in mocking, pitiful grins. Their hair, stiff with blood and bile and filth, hung in inverted fans beneath their heads so the carcasses looked like denizens of some antipodal nether region wrenched above the surface of the earth. Beneath each body stood a metal pail. Jake glanced into one and saw it was half-full of dark blood and brown leaves. A slender breeze—just a momentary breath of air, really—filtered through the trees, and the stench of death washed over them. Then the flies. There were thousands of them. The first insects perched on Jake's hands and forearms. One flew into his open mouth. Jake spat it out and then, before he quite knew what was happening, he had to lean over and empty his stomach. Jared Sweet did the same thing a moment later.

"Jesus H. Christ," whispered Reeves Duncan, surveying the grisly scene. Both arms were missing from the corpse closest to him. At the base of a tree nearby was a pile of dirty clothing. A lumber saw and two hatchets rested on the exposed roots. Next to them sat a single brown head, its features distorted by rot.

Daris's face was ash-gray. "*Holle hath keine Begrenzungen, aber, wo wir sind, ist Holle…*"

"Marlowe," mumbled Doc. He looked sick, but Daris thought he knew why.

"Exactly. We seem to have located your missing Croats, Walter. What's left of them, anyway. I hope to God these men were dead before the saw was employed."

Clarence East stared at the two physicians as if they'd taken leave of their senses; as if perhaps the world at large had taken leave of *its* senses and finally gone stark raving mad, like a rabid dog shivering in the noonday sun. Jared Sweet was wide-eyed and pale, his hands wrapped tight around his saddle horn. Only Edmund Petticord remained impassive. The little man seemed not to notice the corpses. He angled his head to one side and listened to the air. A moment later the rest of the group heard it too: voices to the south, and the sound of a pistol shot. Jake wasn't sure what it meant. But he knew it might mean their pursuers were getting closer. He didn't want to get caught where he was. Not by the sort of people who could do *this*.

Petticord nudged his horse past Jake on the left.

"Still comin'," he said. "Follow me."

He didn't have to say it twice.

✼ ✼ ✼

It took them the rest of the day to make it back to Atcheson.

They spent most of the time hiding. Two groups of riders (or possibly the same group, twice) passed within thirty yards of them during the course of the long afternoon. Crouched behind a fallen sycamore, Reeves Duncan cocked his little .38 and waited for a target to ride into view. But Ed Petticord knew how to go to ground. He'd found a dry creek bed that lay several feet below the forest floor. The horses sheltered there as the men in the posse took turns on watch. Eventually, when the sounds of pursuit had faded, Jake and his companions coaxed and cursed the horses up out of the creek bed. They bulled their way through a mass of vines and briars and into another stand of virgin pines. Here they remounted and pushed toward the east. They rode into town at dusk, tired and filthy, livid with welts and scratches. Daris Kendrick had fallen and bruised an elbow. Jake had caught a hackberry limb just above his right eye and still couldn't see straight. But the vision of the orchard of butchered bodies was still with them. No one complained of his discomfort. No one said a word. When they got to Doc's house, Jared Sweet and Clarence East gathered the reins of the horses and led them around back to be fed and watered. Reeves Duncan left without saying where he was going. Jake, Doc, Daris, and Ed Petticord filed into the kitchen. The house was dark. Standing inside, Jake noticed the glass of the kitchen window was shattered. Silverware and fragments of glass and porcelain littered the wooden floor.

Doc was moving slowly. He wasn't the oldest man in the group, but the horrors of the afternoon seemed to sit more heavily on him than the others. Petticord poked the embers in the fireplace and managed to coax a red flame to life. In the light they saw a message painted on the mirror above the mantel piece. It said:

FIND ROSE ANN

And, on the far wall, another one:

GIVE US THE NIGER

They also saw the Ranger. Captain Jewel Lightfoot sat in Doc's big chair in the corner, staring out from a pocket of shadow. Books and random papers were strewn on the rug around him. The Ranger's square-toed boots were propped on a supine body, and his six-shooter lay in his lap.

Jake edged over to look. The face of the man at Lightfoot's feet was bloody and swollen. His hands were bound behind his back with lengths of what looked like reins, and he had a brown kerchief stuffed in his mouth.

"Evenin', gentlemen," said Lightfoot. He was drinking from a bottle of Doc's best bourbon. His gray eyes were bright. "Y'all look like you was rode hard and put up wet. House got tore up pretty good while we was away. Just as well ol' East wasn't here. We mighta found him swingin' from that cottonwood out front. And don't think your housekeeper's gonna be over to help clean up, Doc, 'cause she done quit. Too many coloreds in the house, evidently. There's a note on the table. But maybe this'll cheer you up. Meet Mr. Ibrahim Solomon."

The room was silent.

"Also known," continued the Ranger, "as the Turk."

They all considered the prisoner. The man on the floor was perfectly still, but he stared back at them with dark eyes that contained unmistakable malice. He focused his gaze on Jake. Jake wanted to turn away, but he found it difficult to do. The prisoner's eyes held his as if their fields of vision were intertwined, like braided rope. The boy felt a sensation of dread run up through his legs into his spine. It was coming, somehow, from Ibrahim Solomon. He knew it was irrational and impossible and yet the force gathered and intensified. Jake fought with all the strength he had to turn away from the Turk's gaze. And when, finally, he yanked his head to one side, severing the connection, he saw his uncle fall. Doc sagged backwards onto the big divan.

"Walter," said Daris. "What is it? What's wrong?"

Doc's mouth twisted with the effort of speech. "I'm afraid...I've been shot."

"Good Lord. Let me see. Why didn't you say something?"

Doc tried to work the buttons of his shirt. Daris sank to one knee in front of him.

"Wanted to get home," said Doc. His voice was barely more than a whisper.

"Lord," said Daris, staring at the blood on his hands. "Lord, lord, lord. Jake, help me. We need to get your uncle up to bed. *Now*."

Found among papers of Jacob J. Hennessey; note on face reads: "*Finely official. We can win local prize with add. of ailerons I bet. Branscomb in Nacog. said to be working on multi-wing beast— possible similar to Zerbe design at L.A. meet. Eben*"

HOUSTON INTERNATIONAL AIR MEET

SEE THEM FLY!

3 days, Jan. 22-24, 1912
Ellington Station

Southern Pacific Railroad; Excursion Rate 32 Cents
Trains Every 20 Minutes

Over 30 Aircraft of All Description

Bleriot Monoplane
Curtiss Biplane
Twining's Ornithopter

$500 Prizes *for Duration, Speed, and Altitude*

Prize for Best Locally Designed Aeroplane or Dirigible

Glenn Curtiss; Louis Paulhan; Charles Willard to Attend

Refreshments Available

SEE THE HUMAN BIPLANE!

16

Lightfoot's Prize

Jewel T. Lightfoot's interrogation techniques were crude but effective. In this case they involved plying his prisoner with one hundred and eighty-proof corn liquor of recent manufacture. The moonshine was supplied by Sheriff Duncan, who'd acquired it, no questions asked, from Dimmitt Evans. It was potent stuff. The Sheriff poured out a spoonful and lit it with a match. Sure enough, the liquid burned bright blue. You had to hand it to the man. Dim Evans might be a liar, a rake, and a bootlegger, but he made a fine product. It was almost pure ethanol.

The Turk fought like a cornered cat. The Sheriff and Jared Sweet had to hold Mr. Ibrahim Solomon's mouth open with a pair of leather belts. They looped one belt around his upper jaw and the other around the lower and pulled as the Ranger squeezed sponge-full after sponge-full of liquor down the man's throat. The Turk tried not to swallow. He managed to spit a fair amount of the stuff out. But he couldn't keep *all* of it out, and after an hour and a half the alcohol started to take effect.

Lightfoot had seen it a dozen times. You could pump whiskey into an Irishman all night and all he'd do was sing. Nine times out of ten, your Dutchman would fall asleep. But most men wanted to talk. Brag. Confess. Commiserate. Curse. Some men felt *compelled* to talk.

While they waited for the corn liquor to take effect, Reeves Duncan went to check on Doc and fetch a pot of coffee. He seemed to be taking his own sweet time, so Lightfoot figured he'd start the questioning without him. He had Jared check the ropes that bound the prisoner to his chair. The Ranger took a couple of steps to place himself slightly behind Ibrahim Solomon's right ear.

"You ready to tell me where you're from?" Lightfoot asked.

"Where I'm from?" said the captive, twisting his neck to look back at his questioner.

Lightfoot scratched a match against the sole of one of his boots and lit up a cheroot. "That's right. Where you're from. That ain't so hard, is it?"

"Oh, no. Not at all. I'm flattered you ask."

Lightfoot nodded. The captive spoke perfect English—with a British accent, in fact. Some men would have been impressed by this badge of refinement. Jewel Lightfoot was not one of them.

"Good," said the lawman. "How about you flatter me some more and give me an answer."

"Ankara, originally."

"Turkey, eh?"

"Bravo, Constable."

"What are you doing in these parts? I don't know if you noticed, but we don't get many Turkans around here."

Ibrahim Solomon winced. Lightfoot realized he was talking too fast. He spat a speck of tobacco off his tongue, tried a different tack. "What're y'all doing with Amos Newton out at the Mill? And why'd you shoot the crazy sumbitch?"

"I didn't shoot him," said the Turk.

"All right. Why'd he get shot?"

The captive smirked. "He was shot?"

Even Lightfoot sometimes grew tired of the petty tortures that accompanied interrogation. *Hard on the hands, for one thing.* Jared Sweet winced as he looked on. Lightfoot wiped the blood off his knuckles with a rag he found in Sheriff Duncan's desk. It smelled of horse flesh and gun oil. He glanced at the deputy. "Son, this ain't gonna be pretty. Why don't you step on over to Doc's and send your boss back this a' way."

Deputy Sweet shrugged. "Sheriff told me to stay with you, sir."

"I'll keep."

Sweet took a long last look at the Turk's broken face before he left.

"Fine young man," said Solomon.

"He's a real lightnin' bolt," said Lightfoot. He went to the window and watched the deputy circle the building, heading back toward Doc McDivitt's place. Doc was hurt bad, according to Daris Kendrick. Gut shot. A slow bleeder. The Ranger had seen plenty of those. Most ended badly. He rubbed at a smudge on the glass. "You know, Ibraham, I ain't no fonder of a beatin' than the next man. I'd just as soon conversate. But you need to realize one thing. You're in Texas. And you *will* tell me why you've got dead bodies hangin' from oak trees out at the Mill, or you ain't gonna leave this room with the same number of organs you had when you come in. If you catch my drift."

Ibrahim Solomon raised his head, tried to focus his eyes. A piece of one of his teeth was suspended in the blood and saliva on the side of his face. He seemed to be digesting this new piece of information. *The bodies.* His captors had found something he hadn't wanted them to see. He raised one eyebrow, winced, licked his lips. He stared at the floor. He exhaled as if he'd decided he no longer had anything to lose. "Ah," he sighed. "The oak trees."

"That's right. My posse found your little butcher shop. Why?"

"Why were they hung from the...oak trees?"

"Exactly," said the Ranger. "Why?"

The Turk was suddenly somber. He tucked in his chin, glanced up at his interrogator as if he was about to ask for forgiveness. "Because they had the lowest branches?" he said.

Lightfoot hit him again. It didn't seem to matter. The Turk laughed like a hyena. Maybe they'd overdone it with the corn liquor. The Ranger wondered if he could find an automobile battery at this hour of the night. Sometimes it helped to connect a man like Ibrahim Solomon to the terminals. By his ball sack.

"Did I mention you're a dead man, Marshal?" said the captive.

"I ain't no *Marshal*, camel jockey. I'm a goddamned Texas Ranger. I drink dust and I piss barb wire. I've tracked Mescalero Apaches through country the devil wouldn't wipe his ass with and I've cleaned my boots on men meaner 'n you. Now tell me."

"Tell you…?"

"The *bodies*. My *compadres* in there saw a dozen dead men hangin' like side meat from a stand of oaks out at the Mill. You're gonna tell me who they were and how they got there and what kinda twisted sonsabitches you and your *amigo* Nageeb think you are. And you're gonna do it before the sun comes up."

Solomon glanced at the desk. The Ranger's pocket watch said eleven-thirty.

"Why not?" he said, and his voice held again those traces of silken menace it had held before the questioning started. Lightfoot was impressed. Most men would have been comatose with as much grain alcohol in their veins as Solomon had. The Turk continued: "You can contemplate the price of your newfound knowledge on your way to the abyss. Your precious Mr. Newton found something, Sheriff. It was something he was very proud of. But it wasn't oil. He drilled into something rigid and unyielding: a metal cylinder of unknown composition, thirty feet beneath the surface of the swamp." Solomon paused to toss his oily black hair up out of his face. "By his own account he ruined six drill bits trying to…how do you say? *Punch through it.* He finally managed to gouge out a little piece of the metal, which he sent to the

Smithsonian Institute, along with a note of inquiry. Never received an answer, as best we can tell. Then he bored a little deeper and found something *inside* the foreign structure. A little...well, how should I put it? No bigger than a kitten. Hairless. Gelatinous. Something like your common garden slug. He wrote off about that too. Again, no answer. Then he sent a telegram to the British Museum, and that message found its way into our hands. There are those of us, Sheriff, who have been waiting a very long time for information of exactly this sort. Amos thought he had something to sell to one of your American carnivals. Your—again, the word. Your *freak shows*, yes? But he left the creature out in the sunlight and it burned to death. *Le pauvre.* This was shortly before we arrived. Turns out he'd found two more of the little pupae that were...not *viable*. In fact, the idiot had destroyed them with his own machinery. These operations have to be conducted delicately. Once my partner and I had established ourselves, we set about excavating the vessel, looking for others of the type inside the metal shell. Amos was cooperative enough. At first. As long as he continued to believe he was in charge, and that we were men of science, sent from abroad to aid him in the recovery and classification of his find. But the charade eventually grew tiresome. The man was quite ridiculous. For example, he proposed to sell tickets to anyone who cared to come out and *spectate*. That was when we started to keep him inside. Well cared for, of course. Plenty to eat. Plenty to drink—and that is plenty, I assure you."

Lightfoot was perched on the edge of Reeves Duncan's desk. He stubbed his cigarette out on the water-stained surface. "You keep talkin' about Amos Newton and I'm gonna cut out your tongue and stick it up your hindparts. Get to the point. Why are you slicin' men up and hangin' 'em from the trees?"

Ibrahim Solomon involuntarily ducked his head. He'd grown wary of the Ranger's small fists. "Sustenance, my friend."

"I ain't your friend. Sustenance for *who*? Or what?"

"You wouldn't understand," said the captive, with an air of exhaustion and contempt.

"Try me."

"For Him-Whom-We-Serve. You see, the young ones, once removed from the chemical baths aboard their vessel, start to grow immediately. They can survive on a variety of fluids. But the Protector has developed specialized tastes. As you may have noticed, he is somewhat different than you and me."

"You mean with the murders?" the Ranger snorted. "I've known some like that."

"Nevertheless, there are physical differences between the…species."

"Good Lord. What are you talking about, Solomon? What is this freak you're killing men to feed? Where's it from?"

The Ranger noted the spark of anger in Solomon's eyes. He didn't like the word *freak* coming back at him. Clearly the Turk was protective of his overlord.

"From a speck in the midnight sky, constable. Not far from a dying sun a billion years from here is a cold little planet that once held dominion over races more numerous than the insects in your swamps."

"Hold on. We got a lotta swamps. I'm gonna have to get my notebook for this."

"Indeed. There are more things in heaven and earth, Horatio, than are dreamt of in your philosophy."

"You might be surprised at some of the things I've seen, Mr. Solomon. Much less what I've dreamed. So how'd it get here? Fell outta the sky?"

The captive shrugged.

"Your creature have a name?" the Ranger persisted.

"Many names. Fiend. Vampire. Nephilim. We call him *Tawuse Melek*. The Peacock Angel. There is a legend among our neighbors in the Sinjar that he and his kind were expelled from heaven—that they fell, wings and all, all the way to hell, and have plotted ever since to reclaim their king's rightful throne from God himself. And they did fall from the heavens, I suppose. That part is essentially accurate, though some of the details are hazy."

"So what are *you* doing with these things? And who's this Nageeb you're traveling with? The Arab."

The captive made a sound that was almost a laugh. "*Arab*," he said. "That's amusing. My companion Naguib is the 111th scion of the Kingdom of the Turquoise Mountain in the easternmost regions of what the British call *Afghanistan*."

"Ain't he a peach."

"The long-dead kingdom, I might add. But it will return. Once we have chastised the Sunni, and the Kurds, we will lift up those who have aided us. It is promised."

"Let that lay for a minute. What is it exactly you're trying to do with these...*things*...that fell from heaven?"

"We are gatherers."

"Of what?"

"Of them."

"Why?"

"Because we are loyal."

"Loyal to what? These—?"

"And there will be rewards. You see, once we recover the pupal females, propagation will be simple. We have our sire. Reproduction is swift. The armies of Tawuse Melek will march before the century is out."

"And you're going to get a *re*ward, huh?"

"Oh, yes. Beyond your mortal imagination."

It was no longer chilly in the room. In fact, the Ranger felt himself starting to sweat. "How about this for a *re*ward? You tell me where that blood-sucking sonofabitch is and I'll let you keep your man parts."

The Turk shook his head. "You can't kill it."

The Ranger stuck his notebook back in his breast pocket. He stretched his neck and shoulders. "Wanna bet?" he said.

* * *

The boy sat watching his uncle die. Walter McDivitt had been resting quietly for several minutes. He woke suddenly and seemed confused by his surroundings.

"Jake!" said Doc, searching for his nephew's face.

The boy was perched on a stool beside Doc's four-poster bed, holding one of his uncle's big hands. "Easy, Doc," he said. I'm right here."

"I've failed you, son."

Jake had to think about this. Words were never his strong suit. "No. That's not right. You never failed me. You took me in."

"I loved your mother, Jake. You know that. I never…."

"Don't talk like that. You're gonna be okay. Daris said—"

Walter McDivitt shook his head. His dark eyes seemed to have sunken into his skull. "Daris is lying. I'll treat you like a man, if that's what you want. I'm shot in the stomach. He won't tell me, but I'm…the slug hit one of my intestines. That's a bad wound. Mortal."

Jake didn't need to be told this. The bed sheets over Doc's torso were soaked with blood. His uncle was shivering even in the warmth of the closed room. "You need Dr. Kendrick?" said the boy.

Doc narrowed his eyes. Dim as it was, the glow of the lamp beside his bed seemed to pain him. "Please. I've left you what little I have. Very little. Use it. Remember your mother."

"Doc?"

"Yeah."

"I shouldn't have doubted you. There's something bad out there."

"Bad." Doc sniffed. "I saw them…on *Samar*. All around us. Monsters. I swear to God, sometimes I still see them. I've known for a long time I was cursed. That I would…bring evil…wherever I went. I knew it when I told your mother I would take you in. I knew it. But I missed her so. And I was alone."

"You're safe here."

"I don't care anymore. Except for you. Get away from this place."

Jake nodded. "I didn't think you wanted me here."

Doc seemed not to hear this last comment. "I'm sorry, son. I'm sorry to leave you with…this…*thing*."

Jake tightened his grip on his uncle's hand.

"Go," said Doc. "Far away. While you can."

"You need water," said Jake. He took the pitcher from the dresser beside the bed and made his way down the hall to the stairs. His eyes were stinging, and he wasn't sure whether to let the tears come, or to hold them back, or how long he'd even have the choice. Downstairs the Sheriff sat at the dining room table, talking animatedly to Edmond Petticord as Clarence East looked on. Petticord had proposed to head up the west bank of the Anahuac by himself to see if he could reconnoiter the Mill from across the river. The Sheriff was attempting to argue him out of it, but the little man didn't seem interested in discussing the matter. Jake tried to form an opinion on the plan, but quickly discovered he didn't much care. He found his way outside and pumped cool water into the pitcher. It was a clear night and he could see the canopies of the oaks in the backyard outlined in the starlight. He heard the soft nicker of one of the livery horses in the barn. He felt a calmness he'd never experienced in this place before, a sense that he had, at last, found home. Doc was hurt and scared and slightly out of his head. But maybe his wound wasn't as bad as he thought. Maybe Daris could do something to get him well and after a month or two things would go back to the way they were, or the way they were only *better*, because now Jake knew he was wanted and that his presence wasn't simply some giant mistake Doc had made years ago and never quite figured out how to remedy.

"Is he resting?" said Daris, poking his head out the kitchen door.

Jake shook his head. "He was, but he woke up. And he's still bleeding."

"I've got something that will calm him. Let me go up with you." Jake started toward the door, but Daris stopped him with an upraised hand. "If there's anything you need to say to your uncle," he cautioned. "You probably ought to say it now."

Jake felt his eyes burn again as he realized what Daris was telling him. He nodded as he looked away. Together he and the black doctor climbed the steep stairs to Doc's room. Jake went first. He stepped inside and found the man called Naguib standing beside the bed, holding Doc's head by the hair. Doc's throat was cut almost to the bone, and the room stank of blood.

The big Arab was drenched in gore. He smirked at the sight of the pitcher.

"Oh," he said, pursing his lips in a grotesque parody of concern. "Too late."

*　*　*

Ibrahim Solomon locked eyes with his interrogator. "I've seen arrogance before," he said. "It tends to leave a man once the Protector—Him-Whom-We-Serve—gets its first taste of his blood. But you misunderstand me. You might be able to terminate the creature's existence, if you work at it hard enough. It does bleed. But then how would you find out where the rest of them are?"

"You're bullshittin' me," said the Ranger. Then, to clarify: "You're a born liar."

"You think it came alone?"

Lightfoot stopped to think. This was almost as difficult for him as running, and the effort was obvious. The Turk emitted a long, unpleasant chuckle. Despite his pain, he enjoyed trifling with the ridiculous little man in front of him. He'd dispatched similar martinets before. French *gendarmes*. Mexican *federales*. This one was going to be a pleasure. And the moment was almost at hand. He just needed to clear his head. The alcohol—*accursed stuff*—was slowing his perceptions. In fact, he was a little unsure of what he was seeing just now. The lawman was grinning back at him.

"Nice play," said the Ranger. "I'd probably say the same thing, if I was in your shoes. But I'm thinkin' you ain't got but the one Protector, Mr. Turk. And I think he's old. And I think if you don't get them female bugs off that space bullet and take 'em somewhere quiet and dark where you can raise 'em up, and have your Protector fertilize 'em, you ain't gonna have you no demon army to follow. No Wars of the End Time. No gold-and-glory *re*wards for sellin' your own kind to the Devil."

Solomon's face contorted with anger and—it was unmistakable—*fear*.

"How—? Who are you?"

The Ranger seated himself on the Sheriff's desk, facing his prisoner. "Thought you'd lost us, huh?"

"You're with the Enemy," said the Turk.

"That's right. You can't hide from the Almighty."

"God is DEAD!" Solomon screamed. "The angel lives!"

"Keep blasphemin', King Tut. Your killing days is over. Whatever y'all was expecting back in '08 was a bust. There's a hole in Siberia a half-mile wide where your last hope went down. Burnt a fair piece of Russia all to cinders, as I understand it. Now all we need to do is put a pound or two of silver in the belly of this last monster of yours, and we'll be done. And by the way: you move again and I'm gonna blow your face out the back of your head."

"Move?"

"You're messin' with them ropes," the Ranger observed.

Solomon nodded, as if he'd expected the threat. He clamped his eyes shut, breathed out his nose. He had to concentrate. He had to focus every fiber of his being on the problem at hand: ending the existence of the preening yokel who lounged on the desk in front of him, examining the ripped skin of his own knuckles. He cursed his predicament. The Ranger had caught him short. He'd underestimated the little man. He'd underestimated the Enemy. What was it they called themselves? *The Brotherhood.* That was it. The Brotherhood was a secret society of Christian fanatics, sworn at pain of death to protect the blood of Jesus's sheep-like followers. They'd spent the last eleven hundred years thwarting Islamic and other threats to their precious cross. They knew the Middle East, of course. Their agents prowled the back streets and low places of Aleppo and Cairo and Constantinople. They controlled the crossroads of Europe and Asia Minor. *But here? In East Texas? In the snake-infested swamps of this kingdom of rubes?* Solomon muttered to himself. He and Naguib had been so close. The operation was almost complete. There was only one way to get it back on track. He was going to have to kill the man in front of him. It wouldn't be difficult. He was about to get some help. The Turk cocked his head as if listening to something in the distance. "Do you know the call of the nightingale, Marshal?"

"Ain't no nightingales hereabouts."

"No," agreed the captive. "I didn't think so."

And again it came: the clear, high notes of a nightingale, from just outside the jailhouse door.

* * *

Naguib moved toward them languidly, a mocking half-smile on his dark face. He tossed his long hair back over one shoulder and slid the bloody dagger back into his belt. Daris pulled Jake behind him. The boy offered no resistance. His mouth was open, but no words came. He felt like he'd lost his senses, as if for the moment all connection with the tactile world had been severed. He simply couldn't form a reaction to what he'd plainly seen: his uncle staring up with lifeless eyes from a puddle of his own blood, his killer standing over him like the worst species of dream.

The big Arab parried Daris's out-thrust medical bag, raised one leg and kicked the black doctor into the wall.

"GO, Jake!" said Daris.

Jake stumbled out into the hallway. He told himself to keep moving. *Help*, he thought. *He needed to get help.* He met East coming up the stairs, slowly but methodically, two at a time. Finally the boy found his voice.

"They killed Doc," said Jake. "Get the Sheriff!"

Clarence East shrugged Jake's hands off his shoulders as if they were cobwebs. He continued up the stairs, walked to Doc McDivitt's bedroom, and found a man with long black hair trying to put his fist through Daris Kendrick's head.

Daris sat slumped in the far corner of the room, one arm bent in front of him to shield his face, his eyes wide with pain and fright. His attacker was bent over him, raining down blow after blow at the defenseless doctor's skull. The black-haired man had several lines of blue writing tattooed on his naked back, and the writing danced and quavered like tiny lines of fire. Clarence East was not a man of subtle thought. But neither was he stupid. He knew and had more or less accepted the salient facts of his existence. He had no education to speak of. He had trouble understanding rapid speech and the workings of most machinery. He knew the exact spot where he was born and was fairly certain he knew where he was going to die; it was, after all, the same place. He was aware that he scared people. He understood why. He hadn't been bested in physical conflict since he was nine years old—which was the last time he'd weighed less than two hundred pounds. There were aspects of the situation he was presented with now that he found puzzling. But here again, the essential facts were clear: an individual he found outlandish and disturbing was trying to kill someone who was, in a rudimentary fashion, East's friend.

What more was there to think about?

East grabbed the stool beside Doc's bed and raised it over his head. When he brought it down on Naguib's spine, the heavy wood splintered with the force of the blow. The

Arab looked up from the floor and snarled something guttural and unintelligible. It sounded like words uttered backwards.

"That's right," said East. He held one leg of the stool in his massive right hand. "This here is *Ochiltree* County."

* * *

Naguib was on him a moment later. East looped one of his huge arms around the Arab's neck and tossed him across the room into the opposite wall, shattering the full-length mirror that stood opposite the bed. Naguib picked up the largest of the shards and flung it at East, gashing the black man's forearm. East didn't have time to examine the damage, though. The Arab lowered his head and drove him out the bedroom door and through the oak banister that ran the length of the hallway. The men fell twelve feet to the wood floor below. It sounded like someone had dropped a piano. East was beneath the Arab and took the brunt of the impact; the black man emitted a brief, sharp bark, and his eyes rolled up in his head. Naguib rose up on his knees and hit him twice in the face and East didn't even raise his hands in defense. Jake had recovered himself enough by now to realize what was happening. He launched himself off the stairs at the Arab. It was a valiant effort, but a failure. The big man tossed him off negligently, almost casually. Reeves Duncan was next. In his panic he picked up the nearest heavy object—a skillet—and rushed out of the kitchen. Naguib backhanded a balcony newel at him and caught the Sheriff in the throat. The Arab smirked. He drew his dagger from his belt and straddled Clarence East's belly. When East tried to focus his eyes, Naguib spat on him. Again the words: harsh, predatory, the spawn of some benighted savage tongue none of them had ever heard or likely would hear again. He pressed the knife to East's throat, searching with the tip for the vein that, once tapped, could never be resealed. At just the moment he found what he was looking for, East stopped struggling.

Naguib was enjoying this: the prospect of death. The certainty of humiliation. He would gut this black giant, then visit the wrath of the Peacock Angel on every soul in the house. He spoke the words to himself. He leaned forward, and a cold smile stretched the corners of his mouth. That's when Dr. Daris Kendrick plunged a hypodermic needle into the soft flesh above Naguib's right hip.

The Arab roared as he whirled to see what had happened.

Daris held up the syringe. Nearly half the brown fluid in the cylinder was gone. The portly doctor's mouth and nose were a bloody mess, and he swayed where he stood. He glanced over at Jake. Even now Daris's instructional instincts were apparent.

"Morphine," he croaked, by way of explanation.

Still groggy, East grabbed his attacker's left wrist. Naguib twisted frantically. He screamed as he felt the first effects of the drug in his bloodstream. He kicked his way out of Daris's grip and stumbled out the back door into the night.

* * *

A look of triumph flickered across Ibrahim Solomon's battered face. He planted his feet and pushed his chair back. Then, cat quick, he swept his right leg across the desk and kicked the Ranger's lantern to the floor. The lantern's glass panes shattered. A blue line of flaming kerosene raced across the pine planks. At just that moment, the door to the jailhouse erupted inward, flung open so hard that it flew off its hinges. Something stood in the darkness outside. Lightfoot squinted, trying to make out the figure. It was big—almost as big as the doorway itself. In the next moment a body fell or was thrown into the room. *Jared Sweet*. His face was almost unrecognizable. The left side of the deputy's skull was caved in, and one of his sky-blue eyes hung like a sweetgum ball from its socket. The young man stared at Lightfoot with his remaining eye. He emitted a soft, almost babyish whimper. He might have been trying to speak.

The Ranger's gun belt was hanging on the far wall. He scrambled for his weapon as Ibrahim Solomon yanked his hands free of the ropes. Lightfoot reached the handle of the big Colt, found the trigger, felt his feet yanked out from under him. He hit the floor and something crashed down on top of him. *Solomon.* The man could move. The Turk slipped one arm around the Ranger's neck, the crook of his right elbow cradling Lightfoot's throat. The Turk squeezed the cradle tight and Lightfoot's face went livid as he strained against the choke. Stale blood pooled in his head. Oddly enough, he had a sudden recollection of his days as a young man, when he'd just earned his star and the life of a Ranger still seemed impossibly hard and glamorous. Captain Bill McDonald told him once: *Ain't but two things can happen when you let a man get in back of you. One means he likes you and the other don't, but chances are you ain't gonna enjoy neither one of 'em.*

He wasn't enjoying this one. The room was brighter now. Something was on fire and in the red light the Ranger finally got a glimpse of the thing that had stepped inside. The figure in the doorway had appeared vaguely human, but this was no longer true. It had begun to change. The bones of its skull lengthened, and a bony ridge formed in the middle of its forehead. Its eyes grew wider. The unholy creature flexed the muscles in its abdomen and the flesh of its upper back seemed to flare out behind it. There were blue veins like a latticework on the pale yellow scrim of the monster's chest and stomach, and now, with a wet, sucking sound, two iridescent screens rose up behind it and spread like the wings of a dragonfly. It was Ibrahim Solomon's Protector. It was Him-Whom-We-Serve. It was a vision straight out of hell.

Sweet merciful Jesus, thought the Ranger.

You will not fear the terror of the night, he told himself. *Nor the pestilence that stalks in darkness.*

Jared Sweet tried to crawl away.

The creature caught him at the door to the cells. It took a step with its left foot—a claw-like, three-toed thing. Then it brought the right foot down on what was left of Jared's head. The Ranger heard a sickening crunch. Blood spurted from the deputy's empty eye socket, and Jared Sweet brought forth the long, keening moan that was the last sound he ever made. The creature lifted him up by the hair. It found the deputy's throat and raked it open with its long teeth. Blood drained from the young man's veins like juice from crushed grapes, flowing down the nightmare vision's arms and bathing its chest. The monster's tongue emerged slowly from its jaws. It was a long, black, triangular organ that separated into a number of thinner filaments, like the waving tentacles of some invertebrate sea dweller. Lightfoot watched as the tentacles wormed their way into Jared Sweet's open mouth and empty eye socket. Another set disappeared into the wound at the deputy's throat. The creature held its prey close. Like a baby at its mother's breast, it started to feed.

Ibrahim Solomon was chanting some obscene liturgy into the Ranger's ear as the creature sucked and chewed at Jared Sweet's body. Dark dots danced in Lightfoot's peripheral vision. The room seemed to contract as the oxygen was squeezed from his brain like water from a sponge. In the back of his mind or the dreadful cellar beneath it he knew he had one chance to do this right and one chance only. He had to kill the evil sonofabitch who was choking him. He had to figure out where Ibrahim Solomon's face was and put a bullet straight through it. Time slowed as Lightfoot angled his sidearm up and back, twisting his wrist to aim the pistol. But the Turk saw what he was doing. He shifted his weight forward and drove the Ranger's face into the floor. Lightfoot could no longer hold his arm up to make the shot. In his last dim moment of failing consciousness, the Ranger put his gun on the floor. He picked it up backwards, with his thumb on the trigger, and tried again. The creature paused at its feeding to gaze down at the two men struggling on the floor. Lightfoot's thumb tightened on the trigger.

The revolver fired.

Solomon shrieked the first syllable of some final interrupted curse. The urgency of his hatred continued, but the Ranger smelled burnt flesh in the air, and the pressure of the choke slowly eased. He knew he'd hit something. He bellied out from under his attacker and gulped at the air, still on all fours. His head ached and he couldn't catch his breath. But now he had the creature's attention. The worm-pale thing dropped the lifeless husk of Jared Sweet and stepped toward the Ranger. Lightfoot tried to turn his sidearm around. He raised it and aimed as best he could at the monster's midsection. He squeezed the trigger again.

* * *

Solomon's face was a mask of blood. Shot through the jaw, he'd rolled sideways off Lightfoot into a puddle of kerosene. Flames danced on his back and shoulders. Though he could barely see, with one hand he found the piece of limestone Reeves Duncan used to prop the jailhouse door open. With his last ounce of animate rage he brought the rock down on Jewel Lightfoot's head. He'd been hoping to crush the little man's skull. As he died, his one consolation was that he might have succeeded.

* * *

Lightfoot heard his gun fire but knew nothing else. He felt himself falling to darkness. *I'm a dead man*, he thought. The jailhouse disappeared and the world went dark and he didn't even seem to mind that everything was moving away from him once and for all and beyond all recompense or capture. He was Jewel Truscott Lightfoot. His time on earth was done and he hadn't even managed to offer himself up in sacrifice as the angels had told him it was his duty and privilege to do. *I'm a dead man.* He remembered that night on the rock outside of Fredericksburg. He remembered that night as if its events had been branded on the back of his brain. He'd hurt one too many people in his life and in the final days of his journey to Hell the Lord had brought him to a vast expanse of granite on the Texas plains. It was a stark place of confession and atonement straight out of the Old Testament, all wrinkled earth and nail-sharp stars, and there He sent Jewel Lightfoot agents of redemption, shimmering creatures impossibly bright and clad in clouds of silver, *swimming* in silver, who offered him the chance of eternal life if only he renounced his attachment to the inducements of earth and swore fealty to a cause that was greater than himself. And he'd tried, Lord. He'd tried for the angels and for the Almighty but the sweetness of the world itself had held him like a snare and now, with the great prize almost his, he was falling into oblivion. The monstrous winged evil he'd been sent to dispatch was at loose among the lambs.

He'd failed his brotherhood. He'd failed his God. The horror reared up before him, impossible and obscene, and reached to take its prey.

I'm a dead man, the Ranger repeated to himself. *Lord into thy hands…*

I'm dead.

* * *

Reeves Duncan arrived a moment later, with Jake just a few yards behind. The little jailhouse glowed a dull orange from within, like a soot-covered ember. The Sheriff noticed the front door was gone. He heard the scrape of wood on wood and a burst of harsh words in a language he didn't recognize. Then a pistol shot. For a moment the Sheriff thought of J. R. Holsan and his Citizens' Committee. Maybe they'd worked themselves up into such a frenzy of civic righteousness that they'd come in search of Clarence East with dreams of castration and murder dancing like demons in their heads. Maybe they were tearing up the jailhouse because they couldn't find him. Bad news if this was the case: he was outnumbered. But the more obvious conclusion was that Captain Jewel T. Legend-of-the-Goddamned-West Lightfoot had lost control of his prisoner. This meant the prisoner might now have a gun. And the Ranger himself might have a bullet burning in his brain.

Another shot.

Reeves Duncan was just a country sheriff, but he knew better than to silhouette himself in a doorway. Best way in the world to get yourself drilled full of lead. Instead he loosened his grip on the little kerosene lantern he held and tossed it into the jailhouse. The glass of the lantern broke and a second sheet of flames illuminated the room. In the sudden glare the Sheriff saw, or thought he saw, something large and incomprehensible standing over Jared Sweet. He didn't stop to think about it. Reeves Duncan was a soft-spoken man. He was hard to rile. He knew this about himself, and he knew also that it was his one great flaw in the eyes of the people he was sworn to protect. But temper wasn't an issue at the moment. The sight of the mutilated corpses hanging in the woods near the Mill had frightened and angered him in equal parts. He'd thrown up twice when they got back to Atcheson. He'd been sweating ever since. Though the vision in front of him made little sense, he knew he was seeing an enemy, and even as he stepped forward he fired both barrels of his old Aubrey twelve-gauge into the creature's torso. The thing gave a wheezing, high-pitched shriek, a sound somewhere between the whine of a cicada and the weird, mourning wail of a panther. Duncan tossed the Aubrey aside, yanked his .38 out of its holster. He didn't have time to use it. The monster moved with amazing speed. By the time the Sheriff figured out what was happening, he was flat on his back and the creature was past him. Another blast split the night. It was

Jake Hennessey, firing after the thing with Doc's old service rifle.

The Sheriff pulled his great bulk up off the ground and entered the jailhouse. Flames danced across the room. The fire had spread to the sheet he'd hung over the window of his office, and the blaze lit a bizarre sight. The office looked like a slaughterhouse. Three men lay on the floor. By the door to the cells was Jared Sweet. He'd been ripped almost in half, and there wasn't much of a face left on his head—only a pulpy mass of flesh, cartilage, and exposed bone. Ibrahim Solomon was sprawled behind the desk. Someone had shot him through the lower jaw. He lay in a glistening necklace of his own blood, staring at the ceiling with lifeless eyes. He clutched with both hands the chunk of limestone the Sheriff used as a doorstop. The closest form was Jewel Lightfoot.

The Ranger opened his eyes, tried to focus.

The Sheriff leaned closer. "Captain. You okay?"

"Leave off," Lightfoot croaked. "I'm dead."

"The hell you are," said Reeves Duncan. "Jake. Over here."

Jake and the lawman lifted the little Ranger and carried him out of the room. The flames on the floor of the jailhouse were attacking the walls. Soon they spread to the roof. The blaze lit up the few structures Atcheson could claim as a downtown, and the heat grew so intense that the Sheriff and Jake had to drag Lightfoot back into the trees. Someone started ringing the bell at the Methodist church—a wild and catastrophic sound at this hour. Neighbors appeared, wincing in the unaccustomed light like night creatures surprised by dawn. Dogs were barking all over town, but it was too late for alarms. The fire consumed everything it could touch. Before it was done with the jailhouse it tried to climb up into the sky like some thrice-damned creature of the underworld, unsatisfied with earth, now clawing at heaven itself.

JAILHOUSE DESTROYED

Night-Time Conflagration
Claims Thousand-
Dollar Structure
Sheriff Confirms
Deputy, Prisoner
Killed in Blaze
Atcheson Teller
November 4, 1911
Page 1, Col. 1

17.

Revenge

Jewel Lightfoot woke up the next morning in the guest room of Doc McDivitt's house. He was sweating profusely, and he smelled of wood smoke and fear. He had a nasty bruise on the left side of his forehead to match the one he'd got on the right in Batson. The back of his head was bloody and swollen, and it was entirely possible his skull was fractured. The insides of the Ranger's arms, meanwhile, were webbed in a sort of metallic blue. It was the oddest coloring Daris Kendrick had ever seen on a white man, and he couldn't help but marvel at it. For almost a minute he traced with his index finger the network of veins and capillaries in Jewel Lightfoot's forearms, as intricate as the canals on Mars the Harvard astronomers had found a few years ago.

"Captain?"

The Ranger jerked himself upright in bed, one hand reaching convulsively to grab for something that wasn't there.

"Easy, now," said Daris. "It's all right. Your pistol is on the bureau."

Lightfoot stared at the black doctor, shook his head, seemed to recover his senses. He eased himself back down on the sheets.

"Close them curtains," he croaked.

Daris clucked. "Told 'em you'd come around. Some men are just too mean to be laid up for long. I didn't mean to startle you, by the way. You were talking in your sleep. Something about a giant rock, and a brotherhood of angels. I made a few notes...."

A blue jay cawed from the live oak just a few feet from the window.

"I may be comin' around," said the Ranger, rubbing his temples. "But I ain't there yet. So you'll excuse me if this sounds…harsh. You need to burn them notes. And you need to forget whatever you heard comin' out of my mouth while I was out. I may not have been in my right mind. *Comprende?* That kind of talk ain't good for a man's reputation."

The doctor pantomimed turning a key to his lips. "Of course. I understand completely. You got yourself a pretty good concussion last night. And a couple of pellets of buckshot in that left shoulder. You can thank the Sheriff for that."

Lightfoot winced. "I reckon I'll live. He kill it?"

Daris drew the curtains and returned to his chair beside the bed. "Not even close, from what I've been told. Jake got off a shot as well. Couldn't tell if he hit anything. It was moving pretty fast, evidently."

"Goddamndest thing I ever saw. Excuse my French. Like somebody left the door to Hell wide open. I need water."

"Right here. Drink as much as you can. But Captain? I need to tell you, Deputy Sweet is dead."

"Yeah," said Lightfoot. "I saw that part."

"The jailhouse is gone. The fire…"

"Didn't even remember the fire till just now. What happened to my prisoner?"

"Also dead. He was shot in the lower mandible with a fairly large caliber firearm—yours, I presume—and apparently bled to death. If he didn't die of the wound, the smoke did the job."

The Ranger probed one of his bruises with the fingers of his right hand. "You sure about that? I needed him alive."

"Quite sure. Mr. East and the Sheriff dragged the body out just before daylight. It was Solomon. I was able to salvage the head, a necklace, and the charred remains of a book of Portuguese verbs."

Lightfoot was silent a moment, considering what he'd heard. "The head?"

"The *skull*, I should say. For phrenological purposes. Having examined his cranial topography, I can assure you Mr. Ibrahim Solomon was criminally insane."

"I feel better already."

Kendrick nodded, licked his chapped lips. "Pronounced occipital ridges," he added.

Lightfoot felt for his pocket watch and realized he didn't have it. *The fire.* Probably wasn't much left to look for at this point.

"I found that book on him," said the Ranger. "Wasn't sure what it was."

"It's almost noon," said Daris. "As soon as you feel up to it, there are some folks who want to talk to you."

The Ranger's eyes widened. "From Austin?"

"Austin? No. I meant the Sheriff, and…I guess. *Me.*"

"Yeah. Alright. Wish I had somethin' to say." The Ranger sat up. "How's Doc?"

"Doc?" said Daris. His voice seemed smaller. "You mean Walter. I didn't tell you that part."

A moment passed. Lightfoot persisted. "Well? You gonna tell me, or do I have to guess?"

"Walter's dead," said Daris, glancing down at the floor.

From downstairs came the clank of an iron skillet on a stovetop. Daris Kendrick said the words again, as if he couldn't help it. His eyes filled with tears, and he placed his head between his hands.

"Walter's dead," he repeated, as if he'd managed so far to keep some part of himself from hearing the news, or comprehending it.

And he wept.

* * *

The Ranger lay back on the bed and closed his gray eyes. They opened again a second later. "Noon," he said. "Goddammit. We gotta get *out there*."

"I think not," said Daris. He paused to blow his nose into one of his monogrammed handkerchiefs. "You're in no condition to travel, Captain. You're in no condition to do much of anything, I'm afraid."

Lightfoot threw off the bed's heavy quilt. "Doctor, you keep makin' the same mistake. You keep thinkin' I'm *askin'*."

WE KNOW YOU HAVE EAST
PUT HIM OUT. OR WE WILL TAKE HIM.

[*Note placed on door of Walter McDivitt's house during early morning hours, November 4.*]

* * *

Edmund Petticord returned to Doc's house caked with river mud and smelling of trees. He said he'd he counted six armed men at the Mill and figured there were more in the woods. There was a shed on the west side of the Anahuac River that seemed to be used for storage of explosives; it was emptied as he watched, and its contents ferried over to the Mill side in an ancient pirogue. He'd paddled himself across the river while holding on to a floating log, then bellied up through tangles of grapevine and speargrass toward the camp. Fifty yards from the mill he saw a massive derrick and a considerable amount of activity, though it didn't seem to be activity related to the production of oil. He'd also seen wheelbarrows loaded with metal containers, like beer kegs, being rolled from the mill house down a path toward the derrick, where a tent was set up.

"Sounds like they found somethin' else," said the Sheriff.

Lightfoot was sitting in Doc's big armchair again. He looked as if he'd just been pulled out of his own grave.

He started to shake his head. Winced. Closed his eyes. "More of the same, most likely. Like I said, the Turk told me there's more of these varmints down in this metal thing your man Newton found. A space bullet, or some such. Little ones. *Pupils*, he called 'em. They probably want to dig up what they can and get outta here. Gettin' a little hot in these parts."

"He called them *pupils*?" said Daris.

"Something like that."

"Any sign of Rose Ann Terrell?" interjected the Sheriff.

Petticord shook his head. "I didn't get any closer to the mill. But no. No sign of Rose Ann."

"I thought you said the girl drowned," said the Ranger.

"Hell, Captain. I don't know what to think anymore. They could have her."

"Sure they could. You're quiet, Dr. Kendrick. Spit it out."

Daris was puffing on his pipe again. "Just thinking. It seems to me, it would make sense for them—this creature, and whoever travels with it—to be headed someplace where they would have a choice as to their next destination."

"In other words?" said the Sheriff.

"A port."

"New Orleans is a port."

"True," agreed the Ranger. "And that thing'd fit in fine in New Orleans. Ripping off heads. Drinking blood. That ain't even illegal in Louisiana."

Jake presumed this was meant as a joke. No one laughed. Not even Lightfoot.

Daris drummed his fingers on the table. "But Galveston's a port too. And it's considerably closer."

"But why a ship?" said Jake. "Where would they be going?"

"Captain Lightfoot relieved Mr. Solomon of his personal effects after capturing him yesterday. Among them was a book—a schoolboy's primer of verb conjugations. The Turk was studying Portuguese."

The others looked on with blank expressions.

"Brazil," Daris explained. "It's the only place in the New World where it's spoken."

"Hallelujah," said the Sheriff. "Maybe that's the answer to our problem. The damn thing's leaving."

"That isn't an answer. That's just the start of more questions."

"And why is that, Doctor?"

Daris gazed up into a wreath of his own pipe smoke. "'Because," he said resignedly. "We can't let it go."

"Why the hell *not?*" said the Sheriff. "I ain't never seen anything I'd like to let go more than this sonofabitch."

The black doctor pursed his lips, made a steeple of his fingers. Even Jake had learned to recognize this professorial affectation. "Sheriff, do you have any idea how big Brazil is? It could swallow Texas like one of your bull snakes eats a frog. Ninety-nine out of every hundred square miles of that country has never even been seen by human eyes. This monster would simply disappear."

"Ain't that what we're aimin' for?" asked East, in his rumbling baritone. It was the first time he'd spoken that day.

"Not the way I see things, Mr. East. Allow me to suggest a set of possibilities. Maybe now that we're pursuing it—have killed one its familiars—this...*whatever it is*, is never going to be heard from around here again. But who else is going to have to live like we're living a year from now? Or fifty years from now? And what if these *pupae*—Latin for *doll*, Captain; a developmental phase in certain insects—can be recovered and brought to adulthood? What if an entirely new species could be established and start multiplying right here on Earth? Beside us. *Competing* with us."

"Feeding on us," said Edmund Petticord. They were all thinking it. The room was quiet. Daris was right, and everyone knew it.

"So how are we gonna kill this thing?" said the Sheriff. "I shot it point-blank last night and it didn't seem to do much other than rile it up some."

The Ranger stared at the ceiling. "I know how I'm gonna do it. A Winchester Model 97 twelve-gauge slide-action scattergun. Two double-action six-shot revolvers, courtesy of Mr. Samuel Colt, a buck knife, and the points of my boots. You wasn't close enough, Sheriff. I'm gonna crawl down this monster's throat and *shoot* my way out."

"Can we get more men?" asked Daris.

Reeves Duncan spat tobacco juice into his coffee cup. "Maybe you didn't notice how the house got tore up yesterday, Dr. Kendrick. I'm thinkin' most of the men around here are just itchin' to string *us* up."

Daris frowned. "Surely there's someone you can call. You're a *sheriff.* This thing has killed four people we know of, counting your deputy, and it came damn close to getting a Ranger last night."

"He didn't come *that* close," said Lightfoot, straightening in his chair. "And more men are just gonna confuse things. We got plenty."

"So it's just us?" said Daris, glancing skeptically around the room.

"Jus' us," said East. It was unclear whether the words were complaint or confirmation.

"Wonderful. And we're going to improvise, like last time?"

Lightfoot shrugged. "You mean *fake it*? Here's what I know. That big ugly is hid up in them woods around the Mill and we can't get to him with anything short of an army. But we ain't got no army, and we ain't gonna *have* no army unless we're prepared to wait, in which case we may lose this thing altogether. I'm thinkin' the neck-breaker, Nageeb, is in charge now, and he's probably trying to wrap things up in a hurry, now that they know we kilt their boss. The way I see it, we need to hit 'em hard and fast, while they're busy doin' whatever they're *doin'.* If this thing is travelin' with its keepers, they ain't got but one road to take. They ain't gonna move overland through the Thicket, and they ain't likely to come through Atcheson, since they know we're here."

"What about the river?" said Jake.

"What about it?"

Petticord chimed in. "I know what he means, Cap'n. They get across the Anahuac, they only got maybe half a mile through the woods to get to good road—the old San Antonio highway runs down to Liberty, and then on toward Houston."

"And if they get on the highway," concluded Duncan, "they're gone."

"Then we gotta stop 'em before they get across the river. I suppose they could swim the horses over. But they gotta keep the ugly covered if they want to travel by daylight, and chances are, the same thing's true of them pupils. Remember? This thing can't suffer sunlight—or *any* light, for that matter. Could be that's why it absquatulated last night: the light from the fire. So if we push 'em down to the river, they're trapped. All they got is the one pirogue, and we can blow holes in that all day. Either that or they move alongside the river, and—Petticord, where'd you disappear to? Stop *lurking*, goddammit. What kinda ground is that?"

Petticord had been thinking. He scooted himself out from underneath one of the end tables. "Not much for traveling. I went through some of it this morning. Swampy. Lotta scrub. I saw two cottonmouths."

The Ranger laughed mirthlessly. "God*damned* East Texas. I don't know if this place is the Devil's armpit or his asshole, but Lord it's some nasty country. Either way, they're in trouble. If we could set up on the far side of the river with a couple of rifles, we could make things pretty hot for them boys."

"Some big trees on that side of the river," said East. "Y'all could hide up in there pretty good."

Lightfoot surveyed the room with a carnivorous grin. "Anybody else know how to shoot?"

"I can shoot a little," said the Sheriff.

"You shot *me* a little," the Ranger confirmed, flexing his right shoulder. The pellets were still in there. Lightfoot had told Daris Kendrick what he could do with his scalpel. "I guess that counts."

Jake leaned forward. "I have Doc's old Krag. That's what I shot last night."

"Hell, we're an army."

Daris was obviously unconvinced. "That's fine, Captain," he said. "But how are you going to push these people down to the river in the first place?"

The Ranger stood and walked to the fireplace in his stocking feet. "If I was Comanch and wanted to flush somethin' out of them woods, I think I'd just set me a fire out there and hope it blowed the right direction. So that's an option. And me and the Sheriff are workin' on what you might call a *contingency* plan."

"Been awful dry in these parts," said Petticord. "That mill would go up like a tinderbox. Might take the woods with it."

"But how we gonna set a fire out there, Ed? We got the same problem with the hired guns watchin' us."

"Sheriff's right," said Lightfoot. "There's that first line of woods, maybe a quarter-mile off the road, then that peters out and you got another two hundred yards or so of logged-out field. You're gonna have to get through that field to get to the real woods—the old-growth stuff where Newton's place is. Yesterday I counted three men watching that road. They'll have twice that many this time, and they ain't gonna be in no mood for house calls. They see us coming and they'll cut us down before we even get close."

"The airship," said Jake. The word seemed to hang in the air like the thing itself. No one quite knew what to make of it.

"Out of the question," said Daris.

"What airship?"

"I said, *it's out of the question.*"

The Ranger held up one finger. "I don't recall as anyone *asked* you a question, Dr. Kendrick. That boy's the same age I was when I started riding with Dan Roberts out on the Pecos. Looks to me like he's old enough to make up his own mind. All I need to know is, what the hell airship is everyone talkin' about?"

The Sheriff spat tobacco juice into a coffee can he held in one hand. "Jake here is an amateur engineer. He and a friend of his, a pig farmer named…"

"Eben Melton," continued Ed Petticord proudly. "They built 'em a aeroplane. That really flies."

"Most of the time," Jake agreed.

"That's dandy," said Lightfoot. "What's your point?"

"The point is," said Jake, "I could fly over the mill and drop something on it. A lantern, maybe. Just like Glenn Curtiss did for the Navy. That would start a fire all right."

The Sheriff shook his head. "I've heard about your aeroplane, son. It's made of canvas, chicken wire, and chewing gum." He leaned to one side of his chair and spat into a coffee can. "These men would shoot you out of the sky."

"They might if they had time to aim. If they knew what was coming. But how are they gonna know? Ten to one, nobody at the Mill's ever seen an airship. Plus the woods out there are so thick they ain't gonna be able to see me for more than about ten seconds at a time anyway."

Lightfoot grunted. "Probably scare the hell out of 'em, is what it'd do."

"But Jake," said the Sheriff, "could you hit it? I mean, could you drop a lantern with any sort of accuracy traveling at that speed?"

"I could hit it."

"Hell," said Lightfoot. "He don't have to hit the building. He just needs to get close to the compound and set something on fire. As long as it's on the north side of the mill, and we got a decent breeze, it's going to take that place out."

"I can do it."

"What do we have that'll burn?"

Jake shrugged. He was feeling confident now. He was starting to get excited. "Like I said, we got a kerosene lantern. We got *two* lanterns. I'll just fill 'em up and light 'em. They'll break when they hit the ground—just like Sheriff Duncan's lantern burned down the jailhouse."

Lightfoot looked at East. East looked at the Sheriff. The Sheriff wasn't sure if he was being blamed or congratulated. He spat in his coffee cup again.

"I've heard worse," said Lightfoot.

"God help us," said Daris.

EXCERPT FROM THE AFFIDAVIT OF DARIS KENDRICK, M.D.
Signed under Oath, February 2, 1912

18. "Thus we had our consilium. The events that transpired next, however, threw all into doubt. I have mentioned previously that suspicions were growing in the community that the deaths in the area were the work of Mr. East. There was but little evidence to support such speculation, and even this was purely circumstantial: East was said to have feuded with the late Josh Turner over the attentions of a local woman, and was known as well to have been involved some months prior in a verbal altercation with the husband of the unfortunate Mrs. Mills. As flimsy as such 'evidence' may seem, men of my race have been hanged in East Texas on less substantial grounds.

19. "The mob arrived at the McDivitt residence just as we were preparing to put our strategy into effect. I was standing on the back steps of the house, just outside the kitchen, when I heard the sounds of argument within. At almost the same moment, I saw two men appear around the corner of the house, as if to stand watch over the rear avenues of egress. I went inside. Clarence East stood in the kitchen. As one might imagine, he presented the classic symptoms of panic: rapid, shallow respiration, enlarged pupils, a marked elevation of pulse. I implored the man—a man to whom I felt considerable gratitude, given the events of the previous evening—not to attempt an escape, as such a course of action might well embolden his antagonists and have the unfortunate effect as well of removing him from his only place of refuge. He nodded, indicating by this silent means of assent that he would comply. And yet now the tumult seemed to be just outside the kitchen door. The voices grew in volume and intensity. A shot was fired—it sounded immensely loud in the house—and East started involuntarily. I tried physically to restrain him, a ridiculous notion, given the vast difference in our musculatures, but this proved unnecessary. Shortly afterward—it is difficult at this late date for me to order precisely the events of that afternoon—I heard Captain Lightfoot speaking from upstairs, and I ventured out into the hallway.

20. *"The situation could hardly have been more desperate. There were thirteen men in the motley congregation, several of whom were noticeably intoxicated, despite the early hour, and all of whom were armed. Their faces told immediately what they had come to do. It is unclear whether they were met at the door or simply entered the house unbidden—a clear case of felonious burglary, given the intentions of this particular group. Sheriff Duncan stood in front of me in the narrow hallway, flanked by young Jacob and Edmund Petticord. Captain Lightfoot commanded the scene from the broken balcony above, his shotgun trained quite deliberately on the mob. I was unaccustomed to seeing anything other than a smirking insouciance on the Ranger's face, but now his patience was noticeably strained. I, of course, knew the reason. Every minute we tarried in town increased the odds of our nemesis decamping from the woods near Nichols Mill. It was easy to imagine the man Naguib and his monstrous alien sovereign already en route to their next port of call, with whatever specimens of young they had managed to salvage from the metallic cylinder, and the prospects of further blood and madness increasing with every mile they traveled. I knew this. I knew of the Ranger's injuries, of his desperation to finish his task, of the dire consequences of letting our quarry escape. And yet here we were, trapped in dear Walter's house, checked in our work by this tawdry rabble!*

21. *"A tall, hatchet-faced man, Mr. J. R. Holsan, later identified to me as the owner and editor of the local*

newspaper, spoke for the group. The mob's demands were unsurprising. East was to be delivered forthwith into their hands for questioning, or they would proceed to take him— by force, if necessary. The Sheriff was additionally required to produce any and all pieces of forensic evidence he had gathered heretofore, along with all notes, papers, etc. related to his investigation. There followed further exposition on the authority of the group, on its constituents, and on Mr. Holsan's communications with certain members of the county's board of commissioners in Gosford.

22. "Mr. Holsan's summation was not without a certain ignoble logic. And yet behind him in the mob I could see the blunt, brutal faces of his followers, the newly-widowed Willard Mills among them. There was hatred in those eyes, and a lust for vengeance that would only be slaked by blood. There would be little questioning involved in any examination of Clarence East by this assemblage! More likely by far would be the prospect of seeing our hulking friend dangling from a rope in the very near future. I found myself taking some solace in the fact that his great bulk would undoubtedly cause his neck to snap upon suspension, ending his struggles mercifully. But then I saw the man Mills staring at me, and I felt an anger rising up inside me that I had heretofore managed to restrain during my visit to Atcheson. Indeed, during my adult life! It would be fruitless, I knew, to try to convince this assemblage of gaping yokels of the real menace they were unwittingly abetting by engaging in this ridiculous spectacle. The situation called, I believed, for subterfuge. I am not embarrassed to say that I supplied it.

18.

The Airship

"I seem to have missed something," said Daris Kendrick. He shivered as he gazed at the complicated mechanism—a sort of winged egg-beater, with wheels—that stood inside one of the several ramshackle outbuildings on Eben Melton's pig farm. "What, pray tell, is the Ezekiel Airship?"

"Yer lookin' at her!" said Eben. He had a tendency to exclaim when excited.

"Indeed, sir. I'm looking, but I'm still asking."

Eben burst forth with that whinnying laugh of his. He plucked off the seal-skin cap his mother had bought him from the Sears catalogue and scratched his matted black hair. "Well, she's an airplane is what she is. Got all buggered up in a windstorm when Burrell Cannon tried to ship her to the St. Louis Expo in 1904. Wind caught her, see? Ripped her right off the flat car! This is our attempt at a resurrection. Reverend Cannon came up with the original design in Pittsburg a few years ago. Modeled it on a description from the Book of Ezekiel! You mind if I ask you a question, Doctor?"

"Not at all," said Daris.

"What happened to your face?"

The black doctor reflexively felt for the scabs on his nose and forehead. "I was recently exposed to the mysteries of the Orient."

"Looks like you was recently exposed to the mysteries of a boot." Again with the laugh.

Daris frowned at the Airship. "Be that as it may. You don't expect me to believe this thing can actually *fly*, do you?"

"Can," said Eben, exchanging glances with Jake Hennessey, "and has. Not far, maybe, but he got her up a coupla times back in 1902."

"How far?" asked Doc.

"How far what?"

"How far has she flown?"

"We don't exactly know!" Eben closed the building's sliding door and started limping toward the next structure, a smaller but similarly decrepit barn. Daris and Jake Hennessey followed. The breeze held competing odors of wood smoke and pig shit. The pig shit was winning. "Jake, whatta you think?"

"I think she probably never went more than a few hundred feet. She's got some nice wings on her, and a light frame, but the reverend had the rotors turning the wrong way. Thought they could paddle the air like you do water. It don't work that way! She probably got picked up and *blown* as much as she flew."

"I beg your pardon," said Daris, trying to keep up with their host. "Did you say 1902? That was before the Wright Brothers flew at Kitty Hawk."

"Sure was," said Eben. "There's folks up in Pittsburg who'll swear to it."

"What's the thing capable of now?"

"She'll sharpen a pencil pretty good if you get them props turnin'." This seemed to be a shared joke. Eben and Jake, who was busy shrugging himself into a leather jacket as he walked, both chortled. "But we pretty much gave up on that one. This here's the real McCoy."

Eben opened the door of the second barn and the wan afternoon light shone on another strange machine. This one stood half again as tall as a man and had a wingspan of over twenty feet. It had six wheels—bicycle tires, evidently; two in front, four in back—and a pair of elegant wooden propellers mounted in the rear.

"The Fair Field Flyer!" announced the pig farmer, shooing a rooster off the near wing. "It's pretty much just our version of the Wrights' Model R, but we rigged it with a set of steering flaps like Glenn Curtiss is using." Eben, famously oblivious to the emotional temperatures of those around him, beamed at his apprentice. No one smiled back.

"What?" said Eben.

Jake Hennessey chewed his lip. "Eben, we gotta get the Flyer ready."

"Sure we do. Air show coming up."

"Not that," said Jake. "I need to take her up. Long flight, this time."

"How long?"

"Out to Nichols' Mill and back."

Eben scratched his wrist. "That's almost thirty miles, round trip. Longer'n anything we've done before."

"Longer," said Jake. "But no different."

"True. But there's weather comin', if I'm any judge."

"That's why I need to go now. Dr. Kendrick, what time do you have?"

"After three," said the doctor. He added, significantly: "Running out of daylight."

The pig farmer laid a hand on the canvas of the near wing. He brushed something small off the surface, and for a moment all they could hear was the grunts of a sow outside the barn. "This is important?" he asked.

"Real important," said Jake. He pulled a pair of brass-rimmed goggles from his jacket and pulled them over his head.

Eben nodded. He seemed to return to himself. "She's as much yours as mine, Jake. You can take her. Just… you know. Be careful."

"I will. It's the same as a flight around the fields. Just further."

"That's right. Just a little further. I bolted the new tank on yesterday. I was cleaning the plugs this morning, so we'll have to put them back in. Then…you know. Fuel her up."

"Can the boy really fly her?" asked Daris.

"He's the only one who has," answered Eben.

"He's done it before?"

"Plenty of times."

"Good Lord," said Daris. "What have you people been doing out here?"

"I don't know." Jake turned away to hide the blush that he knew was filling his cheeks. "*Flying*, I guess."

19.

Naguib

Time to leave. Time to leave. Time to leave.

The thought kept repeating itself in Naguib's brain, crowding out everything else. What had once seemed like the perfect operation was now a shambles. Solomon was dead. As incredible as that fact seemed, one of Naguib's men had seen the body dragged from the burnt-out hulk of the little jailhouse where he'd been held. Solomon had outwitted, outfought, and out-planned a hundred local constables, immigration officials, and petty gangsters over the years. Most of them had ended up dead, with piano wire wrapped around their throats and their eyes gouged out of their skulls. And now, to be tripped up by some ridiculous banty rooster with a badge and a gun bigger than his own head? It was disastrous. Inconceivable. He would be questioned a dozen times when he got home. But there was still time to salvage the operation. The Protector was safe. Slightly wounded, perhaps, but safe, and sated, and asleep in the crawl space beneath the mill's main building. They'd recovered three pupae and were close to extracting another from the interior of the space vessel. And that was enough. That would be four more than they'd had before. And four, he knew, would be sufficient for the purpose. The females would each bear a dozen young within the decade. From these young would come a hundred more, and from them a thousand of the Protector's race—some of them males, the midnight shadows, the drinkers of blood. The Protectors would bring Naguib's people back from the brink of extinction. Back to power. Back to glory.

For now, though, it was time to leave. The coach was loaded. The little girl was aboard, still drugged in a sleep that would last through the first feedings. He had to get the Protector and its future mates to

Galveston. There they'd board a ship for South America, as Solomon had planned. The arrangements were made. He'd spit one last time on this accursed land and sail to a place where the next generation could be nurtured in isolation until the time was right. For return. For revenge. He had only one regret. He wished he'd had time to kill the little Ranger as he had that pitiful scarecrow of a town doctor. He wished he'd had time to kill them all: the boy; the Nubian; the fat sheriff; the accursed black man with the filth in the glass vial. Time to leave. But maybe there'd be a chance still to pay them back for the death of Ibrahim Solomon. He would watch for it. The Protector was still with him. And with the Protector, all things were possible.

20.

Nichols Mill

The Flyer was sluggish today.

The airplane shuddered and bounced over ruts and anthills in Eben's back pasture as Jake slowly brought her up to speed. At one point he could have sworn the little twelve-horsepower engine was missing on one cylinder, but thirty seconds later it seemed to be running fine. He soon forgot about it. Jake felt a familiar sense of elation as the plane climbed up into the air, her long wings trembling in the air. The sensation never failed to amaze him. The spruce slats of the frame shook as he guided the aircraft over the line of scrub oaks on the far side of the field. He pushed the stick to the left and pressed on the rudder pedal and the Flyer slowly banked to the west. He looked back over his shoulder and saw Eben lumbering across the field, waving his seal-skin cap maniacally, as if he wanted to join him. Further back stood the squat, dark figure of Daris Kendrick, staring up at the sky with both hands held to his head, apparently immobilized by the entire experience.

Jake crossed over Kneeland Ware's empty cotton fields, brown and littered after the harvest, and veered northwest along the Saratoga road. It was a chilly, overcast day, with a breeze blowing from the north. He was staying low, at about forty feet, to conserve fuel, but even at this altitude his nose was running and the wind stung his cheeks. The lanterns he and Eben had tied to the left wing strut glowed dully against the gray sky.

As he approached Evan Flood's place, Jake was surprised to see a group of riders heading out of town. He wondered for a moment if they could be Captain Lightfoot and his friends, but this was a bigger group. He saw Willard Mills on a big bay mare, leading the posse, and he recalled what he'd heard back at the house. This was the group Daris and the Sheriff had maneuvered into a frontal assault on the Mill. They'd let on as how the men on Amos Newton's rig crew were labor activists from up north—foreign anarchists bound and determined to preach the gospel of atheism and violent rebellion to the state's dusky laborers. These men—Wobblies, most likely—had murdered poor Amos. They'd hit the jailhouse the previous night to rescue Clarence East, who was prepared to testify against them, and they'd burned down the building and killed Doc and Deputy Sweet in the process. The bodies were right upstairs, if anyone cared to take a look. It was a risky, outlandish plan. Jake was astonished to hear the lies coming out of Daris Kendrick's mouth, elaborate fabrications somehow made plausible by that elegant, sonorous voice of his. But the Sheriff backed him up, and Jewel Lightfoot, still holding his shotgun and still quite visibly disgusted by the mob who'd entered Doc's house by force, acted like it was flat-out obvious who'd been doing the killings around Atcheson.

Far-fetched as it seemed, the plan seemed to be working. Jake recognized J.R. Holsan in the group below him, and Willard Mills and Fletcher Cobb. Two of the men on horseback pointed up at the Flyer. Jake grinned in spite of himself. He always liked to see that. *The admiration. The wonderment.* It made him feel superhuman somehow.

It took Jake ten minutes to reach the turn-off to Nichols Mill. As he approached the expanse of old-growth oaks and pines he saw a man stand up from behind a tangle of bushes and shade his eyes, as if he couldn't quite believe what he was seeing. Jake reached down and tried to loosen the knot that held the nearer of the lanterns. He'd practiced doing this on the ground so he could do it without looking. Now, though, it didn't work. The knot wouldn't budge. Jake realized that if he didn't get the thing untied quickly he was going to miss his opportunity. He was traveling at an incredible speed—over forty miles per hour, as near as he could tell. He looked to his left and watched his fingers work the knot. Finally he solved it. There was still nothing under him but trees. He climbed a little, and that's when he saw the clearing hacked out of the forest. In fact, the word *clearing* didn't quite capture the destruction. The land was simply scalped of all vegetation. Dead trees and portions of trees were heaped in random piles, their rust-colored foliage rotting into the earth, and the red clay beneath lay exposed to the elements like an open sore. Scattered among the mounds of dead trees were irregular lengths of steel pipe and abandoned drill bits, discarded engine blocks and metal objects of various shapes and sizes, all rusted and forlorn. It was a wasteland carved out of the middle of the Thicket, a sort of canker invisible to anyone but God and the birds. And now Jake. In the center of the desolation stood a massive wooden derrick, maybe fifty feet tall, listing at a fifteen-degree angle. The structure was reinforced with rusted metal pipe and brackets and anchored by means of cable to a huge bald cypress at the edge of the clearing. A steel girder protruded from the framework of the derrick, and a dozen ropes hung from pulleys on the girder to something in a hole in the earth below it. The clearing was several acres wide, and most of it was filled with dark fluid. In the center of this black swamp was a conical excavation walled off from the fluid by a berm of red earth. Something silver and smooth glinted at the bottom of the excavation.

The Flyer crossed the ruined land at a height of no more than forty feet. Jake actually locked glances with a long-haired, shirtless man, sunburned and streaked with oil, who was pushing a wheelbarrow of earth out toward the center circle. The boy was so absorbed in analyzing what he was looking at that it took him a few moments to realize he'd found his target. Whatever was going on in this ulcerous clearing, the excavation below him was clearly the focal point, and that lake of oil and mud was going to burn fast and hot.

Jake nosed the Flyer higher to avoid the line of trees on the southeastern edge of the clearing and soon he was over the brown waters of the Anahuac River. For a moment he looked for his friends. They were supposed to be down there somewhere, deployed to cut off escape from the Mill, but he didn't have time to hunt for them. He began the awkward process of banking the Flyer for another pass at the camp. As he flew, he wondered whether it would be better just to hold on to the lanterns and report back on what he'd seen. The notion of setting the woods on fire was so repellent to him— so contrary to his notions of prudence and good order— that for a moment he wondered why he'd ever volunteered to help. But this was only for a moment. He remembered that orchard of butchered corpses dangling by their ankles somewhere in the thickets beneath him. He remembered the sight of his uncle, dead in a lake of his own blood, and he recalled with utter clarity the eerie, cataclysmic wail of the thing that had bolted out of Sheriff Duncan's little jailhouse like an animate nightmare. He knew he had to do something more.

As Jake crested the trees on his second run, throttling back so he could take dead aim, he thought he heard the Flyer's engine backfiring. It turned out to be worse. The man he'd seen earlier had set his wheelbarrow down. He held a shotgun to his shoulder and Jake saw the gun kick as he fired again. A moment later the canvas of the Flyer's lower left wing split in three places. One of the guy wires was severed. Jake could feel the wing dragging. Worse, he'd lost the near lantern, and the remaining lantern was damaged. A tongue of flame had escaped from one of the broken panes and was licking at the sailcloth on the underside of the still-intact upper wing. Jake glanced over again, trying to unfasten the knot that held the intact lantern, and the plane drifted left.

A sudden gust of wind slapped the aircraft like a toy and pushed it into the derrick; the crippled left wing clipped the steel of the structure and the impact sheared the wing in two. The Flyer pinwheeled violently and slammed, tail-first, into the vast soup of mud and oil.

✻ ✻ ✻

Jake untied himself from his seat. He was okay. His nose was bleeding, and he'd scraped up his left hand, but he was otherwise unharmed. It only took him a moment, though, to realize the danger he was in. The aluminum cylinders of the Flyer's little engine were white-hot—and they were now only six inches from the surface of the oily pool. Jake floundered out into the muck, trying to get away from the plane. It was maybe four feet deep, though the bottom was uneven and once he slipped into mud up to his eyes. He tore off his goggles. His leather jacket, wool pants, and boots, all now thoroughly soaked, felt like twenty pounds of additional weight. Finally he hoisted himself onto the berm and pulled himself up, only to find himself staring up into the barrel of a gun. It was the Wheelbarrow Man, grinning at him from under the grit and sweat that covered his face.

"That's right," he rasped. "Come on outta there, bird boy. Raise your hands where I can see 'em."

"We got a problem," Jake gasped. His panic robbed him of breath.

The man looked like he hadn't eaten in weeks. He flashed a gap-toothed grin. "*You do*, maybe. Come out to spy on us, didya? We heard you might be comin'."

"Listen to me. The engine in that thing is still hot. *Very* hot. And it's sinking. It's just about to hit that oil. When that happens, this whole place is gonna go up in flames."

The man glanced out at what remained of the aircraft. His eyes traced a rapid circuit of the earthen berm. Jake followed his gaze. It was worse than the boy had thought. At various locations Jake could see sticks of what looked like dynamite fastened to the outer walls of the berm, all connected by a common detonator wire. Someone was planning to blast the whole place to oblivion, burying the metallic object at the bottom of the hole beneath several tons of earth. The man's eyes widened. He dropped the shotgun, took two steps backward, and started to run.

He didn't get far. The man stumbled over a tangle of discarded wire and fell head-first over the lip of the berm. As Jake watched, he slid several yards down the steep slope toward the metal structure in the center of the man-made crater. Jake realized now that the structure—object—*vessel*—was larger than he'd originally thought. He suspected only a small part of it was visible at the bottom of the crater. There was something about the thing that he found majestic, almost irresistible. Even in the dim light of that overcast afternoon the metallic skin of the object seemed sleek, almost liquid in its composition. Jake wanted to ease himself down to it to feel its sides, to locate the rivets he couldn't see but knew had to be there on the surface of the vessel. But he had other things to think about. The Wheelbarrow Man was trying to claw his way back up the oily slope. It wasn't working. The harder he tried, the faster he slid backward toward the bottom of the crater, and the hole in the metal vessel. He ended half in, half out of the cylinder. He was clearly hurt. Now he sounded desperate as well.

"Hold on!" said Jake. He knew he couldn't hazard a descent himself. He might never get back up. He peered around him for a length of rope—a long pole—anything he could use to help the man.

"Get me OUTTA here!" shouted the Wheelbarrow Man.

As he did so, he tried to pull himself out of the aperture. But just then something seemed to seize him from below. Wheelbarrow Man screamed. He gripped the smooth sides of the vessel with both hands but was pulled further in. Another scream—higher-pitched, this time. Jake looked back just in time to see the man's head disappear into the hole. Jake wasn't sure what he'd just witnessed. But he didn't have time to think about it: just then, the Flyer settled further into the ooze, and the oil caught fire.

Jake ran like he'd never run before: off the berm, over the rickety wooden walkway between the berm and solid earth and then into the woods. He tore through several yards of grape vines and hackberry trees. He could hear gunshots now, off to his right, but he didn't have time to figure out who was firing or why. He could see an end to the trees in front of him and he came to a bluff just a few feet over the river. Before he could make up his mind to jump, the world behind him convulsed in fire and thunder. Suddenly he was flying again, tracing an involuntary arc in the sky toward the muddy Anahuac River.

* * *

A hundred yards upstream, on the reedy west bank of the Anahuac, Jewel T. Lightfoot, Reeves Duncan, Clarence East and Ed Petticord watched box turtles arrange themselves on the trunks of fallen trees in the river. The afternoon was overcast and cool and it looked like it was raining off to the north: the current was picking up, and the Anahuac had turned from brown to yellow. There was a sort of shimmer in the clouds like lightning, but the trees were too close for the men to see much of the sky. They listened to woodpeckers rapping at the hardwoods around them, and occasionally they heard their horses cropping grass from where they were tied in a clearing twenty yards from the river. The men had been sitting for almost an hour. There was no sign of activity on the opposite bank, and the inactivity was starting to tell on them. Afternoon was edging into early evening. The light was growing thinner. There was no avoiding the thought. Night was coming.

Ed Petticord reached up and caught a grasshopper in mid-flight. He'd started to pluck off the insect's tiny legs when he heard the whine of an engine. He popped the grasshopper in his mouth and motioned to the others. From somewhere northeast of their position came the drone of what they knew instantly was the Fair Field Flyer. It grew stronger, then faded away. Lightfoot looked over at the others and shrugged. There it was again—the engine sound, just for a moment. They heard a shout from what seemed like a great distance away, then nothing for several minutes. A single gun blast. *Shotgun*, most likely, though from here it sounded like a child's firecracker. A second blast. Then shouting.

Clarence East watched Petticord chew. "You that white man eats bugs," he said.

The little man swallowed. "Reckon so."

"Why you eat them bugs?"

Petticord shrugged. "Get hungry," he answered.

Sheriff Duncan stood up from his hiding place behind the trunk of an old oak. Lightfoot shook his head emphatically and signaled him to get down again. Just then they heard a huge explosion. The blast was strong enough to send the turtles scrambling into the water. A cloud of dark smoke boiled up and over the trees.

* * *

The green coach appeared on the far bank of the river three minutes later. The driver of the ungainly conveyance was just a shade over six feet tall but as broad as a door, dark-skinned, with a hatchet-like face and jet-black hair that streamed down his naked back like an Indian's. *Naguib,* the Ranger whispered to himself. It was his first time to see the Arab, but he knew it was him. Two other men followed the coach. Just shy of the river bank, Naguib reined the gray horses to a halt. The animals danced sideways in their harness till the big man clambered down from the bench and cut the traces. Still harnessed, the horses moved awkwardly along the weedy bank into the trees. Naguib's helpers had already started to work. The two men inserted jacks under the axles, cranked them up, and started prying the wheels off the coach.

* * *

More smoke. Edmond Petticord watched the black column climb up into the sky. Tendrils of haze came creeping out of the woods on the far bank. He fought off a cough, buried his face in his jacket. He was tired and hungry. He wished he could find another grasshopper. A grub. Maybe a handful of ant eggs. Anything to cut the tension.

* * *

The coach now stood on a set of much smaller wheels, roughly ten inches in diameter, that had been concealed behind the outer set. Naguib and his assistants went to the rear of the vehicle and shouldered it down the gentle incline into the river. The vehicle wallowed in the muddy water but quickly righted itself. Reeves Duncan exchanged glances with the Ranger. The damn thing *floated*. That's how they planned to get their inhuman cargo across the Anahuac.

Clouds of black smoke began to drift over the river.

As they watched, Naguib drew a revolver from the waistband of his trousers. The Arab moved behind one of his assistants, a bearded, heavy-set man with a red kerchief around his neck. The man was looking back up the trail toward the millhouse when Naguib put the gun to his head. A red mist burst from the heavy-set man's skull, and he dropped instantly. The third member of the group, a skinny Negro clad in a shirt and shoes but no pants, was holding a rope attached to the floating coach. He saw the murder and turned to run, still holding the rope. The big man dropped him with a single shot to the back.

Jewel Lightfoot had seen enough. This wasn't part of the plan. The plan called for concealment until the enemy actually started to cross the river. But the Ranger wasn't accustomed to watching cold-blooded murder. He broke cover and strode to the weedy bank. There he settled himself on one knee and cocked the Winchester's hammer. This much was clear. Less clear was the manner in which the Arab sensed the sudden threat. Perhaps some secret vibration of earth or air alerted him. Maybe the howling unholy gods he worshiped whispered in his ear. Whatever the impetus, the big man whirled to face the Ranger. Lightfoot sighted down the barrel. In the split-second before he pulled the trigger, though, another explosion ripped the sky. And another. The Ranger refocused just as Naguib fired his big pistol. A slug tore through the Ranger's skinny calf, spattering blood on the weeds nearby. He fought the surge of adrenaline that flooded his head and arms. *No sense gettin' mad,* he told himself, *when you've still got shells.*

Captain Jewel T. Lightfoot had once shot the left eye out of an Apache scout at seventy yards. Hitting this outlandish hunk of buffalo turd with a scattergun at fifty was not going to be a challenge. He set himself again and took dead aim. Naguib's second round whined past the Ranger's cheek and buried itself in the trunk of a cedar elm behind him. The Arab was moving now, retreating up the far bank into a curtain of smoke, his ponytail of black hair bouncing behind him. Lightfoot fired. The buckshot slammed into the big man and seemed to push him into the smoke. The Arab disappeared.

✧ ✧ ✧

Jake Hennessey clawed his way up on top of a fallen tree that extended several yards into the river. He spat out of a mouthful of the muddy warm water of the Anahuac. He wished he could swim. He wished a hundred things. But he realized the first thing he needed to do was get to shore. *The far bank.* He could already feel the heat of the fire behind him. Unfortunately, the far bank was seventy-five feet away. Jake wasn't sure he could make it. In fact, he wasn't sure he could move. Mostly what he wanted to do was rest. *Sleep. Stop moving.* Because maybe if he closed his eyes just for a moment he could open them up again later and all the events of the past few weeks would have disappeared. His uncle would be at home again, reading by the fireplace, and Jake would have a chance to say everything he wanted to say. But then the air thudded with the force of a new explosion, and Jake realized he was wet and cold and alone. A tree limb the size of a sofa splashed down in the water beside him. Birds darted overhead, fleeing downriver. Jake reached down and pulled off his brogans. He was going to have to swim.

* * *

The coach drifted out into the muddy river and rotated as it caught the current. The Sheriff and Edmond Petticord stood up. The coach floated past them, moving toward the middle of the stream. It wasn't moving fast, but it was definitely *moving* on the swelling river. Riding the current, it would soon reach the ruinous mire that was Sour Lake, all cypress trees and spatterdock pads. Only a few miles beyond the swamp stood Atcheson; and beyond Atcheson lay the last fringe of forest before the land flattened to meet the warm gray Gulf of Mexico. The men could see the orange of the flames now through the trees on the far bank. The slender breeze that had been blowing disappeared, and the air was heavy and still. A thick black haze obscured the sky. Lightfoot turned on his heels and went hobbling back into the underbrush toward where they'd left the horses. He was favoring one leg and the Sheriff thought he saw blood on the back of the Ranger's left boot. Petticord glanced over at him, but the Sheriff just shrugged. Both men started walking along the shore, parallel to the course of the floating coach. East followed a few steps behind, his massive dark arms tucked into the front of his overalls.

That's when it started to rain.

* * *

The coach materialized out of the haze like a dream, drifting in the gentle current. It approached by inches. Finally, when it was still eight feet away, Jake lurched forward into the river, slapping at the surface, spitting water. He felt like his heart was about to jump out of his chest. The water closed in around his head and he felt himself slipping deeper until he touched one of the coach's tiny wheels. He shoved an elbow up on the frame and held on tight. Then he inched himself up onto the frame and out of the river. He stood up on his shaky legs, water pouring out of his trousers, and was surprised to see Reeves Duncan gazing at him from the far bank.

The Sheriff was saying something, but Jake couldn't hear it. Lightning lit up the world, and a peal of thunder rolled over the river a moment later. The boy's ears were still full of water. He felt like his entire *head* was full of water.

But he waved back.

"I'm FINE!" he shouted. "I'm safe!"

Lightfoot reappeared from the woods with a lariat. The wiry Ranger was limping but he trotted to the bank of the river, set himself, and cast the loop overhand toward the nearest corner of the coach. The lariat looped around the brass orb atop one of the corner posts, and Lightfoot yanked it tight. The sheriff and Petticord joined him.

"Bring it in!" spat Lightfoot. Rain dripped off the back of his hat.

Hauling on the rope as hard as they could, the three men managed to hold the vehicle against the current. Getting it to shore was going to be another matter.

* * *

Jake felt the presence of the creature before he saw it. The coach began to shudder as something struck it from within. The wood of the green panels splintered, and squealed, and finally the port-side door burst open. There was a pause of several seconds before a long pale appendage emerged from the cabin and moved experimentally along the wood of the exterior. It was as wide as a man's hand but twice the length, with thin black claws at the tip of each finger and on the back of each knuckle.

Jake watched, simultaneously fascinated and terrified, as the monster's head appeared outside the cabin. It was a viscous, grub-like gray, and it glistened in the weak light, fearsome, abysmal, and antithetical to all good reason. Oddly, unbelievably, the thing's face began to change shape. Its small head grew longer, and a vertical ridge of bone or cartilage in the center of the forehead appeared and grew larger as Jake watched. The thing's lifeless black eyes peered up into the early evening sky. It seemed to wince at even the hazy half-light of dusk and rain and oil smoke that surrounded them. Any schoolboy could tell you there were eight planets in the solar system—each more frigid and desolate than the next. Though the word *hell* had been used in describing the creature, Jake knew reflexively that this thing haled not from any realm of fire but from featureless voids and fearsome cold, from worlds as hard and unremittingly dark as the shadowed face of the moon.

Then it saw Jake. The creature hissed, and its chest began to expand. It pulled itself up onto the cabin roof with one arm and a leg and moved toward the boy, creeping on all fours like some oversized insect. A pair of purplish iridescent wings rose and spread behind it as it came.

Jake couldn't help it. He screamed.

Unphased, the creature lifted one of its clawed fingers and extended it toward the boy's throat. The gristly digit came within a foot of Jake's face. Six inches. Jake leaned as far back as he could over the river as the thing in front of him cocked its oblong head. It opened its horror of a mouth to reveal two rows of small but sharp brown teeth and a glistening black tongue. The tongue seemed almost sentient. It flicked and curled outside the nightmare's mouth, a ropy obscene tumescence that momentarily separated itself into a dozen slender strands before it reintegrated. It seemed like an hour but was in fact only a moment before a ragged volley of gunfire erupted from the shore. Four rounds tore into the creature's shoulder and head. Now it was the monster that screamed, anguished by the slugs ripping its fibrous flesh but pained perhaps as much by the surprise of the attack, at its sudden realization that it was exposed to its enemies. Clearly even the radically diffracted light of this murky evening was enough to disorder the thing's senses. It scuttled backward over the roof of the cabin and disappeared into the coach.

* * *

The Ranger stuck his Colt in the waistband of his trousers. "That's enough, goddammit. *Pull.*"

And they pulled. They pulled until their arms burned and the flesh of their fingers and palms was raw. But it was only when Clarence East spat on his giant hands and took hold of the rope that the four men began to reel the coach in toward shore. It came slowly, but it came. The vessel finally grounded itself in the mud. Lightfoot drew his revolver again and stepped onto the narrow railing, then up onto the fractured roof of the vehicle. Jake was lying on the far side of the coach. His eyes were wide and he was breathing hard; he tried, but failed, to speak. The Ranger turned to signal his companions and at almost the same moment, the door on the shoreward side of the conveyance was shattered from inside.

The monster was over seven feet tall, but it moved with startling speed. The face was a blunt and tragic imitation of something human, with a huge, ridged forehead, black eyes, and a gaping hole for a mouth. It caught East by the hair and pulled him with it toward the water.

Lightfoot sprang down from the coach and wrapped his free arm around one of East's legs, bracing to hold the big Negro on the bank. The Sheriff couldn't see a clear shot. He flipped the double-barreled Aubrey in his hands and swung at the thing's head instead. East twisted and thrashed and finally broke free; his scalp hung like a bloody cap from one side of his skull. But now Lightfoot was in the creature's grasp. And as quickly as Reeves Duncan could figure out what was going on, the monster yanked the Ranger into the mud and reeds at the edge of the river. Lightfoot fought to his feet, looked down and fired twice into the creature's eyes. The thing recoiled, shrieked, then whipped its long arms around the Ranger's ankle and dragged him under the water with it. East grabbed the Ranger's shotgun and vaulted up onto the coach. The water roiled and bubbled in three different spots, but there was no other sign of the Ranger or the creature for almost a minute. When, finally, a white face broke the surface, its gray eyes were wide with shock, and the lower jaw was missing. It was Lightfoot. His hand reached out of the river as if to grab the sky, as if that low gray blanket held substance enough and solace to hold a man up when he fell. Before anyone on shore could help, the Ranger disappeared again, his disfigured face and fingers pulled back under the water.

Reeves Duncan gagged. He was embarrassed by the sound, and maybe as much out of shame as of rage he fired the twelve-gauge again and again at the water around where Lightfoot had surfaced. He almost certainly hit the Ranger himself, but it was too late for that to make any difference. East saw something moving downstream and fired as well. The two men followed the ripples on the surface another hundred yards south. It was raining so hard now that they had to shout to each other to be heard. Not that there was much to say. The Sheriff and the big black man floundered out into the mud and ruined cypress trees where the Anahuac emptied into the swamp of Sour Lake. They fired as they went, reloading as they moved, raking the river with lead until finally they stood chest-high in the broad brown swamp and there was no way to advance. Reeves Duncan stopped counting at twenty-nine shells. Nothing came up. Jewel Lightfoot was gone.

* * *

"Jake? You okay?"

The boy opened his eyes to find Edmond Petticord bent over him, his face just a few inches away. "What happened?" Jake mumbled. He coughed up a mixture of brown water and cinder-black phlegm. He blinked his eyes against the cold rain.

"It took the Captain," said Petticord, oblivious to Jake's coughing spasm. "Just *took him*. Down into the swamp. The Sheriff and East went after it. Told me to mind you. I think we got some other problems, though."

Jake wiped his mouth and nose on his wet shirt. "What? What problems?"

Petticord nodded at the green coach. "See for yourself."

Jake picked himself up off the grass and followed the little man onto the coach. Even with the oil smoke heavy in the air, the cramped cabin stank of filth and rotting flesh. They opened the far door to let in the last light of evening. Against the rear interior wall stood four metal canisters, possibly aluminum, each about three feet high and the diameter of a big man's embrace. Petticord pointed, and Jake squatted down for a better look. Each of the canisters had a thick glass portal, and through each portal Jake saw a slug-like body floating in an amber fluid. He looked closer at the creature in front of him. It was turnip-white and smooth-bodied, with tiny fin-like appendages—*arms? wings?*—folded to its side. It took the boy a moment to recognize the other shape in the canister. What he'd initially thought was some multi-legged sea creature was, in fact, a human hand. It was missing two of its digits, and there were ragged holes where something had been chewing at the soft web of flesh between the thumb and forefinger.

Suddenly the little creature opened its eyes. It stared at the boy through the glass, then hurled itself against the portal with an audible thump.

Jake fell backward on the floor of the coach.

"They're perky," said Petticord.

"Good Lord," Jake croaked. "I guess these are the young ones." He paused to catch his breath. "Ugly, ain't they?"

Petticord nodded. "Like baby cicadas. Only they got teeth."

"We gotta get rid of these things. Did you say there was some sort of storage shed over here? With explosives?"

"That's right," said Petticord. He was still staring at the monster that floated in the nearest canister. It was dormant again. Its black eyes were closed, and it floated tranquilly in the yellow fluid. "They kept the dangerous stuff over here."

"Where is it?" Jake demanded. Petticord was a dream-addled man, easily distracted from the task at hand. Jake had the disturbing thought that his companion might actually be entertaining the notion of letting one of the creatures out of its container. *Just to see what might happen.* A man who ate bugs and carried corn snakes around in his pants couldn't always be trusted. But the anxiety in the boy's voice roused Petticord from his reverie. He led Jake back up the bank of the Anahuac and into the scrub oaks and hackberries to a rough-hewn shack, six feet by nine feet, thrown together with scrap lumber and too many nails. There was no more dynamite. *Probably used their entire stock to wire the berm*, Jake thought. But in one corner, behind several lengths of knotty pine, stood several jars labeled BLASTING OIL. This was nitroglycerine unmixed with any buffering agent, and thus extremely volatile. Jake knew blasting oil was considered too unstable to be used for much of anything these days, which was why dynamite had mostly taken its place. But it would do for the task at hand.

"Let's load this in the coach with the canisters. Careful. Don't even *walk* fast, Mr. Petticord. This stuff is jumpy. One jolt and…"

He didn't have to finish the sentence. They each took two of the jars and gingerly made their way back to the coach. They placed the jars on the splintered roof. Jake lowered himself into the cabin again. He meant to situate the blasting oil between the metal canisters. But he noticed something else in the dim chamber.

"Mr. Petticord! I need some help here."

Jake pointed to the ragged bundle in one corner of the enclosure. Protruding from a bundle of dirty blankets was a mop of red hair. Petticord stepped down into the cabin and together he and Jake tore at the ropes around the bundle. They separated the blankets to reveal a little girl, naked and as pale as the moon. It was Rose Anne Terrell. Blue bruises covered most of her upper body. Her eyes were open, but she was stiff and cold. The two men passed the little body out of the coach and onto dry land.

"She ain't been eatin' much," said Jake, kneeling over the girl. "But she's breathing."

The voice that responded sent a dull chill through the boy's limbs. "Of course she's breathing. We'll need something to feed the young."

Jake tried to stand. It was then that he felt the blade against his throat.

"Call your friends," said the voice. Jake could see blood smeared on the dark arm that held the knife. He knew without looking that it was Naguib, the longhaired man he'd seen standing over Doc the night before.

"No need for that!" said another voice. It was Reeves Duncan. He and East appeared out of the woods a few yards away, with their weapons trained on the Arab.

"Drop the guns," said Naguib.

The Sheriff shook his head. His face was flushed a bright red, and he was breathing like a winded bull. But he gave no sign of backing down. "Not a chance, friend."

"Drop!" said the Arab. "Or I cut the boy's throat. Like a goat."

"I seen what you did to them fellas a while ago. You'll butcher him anyway."

Naguib emitted a nasty little chuckle. "Yes. Maybe you learn. So. Hand me one of the weapons, and I let the boy go."

"And the little girl," said the Sheriff. Jake saw East glance down at the naked figure of Rose Anne Terrell, still unconscious on the grass. East wasn't looking so good. His scalp hung like a lopsided cap from one side of his head. Blood ran down into one of his eyes.

The big brown-skinned man pulled Jake closer, pressing the flat of his knife hard against Jake's Adam's apple. "Not the girl," he said. "We have use for her."

The Sheriff spat to one side. "I'm sure you do. But she stays with us. You want to catch up with that thing you been feeding, you'd better get moving. It's got up into Sour Lake, and it didn't seem to be *waitin'*."

The comment seemed to hit home. Naguib's eyes glittered with malice. "Take the girl," he grunted. "Now give me the gun."

The Sheriff and Clarence East exchanged glances. East stepped forward with the Ranger's Winchester. "Open it," said the Arab. "That's right. I need it loaded. Put that box of shells on the coach. Now hand me the weapon. Slowly."

As soon as Naguib's right hand closed around the shotgun, he trained the weapon on the Sheriff. With his knife hand he shoved Jake to the ground. Naguib backpedaled toward the river and climbed onto the coach, keeping his gun leveled at the lawman all the while. He ducked his head quickly into the cabin to verify that its metal vessels were intact. He was focused so intently on maintaining his stand-off with Reeves

Duncan that he didn't seem to notice the jars of blasting oil standing on the roof of the coach.

"Push me off," the Arab commanded.

No one moved.

"Push me off, you sons of whores. Or someone dies."

"You ain't gonna get far," said the Sheriff. "You know that, don't you?"

"Far enough."

East and Petticord and Jake advanced and grasped the rail of the coach. They planted their feet and shoved it out into the current.

Naguib stood on the narrow rail as the vehicle floated lazily downstream. Ten feet. Twenty. He was smiling.

"Sheriff," hissed Jake, keeping his voice as low as he could.

"Yeah?"

"There's nitro on the roof of that coach and I don't think he knows it. We need to turn tail and run."

"Run? But he'll *shoot.*"

"That's gonna be his problem."

The Sheriff glanced sideways at Jake. He could see East and Petticord had understood the exchange. He nodded slightly, then spoke as calmly as he could. "Everybody," he said. "We move on three. One…two…*three.*"

Naguib was pleased to see the men run. He'd counted on killing at least one of these meddling idiots, even if only with a parting shot. Now they were making it easy. He sighted down the end of the barrel, found the big black man's spine, pulled the trigger. The hammer flicked forward. The shell detonated. The man called Naguib, 111th scion of the Turquoise Kingdom, sworn vassal of the Protector, blew himself and his treasures into a thousand pieces.

NINE KILLED IN WELL
FIRE HOLOCAUST

Ins. Commissioner
Calls Catastrophe
Worst in Oil
Field History
Cause of Fire
Linked to Labor
Agitators

Atcheson Teller
November 9, 1911
Page 1, Col. 1

21.

Pursuit

It may be impossible for us to comprehend the early 20th Century's fear of fire. Fires still kill people and damage property, but the destruction they cause today is minor compared to the results of the conflagrations that took place in the United States in the fifty years following the Civil War. The largest of these was the Chicago Fire, in October of 1871. At least three hundred people died in the disaster. Another ninety thousand were left homeless. Frederick Law Olmsted, who wrote a famous and not-altogether flattering account of his travels through Texas in the 1840s, and later won fame as a principal designer of New York City's Central Park, visited Chicago shortly after the Fire. He estimated that "the houses burned, set ten feet apart, would form a row *over one hundred miles in length.*"

Though not as destructive, there were similar large fires in Baltimore and Boston in these years, as well as a vicious blaze that raged through Galveston in 1885. Conflagrations hit small towns in Texas as well, literally wiping such communities as Elmina, Newtown, and Olive off the map. Much of the damage caused by the apocalyptic 1906 earthquake in San Francisco was in fact a result of fires that started in the wake of the tremors. The results were appalling. "The total value of the property destroyed," wrote a stunned Texas Commissioner of Insurance William J. Clay of the San Francisco disaster, "is estimated at more than $300,000,000, and the loss to fire insurance companies exceeded $225,000,000. This amount, it will be seen, is nearly double the total surplus of all fire insurance companies reporting to this Department. In all the history of fire insurance no condition approximating this one has arisen. It is estimated that the loss was sufficient to exhaust the surplus earnings for the last thirty-six years of every company doing business in the United States."

Jake Hennessey's oil fire destroyed several square miles of old-growth timber on the east bank of the Anahuac, then spread south toward Atcheson, only petering out when it hit the cotton fields Joe Fuller was holding fallow for the winter. In all, according to contemporary accounts in the *Teller*, the blaze burned seventeen thousand acres of the Big Thicket, killed one bull and a dozen pigs, and displaced thirty-one people.

Reeves Duncan and a team of townspeople eventually found ten bodies in and around the Mill and excavation site. It was a damn shame the men of the Mill put up such resistance to the posse who'd ridden out to investigate, the Sheriff observed. To anyone who listened, he repeated his suspicions that Amos Newton's rig crew was rife with I.W.W. syndicalists—desperate characters with low morals and violent ideas, fully capable of mistaking a nigger for a fellow human being and God only knew what other acts of sedition and mayhem. There was ample evidence, he added, that they were responsible for the grisly killings around Addison.

Some of the other remains recovered from the charred remains of the Mill and its outbuildings were only barely identifiable as human. The smallest of them, it was pointed out, didn't look human at all. The Sheriff took care of these items. Fire could do horrible things to a body, he said. He buried the scraps of bone and gristly flesh—and two sets of tiny, needle-sharp teeth—deep in the Thicket, some fifteen miles north of Atcheson. None of the searchers from town ever found the scorched remains of the butchered Croats who were hung upside down from the oak trees out on the Newton tract. The Sheriff and Clarence East buried what little of these bodies they could locate—a few blackened bones, some teeth, a mostly-intact foot. There were some deaths it was pointless to discuss. Or report.

* * *

Jewel T. Lightfoot was apparently unmarried and childless, but he did have a brother who thought highly enough of him to request that his body be sent by rail to San Angelo, where he was to be buried in a family plot just south of the Concho River. Funds to pay for transport would be advanced. The sheriff never met this brother, a Mr. Gideon P. Lightfoot, because he communicated by telegram. In the irregular days following the fire, Reeves Duncan did what he could as well as he could. He sent back a message that the Ranger's body hadn't been recovered yet. He promised an update as soon as additional information became available. Only much later did he wonder how news of Captain Lightfoot's untimely demise could have reached San Angelo so quickly.

Sheriff Duncan wasn't sure how to explain the Captain's death to the bespectacled little bureaucrat who stopped in to see him a week later. The stranger's card identified him as Colonel Deak Ross of the Texas Rangers. The man didn't look like a Ranger. He had a smooth, shiny complexion, a neatly-groomed moustache, and callous-free hands. Nonetheless, there was the badge: just like Lightfoot's, carved from a silver Mexican *cinco pesos* coin. Colonel Ross stated that he'd been sent to investigate reports of violence in Atcheson and the surrounding area on account of a letter written to his superiors by state senator Sinclair "Sink" McClellan of Houston. Senator McClellan had himself been contacted by a Dr. Darvis Kendrake, a man of some importance in the district, despite his African ancestry.

Reeves Duncan told the colonel what he hoped to be true. Something awful had been at work in the Thicket. Good people were dead as a result. Maybe the bravest of the fallen was that banty rooster Captain Jewel T. Lightfoot, who had made the ultimate sacrifice while performing a last great service for the State of Texas.

"I'm afraid I don't catch your meaning," said the Ranger. "How's that?"

"Something awful?"

The Sheriff was getting used to this particular lie. He barely hesitated. "Reds, Colonel. Bunch a' goddamn labor agitators, and murderers among 'em. I was thinking you mighta seen the newspapers."

"And you say Jewel Lightfoot was here?"

"Of course he was here. State sent him down. Department of Insurance, Statistics, and History. I thought that's why *you* were here, to tell you the truth."

Deak Ross wiped his spectacles with a precisely-folded handkerchief. His cheeks glowed a brighter shade of pink. "Captain Lightfoot was relieved of his duties three years ago, Sheriff. He is no longer a Ranger, and as far as I know is not affiliated with any agency or bureau of this state."

"Relieved?" said the Sheriff.

"His mental faculties were deemed to be unsound."

Reeves Duncan wriggled his neck around in his collar. "You mean someone thought he was…?"

"Batshit crazy," said the pink-faced man, with a trace of exasperation in his voice. "That's exactly what I mean. And not just *one* someone but several—and more importantly, several that matter. Captain Lightfoot was working on a very curious case a couple of years ago and lost a particular friend at around the same time. The rigors of duty seem to have hindered his faculties. He claimed to have met up with a band of angels on top of Enchanted Rock in November of 1908. *Seraphim,* is what he called 'em. Said they anointed him to fight the enemies of God. That he was a member of a sacred brotherhood and therefore no longer subject to civil authority. Started injecting himself with a solution of suspended silver to 'purify his blood.' Turning himself into a weapon of Christ, or some such thing. I don't suppose I need to remind you, Sheriff, that this is the twentieth century. Where is the scoundrel? Last we heard, he'd taken off for the Holy Land on some sort of pilgrimage. If he's holding himself out as a Ranger still…"

"He ain't holdin' himself out as nothin' anymore," said the Sheriff. "Like I said, Colonel. He's dead."

The tidy official grunted with surprise. "Dead. Of what cause?"

"Well, he… He drowned, I guess."

"You guess?"

For a moment Reeves Duncan contemplated telling everything he knew. Mysterious deaths. A metallic *space bullet* of some sort buried in the mud near Sour Lake. Beer kegs with flesh-eating bugs the size of catfish in 'em. It would be a relief to let the world in on the secret. Pass the cup. Let someone smarter than he was figure out what the hell had happened in Ochiltree County the last few weeks. But the moment passed. *Tell everything he knew?* Hell. He didn't *know* what he knew.

The Sheriff coughed. "He drowned, Colonel. Trying to cross the Anahuac River with me and a couple of other men, heading into the camp. There was a citizens' group—"

"A mob?" asked the official, wrinkling his nose at the thought.

"Yessir. A *mob* is right. They was headed for the Mill from the other direction as us, from the town side, on a tip. Run into gunfire before they got within a half mile. They shot back, and I gather all hell broke loose. They managed to push the Mill gang back into the woods. Into the path of the fire, as it turned out. You said you heard about the killings hereabouts."

"I have indeed. I was dispatched to take a first-hand look at the situation. But the labor camp was…I gather…*destroyed?* By the fire?"

"Hard to tell exactly what happened, but it looks like they got careless out there. Oil fire spread out into the woods and kept going. No survivors."

"Destroyed," the Ranger concluded to himself. "Then the problem is solved. And we have a few less bomb throwers to worry about. Am I right?"

Reeves Duncan nodded. "Exactly right."

The little man gazed for several moments into the sheriff's eyes, seemingly pondering whether or not to believe what he was hearing. "Thank you, Sheriff. I'll be heading back to Austin now."

"Thank *you*, Colonel."

"For what?"

The Sheriff shrugged. *For believin' that ridiculous load of horse shit I just dumped on your head,* is what he wanted to say. "For comin' out to check on us, I guess."

The colonel allowed himself another brief look at his surroundings. Atcheson, Texas. Population 404. He reached up his small hand and slapped a mosquito off his cheek. "It's my pleasure, I assure you. Now, if you'll excuse me, I have a train to catch."

* * *

Reeves Duncan wasn't lying when he said the problem was solved. Not exactly. The Sheriff had struck the creature several times with the butt of his rifle. Lightfoot shot it twice in the eyes with his service revolver. With those goddamned *silver bullets* of his, for what it was worth. The Sheriff and East had pumped almost thirty shells into the river where they'd last seen the thing on the day Lightfoot died and they must have hit it once or twice. So they might have killed the beast. Shoot. They'd *probably* killed it. It wasn't a ghost. It was flesh and blood, and flesh and blood could always be trumped by fire and lead. True, nobody had seen the carcass. Ed Petticord had made it his personal mission to scour the banks of the Anahuac ever since. He seemed to be out there more or less continuously, at least as long as the sun was up, but so far he'd seen no sign of either the creature or the Ranger. But the lack of a body didn't prove anything. There was no way to know if the creature—the *monster*—whatever it was—would have floated to the surface in death, like a man, or simply settled to the bottom and been devoured by the catfish and turtles that thrived in Sour Lake. So the Sheriff was tempted to believe the monster was dead. Every inch of him wanted to believe it. But in all the burnt-black land and tannin-stained waters there was no sign of the creature Reeves Duncan thought about night and day.

※ ※ ※

They buried Doc in the Methodist cemetery.

A hundred and twenty mourners turned out, some of them men who'd entered his home by force only two days before. Daris Kendrick put thirty-eight stitches in Clarence East's head to hold his scalp in place, then returned to Houston to attend to his medical practice. Jake went back to school. The newspapermen left town, and things started to return to normal. Then, a week after the visit of the Ranger colonel from Austin, the Sheriff heard a desultory remark from Dim Evans. Seems a man named Morris who lived a few miles down the river had found three of his hogs torn up. Damnedest thing he'd ever seen. Couldn't say if it was gators or some kind of cat. Reeves Duncan shrugged. "No tellin'," he said, as nonchalantly as he could, and went about his business. But that evening he rode out to inspect the carcasses. It was just as Dim had reported: the hogs were ripped to pieces, their blood drained from their bodies. Same thing happened to a steer two days later just a little further down the Anahuac, not far from where it met up with the Trinity and continued south toward the Gulf of Mexico.

※ ※ ※

That weekend Reeves Duncan, Jake Hennessey, and Ed Petticord set out with the county's dogs in search of the creature. The Sheriff told the county commissioners that he was after a man named Naguib, a reputed anarchist and bomb manufacturer whom he suspected had shot and killed Amos X. Newton and set the fire that killed the men at Nichols Mill. How the perpetrator had managed to escape the conflagration was unclear. A contemporary account in the *Teller* stated: "Sheriff Duncan is confident he will apprehend this foreign-born assassin, a crafty and notoriously bloodthirsty Mussulman, and he calls on the citizenry to assist where possible." A description of the alleged perpetrator followed, along with a note that two local citizens who attempted to volunteer for the posse were rebuffed, on account of the sheriff's desire for "stealth and secrecy of movement above all, which can best be achieved by limiting the number of men in the deputation."

Clarence East joined them six miles south of Atcheson. It was unclear whether Willard Mills and his vigilantes were wholly satisfied that East was innocent of the killings before the fire at Nichols Mill, but no one wanted to test the matter. East was kept secluded in Ed Petticord's house. Very early on the morning after Reeves Duncan's departure, the big black man set out on foot to rendezvous with the Sheriff and his unimpressive posse.

After three weeks the County wanted its bloodhounds back and the Sheriff couldn't see a way to refuse. They weren't doing much good in the rain anyway, and they ate more than their share of provisions. Reeves Duncan returned the dogs. He resigned his commission by means of a brief and somewhat cryptic note to the county judge, and rode south to rejoin his companions. East caught catfish to supplement their diet, but they subsisted mainly on squirrel, salt pork, and, as Jake Hennessey wrote in his journal of the expedition, whatever "semi-edible greens" Edmund Petticord could scavenge from the countryside.

They all devoted considerable thought to quitting. Jake wondered on numerous occasions whether they'd lost the creature altogether. They suspected that once the thing got to the Gulf, there would be no way to stop it anyway or even to figure out which way it had gone. But for all their doubts, they kept moving. Jake kept a sporadic and not entirely satisfactory diary. An entry:

December 9. Cold tonight. We are on the beach & there is no cover, so the wind is fierce. More rain today and later sleet. Mr. P is worse. He coughs most of the night. He seems to weigh no more than a cat, but will not complain. The sheriff rode north a mile or two but saw no sign of the thing we track. East says maybe it is tracking us.

☼ ☼ ☼

They caught up with the creature on the brown shore of Trinity Bay. On Tuesday the rain turned to sleet again and the next morning they woke up in frost-coated bedrolls under flurries of wet snow. That Friday, though, the wind shifted to the south. The sky softened and the temperature climbed.

They lured the thing out of the estuaries with a wounded goat, cut just deeply enough on one shoulder to get the blood flowing. It was almost three-thirty in the morning when Petticord heard the animal's screams. He tossed a fistful of sand at East, but the big man was already awake. Sheriff Duncan sat up and reached for his rifle. Jake and East followed, each with their own weapons.

They found the creature lapping at the goat's severed head. The monster was weak and barely recognizable. It was a mass of mud and filth, its broken wings dragging behind it, now looking more like long tentacles. Black eyes glared from its chitinous oblong head.

They pumped slugs and buckshot into the monster as fast as they could fire and reload. The creature changed colors, according to East's account, from gray to white and back again. Its face changed shape, the features pulsating like small hearts. After ten minutes of firing, the creature screamed and lurched and finally went still. Just before dawn, though, it stirred and started to crawl toward the bay. East was closest to the thing. He took one of the shotguns by the barrel and smashed it over what remained of the monster's head—once; twice; so many times that he cracked the stock and bent the barrel of the weapon. Even so the creature shuddered and inched toward the water. It was only when the first rays of the sun struck it that it went still again.

The sun rose quickly. By nine-thirty that morning, the temperature was almost sixty degrees. Seagulls and terns circled overhead. The skin of the creature began to turn black, and a sickly yellow smoke rose from its carcass. Clarence East tossed his broken weapon aside. The big man walked down to where little waves of coppery surf were rolling in on the beach. He sank down in the sand, stared out at the bay, and started to cry.

DROP KICKER IS
MAN OF THE HOUR

*Kicking, Especially Good
Drop Kicking, the
Backbone of Game*
Rockne Explains
Importance of the Art

Atcheson Teller
December 14, 1911
Page 1, Col. 3

22

Post-Script: The Atcheson Horror

The most tantalizing aspect of the deaths in and around Atcheson in 1911 is how little we know about them. What exactly did Amos X. Newton find beneath the sloughs north of Sour Lake? If the metallic cylinder Jake Hennessey saw was in fact a space vessel of some sort, where did it come from? When did it arrive on Earth? And where is it now? I'm fairly certain I have pinpointed the portion of the Old Newton tract formerly occupied by the Nichols Mill. Unfortunately, the land is privately owned, and its owner is not congenial to sightseers. He has so far rebuffed my requests for entry onto the land, though to be fair I have not been entirely forthcoming about the reasons for my curiosity. I suspect that whatever Amos Newton found, and Jake Hennessey saw, lies buried still beneath the East Texas mud that fell in on it after the berm surrounding the excavation was destroyed almost a hundred years ago.

And what of the men (can I call them "thugs"?—ethnically and religiously inapposite, I know, but behaviorally apt) known as Solomon and Naguib? What cryptic and traitorous clan sent them forth with the monster to supervise recovery of the things contained in the metallic cylinder buried in a slough of the Big Thicket? Daris Kendrick was able to trace the name *Tawuse Melek*, one of the terms Solomon used to describe the monster, to the beliefs of the Yazidi sect of northern Mesopotamia (now Iraq). Considered by their Muslim neighbors to be devil-worshippers, and unclean, the Yazidi are obsessively closed-mouthed about their religion;

indeed, fraternization with outsiders is punishable by death. This particular aspect of the group was illustrated by the stoning death of a teenaged girl by members of her own family in 2007. Apparently the girl had become romantically involved with a young Muslim boy—a major transgression. Captured on a cell phone camera, images of the chaotic homicide circulated around the world on the Internet in ensuing weeks.

The cult's belief structure is dominated by the figure of *Tawuse Melek*, the "Peacock Angel," a winged deity supposedly cast out of heaven by God for refusing to swear allegiance to man. Defenders of the Yazidi faith proclaim the creed to be peaceful in all respects. Perhaps it is—periodic stonings notwithstanding. But there is a barely-repressed rage evident in the texts of its apologists toward the Mohammedans who have long persecuted the sect—particularly in the 19th Century, when Constantinople sent its secret police out to murder and intimidate Yazidis in Turkey, Syria, and northern Iraq for their lack of zeal for the teachings of the Prophet.

Daris Kendrick theorized that Ibrahim Solomon was a disciple of some Yazidi splinter group, a secret society bound to service of its vision of the Peacock Angel in hopes of gaining some final and decisive advantage over their numerous Islamic tormentors in the Middle East. If such were the case, the group's violent and laborious quest to locate and recover others of the monster's species—the pupal forms of the creature unearthed by the luckless Amos X. Newton—takes on a decidedly sinister, possibly even millennial, cast.

By the same token, whose interests did Jewel Lightfoot represent? Even assuming he did in fact operate under the secular auspices of the Texas Department of Insurance, Statistics, and History, the most powerful and, to this day, the most mysterious of the state's executive agencies, the notion that his mission was a purely economic one—i.e., to snuff out the financial threat posed by the monster—seems unlikely. Loyalty to secular duty is one thing. A belief strong enough to inspire a former Texas Ranger to inject himself with a solution of suspended silver—and to speak openly of his conversations with angels on a colossal hunk of granite in western Gillespie County—is quite another.

Silver was a popular anti-bacterial agent in the early 20th century; indeed, before antibiotics became widely available, silver was commonly employed by physicians to fight infection. Country folk sometimes kept a silver dollar in their milk pails to keep the milk from spoiling. Silver has also traditionally been considered a sacred substance and, as such, an effective weapon against all manner of evil. So-called "naturepaths" even today prescribe colloidal silver to fight microbial infection. Internal consumption is officially discouraged, as accumulations of silver in the blood can lead to the bluish tinting of the skin known as *argyria*, and in larger concentrations has been linked to nerve damage and mental disorders. To his dying day, Daris Kendrick was convinced silver was in some measure toxic to the thing he called the Atcheson Horror. By injecting the metal into his veins, Jewel Lightfoot had in effect made himself a sort of poison pill, a suicide weapon against the thing that killed and apparently consumed him.

＊ ＊ ＊

Fortunately, some questions do have answers. Though I have altered their names and various details of their identities, the individuals who populate this story were real. They left tracks. We know what they made of their lives.

Rose Anne Terrell survived her kidnapping with her health intact and her memories mercifully vague. She seemed to have spent most of her captivity either unconscious, presumably drugged, or in concealment. She may never have known what was planned for her. Certainly she recovered from whatever trauma she suffered. Rose Anne graduated from Texas Women's College in 1926 and worked as a nurse for thirty-four years in Dallas's Parkland Hospital. Her obituary, published in 1975 in the *Dallas Morning News*, indicates that she was survived by four children and eleven grandchildren and that she had traveled to twenty-four countries in the course of a productive and interesting life. With presumably unintended irony, the author of the obituary noted that Rose Anne was "fond of tall tales and mysteries." I sometimes wonder if this was because she was a participant in one of the greatest of them.

☆ ☆ ☆

Reeves Duncan had seen enough. He told Jake Hennessey it wasn't so much the horrors involved in fighting the creature that turned him from peacekeeping as it was the way his own community seemed to turn against him in those dark days after the killings. In June of 1912 he moved west to Burton, where he had kinfolk who helped him buy a dairy farm. It wasn't a big piece of land—thirty-nine acres, according to Washington County records. Family members say he never talked about his days in law enforcement. He was no great shakes as a farmer, but he married late in life and sired two sons. One of them, his namesake, died at the age of seven. The other eventually became the president of a mutual insurance company that catered to the Czech-American inhabitants of that region. The company was mildly successful for many years, till the widely-trumpeted Senate Bill 14 finally put an end to the rate-setting freedoms enjoyed by the state's farm mutuals. Still, thanks to Sheriff Duncan's son's civic activities and philanthropy in the area, there is a Jared L. Duncan Little League baseball diamond in Washington County that is still in use to this day.

☆ ☆ ☆

Edmund Petticord resisted the siren song of conformity all his life. Though he never held a paying job, he nevertheless went on, to the astonishment and irritation of many of his neighbors, to a distinguished career as an amateur botanist and backwoods philosopher. In his sunset years he became a sort of mascot for the Texas preservationist movement that coalesced in the 1970s to save what remained of the Big Thicket. He was an acquaintance of Senator Ralph Yarbrough and Supreme Court Justice William O. Douglas. He led numerous botanical expeditions into the heart of the woods and at the age of eighty-seven was the subject of a feature article in *Smithsonian*, the official publication of America's premiere scientific institution. He died seven years later, childless but happy, and was buried by his lone relative, a nephew who was himself nearing eighty, at an undisclosed location northeast of Atcheson. He apparently never breathed a word to anyone about the Atcheson Horror, or his part in running it to ground.

* * *

East's story is less edifying. In December of 1911 the big man went to live with Daris Kendrick, who tended to his ruined scalp and was eventually able to find him work as a cotton jammer at the Port of Houston. He eventually married, and fathered two daughters and a son. But he was never able to put down roots, and he developed a drinking problem that stayed with him until the day he died in an automobile accident near Dickinson in 1926. His son, Alfred Taylor East, achieved a measure of fame as a band leader and music teacher. In 1949 he took the reins of Hempstead College's celebrated marching band and held them for nearly thirty years. He once remarked to a student biographer that his father suffered from nightmares all his life. Alfred's son, another Clarence, served three terms in the Texas Legislature in the 1980s before returning to a private law and lobbying practice in Houston. He currently represents a number of professional athletes, including the quarterback of the New Orleans Saints. He politely but firmly declined to comment on my depiction of his grandfather or any of the events recorded herein.

❊ ❊ ❊

Daris Kendrick died during the Camp Logan riot that convulsed Houston in August of 1917, when black soldiers stationed in Harris County "mutinied" in the face of repeated insults from the local populace. Kendrick was miles away from the fighting at the time. He was tending to a white man named Henry Baggot, a greengrocer who had collapsed on Walker Street as he walked home from work. A nervous police officer saw Kendrick bent over the man and assumed the worst. He ordered the black doctor away from his patient. Kendrick refused, of course—whereupon the policeman shot him in the back of the head at point-blank range. Houston's foremost African-American physician left behind a wife and daughter, a thriving medical practice, and, according to a contemporary newspaper account, "fifty-three boxes of notes and anatomical specimens." It is a measure of the times that while nineteen black soldiers were court-martialed and eventually hanged in the months after the Camp Logan riot, the policeman who shot Daris Kendrick received no punishment at all. I have often wondered if pieces of the "Atcheson Horror," as Kendrick called it in one of his letters to Jake Hennessey, were in those fifty-three boxes, and what, if anything, might have been learned from such fragments.

❊ ❊ ❊

Slender, raven-haired Jacob Joseph Hennessey was eighteen and a freshman at Texas A & M University when the First World War broke out. Three years later, when the United States finally entered the conflict, goaded by German U-boat depredations in the North Atlantic, Jake volunteered for the Army Air Corps. He flew nine missions in France before losing his airplane and his left ear in a dog fight over Alsace in 1918. Back in the States, he studied mechanical engineering at Georgia Tech. There he met a soft-spoken, green-eyed girl from Savannah and married her three weeks later. The couple had one child, my grandfather Charles. In 1924 Jake began a distinguished career with the Lockheed Aircraft Corporation, where he had a hand in designing such storied flying machines as the Vega, the Orion, and the P-38 Lightning.

Though he never spoke publicly about the Atcheson Horror, it seems likely that Jake disclosed at least portions of the story to the United States government. My grandfather mentioned on more than one occasion that his father was involved in research conducted by the Department of Defense on the possibility of alien visitation of Earth. But Jake Hennessey always publicly denied not only the possibility that so-called "UFOs" were real, but also that he was involved in any project dedicated to *proving* they weren't real. If I write with any sense that I am disappointing the past, it is because I suspect my great-grandfather might disapprove even now of any discussion of this episode in his life. And yet Jake Hennessey kept his journals from the period, and made sure they were safe, and was careful to hand them down to his son—along with a handful of newspaper articles and the mold-speckled affidavits of Clarence East and Reeves Duncan, copies of which I have on my desk as I write. Clearly he recognized that the story needed to be preserved, if not disseminated.

✳ ✳ ✳

The remains of the Atcheson Horror were donated by the County Sheriff's office to the Ochiltree County

Preservation Society, which for many years had an office and a sort of makeshift museum on the third (and later, parts of the second) floor of the courthouse in Gosford. In October of 1964, the *Teller* ran a Sunday feature titled "REAL LIFE TREASURES RIGHT HERE AT HOME," in which the author catalogued some of the items on display in the museum. The list included several Civil War-era firearms and a set of deck chairs from the old Turkey Creek Spa. There was also something called "the desiccated remains of a giant squid," reputedly found at Bolivar Point in 1911 by Sheriff Reeves Duncan, young J. J. Hennessey, and "their colored man, C. East." These remains have since disappeared, though no one I've talked to remembers exactly when. All that survives is an ancient photograph of the three men posing stiffly in front of a mass of blackened carcass.

While the accounts given by the men regarding the creature's physical characteristics diverge in certain respects—the monster's height, for example—they agree on the general hue and consistency of its carcass. All stated that the thing was hairless, and at least somewhat translucent— the greenish-black outlines of its veins and internal organs were clearly visible. East said it was "white like a grub worm." Petticord described the thing's body as mushroom-like, but as tough as suet. Daris Kendrick eventually examined a scrap of tissue forwarded to him by the Sheriff. In his affidavit, he compared it to the fibrous flesh of a mussel or scallop. The little doctor also sent Jake Hennessey a set of notes, evidently based on the field observations of his companions. The monster's head was much larger than ours, dominated by lifeless black eyes and a distended set of jaws containing prominent, elongated incisors. (Kendrick speculated that the teeth were used for killing and shredding rather than chewing, and that the creature subsisted largely on fluids rather than flesh—a vindication of sorts for Walter McDivitt's "vampire" theory.) There were two sets of claws on each hand and a large, chitinous single claw—possibly for ripping the flesh of its prey—on each of its inner forearms. While there was but little of the brain left to examine after East's final assault on the creature, the stomach was intact and yielded semi-digested fish, frogs, and part of what appeared to be a nutria, a large and particularly unattractive rodent now common in southeast Texas and Louisiana. Also retrieved from that organ was a gold-plated bracelet with the name DALCHAU inscribed in Gothic script, and a five-pointed silver star, that iconic badge of the Texas Rangers.

Two silver slugs were found in the creature's head, encased in a clot or "knot" of putrefying flesh. This was the evidence that led Daris Kendrick to conclude Lightfoot had been right: silver was toxic to the monster, intensified by its body's tendency to incorporate—to *draw inward*—the substance. If the creature consumed portions of Jewel Lightfoot himself, as seems likely, it ingested flesh and blood thoroughly dosed with the solution of silver the Ranger was said to have injected himself with. This surely contributed to its demise. It also seems that at death the creature basically disintegrated. It devolved into mass of ropy, intertwined filaments, with the head and face subsiding into the body like a house sliding into a sink hole.

The human body is mostly water. The creature's body was primarily liquid as well—perhaps to a greater extent. Aside from the oblong cartilaginous structure of the head, there were few fixed skeletal components. It is possible the creature's high fluid content helped it change shape. While the men who killed it weren't sophisticated enough to examine or even to locate the components of its nervous system, it seems likely it was more highly evolved, and probably less centralized, than our own. The notion that the monster was a shape-shifter was flatly dismissed by Daris Kendrick. Perhaps it ought not to have been. We know a variety of terrestrial creatures can alter their appearance more or less at will. Members of the cuttlefish family, for example, can display up to thirty distinct shades of color per second through neural manipulation of their pigmented chromatophores. Changes in morphology are possible as well. The flying squirrel extends its fleshy membranes to turn from rat to kite; the puffer fish can enlarge itself to twice again its resting size.

* * *

The photograph taken that afternoon in 1911 depicts three individuals (Petticord is not in the picture, either because he was too ill to pose or because he was the photographer) wearing suspenders, open-collared shirts, and hats that partly shade their faces. They are clearly exhausted. East's shirt is torn at the left shoulder. They kneel beside the obscene carcass, and the newsprint records their names but not the obvious questions. *How did a giant squid manage to find its way into the Gulf of Mexico? Why would three men from a town fifty-three miles inland have seen fit to scour a lonely beach for giant squid with shotguns at the ready?* And, finally, *Why do the men seem so discouraged by their discovery?*

Over the past several months, I've spent hours looking at the *Teller*'s grainy reproduction of this photograph. I've tried to figure out whether my telling of the story behind it would meet with the approval of my great-grandfather, Jake Hennessey; or of Sheriff Duncan; or of Clarence East.

The truth is, I don't know. Because what I see in the dark eyes that stare out of that picture is fatalistic. It is, at bottom, an acceptance that no sane man will ever quite believe the things they know they've seen. And that I have now divulged. But there is solace in the truth—and even, I think, in the attempt to locate the truth. I have visited the gravesite of Leonard Dalchau. His marker stands in a Lutheran churchyard in Schulenburg near the weather-scarred headstones of his parents. I left the schoolteacher's bracelet there. In the State Cemetery in Austin there is a granite memorial for Texas Rangers who died in the line of duty. Not far from that marker, in the shade of a giant live oak, I dug a shallow hole in the grass and placed inside it Jewel Lightfoot's five-pointed star.

Daris Kendrick never actually saw the creature that haunted the sloughs around Atcheson. There is a trace of skepticism in everything he wrote about it. But he was, as usual, wide-ranging in his consideration of the conflict in which he participated. He speculated that the Atcheson Horror was neither the liberating angel its familiars took it for nor the demon Jewel Lightfoot held it to be. Rather, he said, the Horror was quite possibly an advance soldier of some fearsome army from elsewhere that had not yet made its way to Earth. If such was the case, he added, conflict was sure to follow. The war to come would be a battle of species, not of theologies—a struggle that would require mankind to unite to defend the biological niche on this small blue planet we have always assumed was ours by right. May the souls of those who died in 1911 know they are remembered—by a few, at least. May they rest in peace. And may the rest of us find the strength to fight as they did when catastrophe descends again upon us from the bright expectant stars.

The End

Made in the USA
Lexington, KY
21 October 2018